PRAISE FOR *MONSTE*

"Back and forth, through time and space, we examine the human propensity to love, to fail at loving, to love again . . . On this tumultuous mapping of American magic, we find ourselves at the center. [*Monster in the Middle*] boldly tells us: You are here."

—*The New York Times Book Review*

"Yanique brilliantly unifies the novel through her scintillating, consistently lyrical language, whether using lampoon, introspection, or tense social drama."

—*Los Angeles Review of Books*

"A genre-defying multigenerational love story that moves fluidly across time and geography . . . Yanique narratively excavates how our family origins influence our aptitude for intimacy."

—*O, The Oprah Magazine*

"Yanique is a writer's writer, one of the most inventive and talented stylists of her generation. . . . [She] explores the way love can echo along the corridors of history, through police brutality and a pandemic, deftly weaving and juxtaposing the trajectories that make love possible."

—*Vulture*

"The story of one couple is magnified and layered through the histories of the generations of lovers that preceded them. Spanning decades and geographies, this novel reveals on every page how love can persevere and take shape over time and space."

—*The Boston Globe*

"In this unique novel blending recent history with a touch of magical realism, love is a multigenerational phenomenon. Moving from California to the Virgin Islands to Ghana and back again to the United States, Yanique maps how one couple's connection is influenced by the family lore and legacies that precede them . . . the voyage is one worth taking."

—*The Atlantic*

"Themes of race, religion, class, and education appear throughout this ambitious novel, but its abiding focus is on the intimate, and the way broader social forces can impinge upon it. . . . Reality assumes a surreal tinge, and the fluidity of narration, across time, space, and character, imparts an epic register to the intimate encounter between Stela and Fly." —*Harper's Magazine*

"*Monster in the Middle* manages something extraordinary—it's a truly unique story about love, specifically Black love. In Yanique's telling, it's not 'boy meets girl,' but 'two people meet, and thousands of years of family trees, values, and experiences converge.' . . . transporting and deeply emotional." —*Glamour*

"Each of Fly and Stela's stories could stand on their own, but when the two finally meet, it's simply perfection. The novel brings us through 2020—and the ending left me truly speechless." —*Hey Alma*

"At a recent book event, Tiphanie said this book is kind of an embodiment of the phrase 'when you marry someone, you marry their whole family.' At its core, this book is about belonging, and the tension between being held and being kept. Delectable." —*Magic*

"Unique and memorable . . . A rich and honest examination of family histories, cultural disconnection, and the way people fall in love." —*Kirkus Reviews*

"Soft and intricate with no detail wasted. Readers are lured into the themes of self-discovery, acceptance, and trauma, with an ending well worth the investment." —*Booklist*

"Yanique inventively juxtaposes the start of a new relationship with family histories in this sumptuous saga. . . . Each arc reads as an evocative short story and an episode in the two protagonists' complex set of unraveled connections. This introspective exploration of first and lasting loves will hit the spot with fans of character-driven family dramas." —*Publishers Weekly*

"Tiphanie Yanique's *Monster in the Middle* is a compelling exploration of how we become who we are and how we manage to find our way to love. In her lyrical prose, the myriad possibilities of being—the accidents of birth, of sex, of race and geography, the choices we make, our compulsions—coalesce into something that feels, gloriously, like destiny."

—Natasha Trethewey, Pulitzer Prize–winning author of *Memorial Drive*

"*Monster in the Middle* is as boundless as it is affecting. Yanique's prose leaps with possibility, as her characters live and laugh and fight and love. Yanique captures romance from its peaks to its craters, deftly weaving whole worlds from everything in between."

—Bryan Washington, author of *Memorial*

"A total wonder. Utterly original and structurally thrilling. I am in awe of this novel and Tiphanie Yanique's masterful storytelling. This feels like a modern fable, a contemporary folk ballad full of unforgettable characters who, by the end, felt as familiar to me as family. What a gorgeous ode to love and its power."

—Brandon Taylor, author of *Filthy Animals* and *Real Life*

"Tiphanie Yanique is one of our very best writers. This book is another marvel, expertly mixing voices and styles, even structures and traditions, to capture the way lives naturally flow together and apart over time . . . *Monster in the Middle* is a book to study and savor."

—Matthew Salesses, author of *Craft in the Real World*

MONSTER IN THE MIDDLE

ALSO BY TIPHANIE YANIQUE

Land of Love and Drowning

How to Escape from a Leper Colony

Wife

MONSTER IN THE MIDDLE

TIPHANIE YANIQUE

RIVERHEAD BOOKS
NEW YORK

RIVERHEAD BOOKS
An imprint of Penguin Random House LLC
penguinrandomhouse.com

These stories have been previously published, in slightly different form, in the following publications:
"Oakland Gomorrah," *Agni* (2013); "Extermination," *Hunger Mountain* (2019); "God's Caravan," *The New Yorker* (2019); "Other Women," for *The Book of Men: Eighty Writers on How to Be a Man*, edited by Colum McCann (2013); "The Special World," *The Georgia Review* (2019) and *The Best American Short Stories* (2020); "The Living Sea," *The Harvard Review* (2020) and *The Best American Short Stories: O. Henry Prize Winners* (2021); "Monster in the Middle" (as "An Introduction to the Monster"), *Kweli Journal* (2017); "Belly of the Whale," *The Caribbean Writer* (2021); "Experiential Studies," *Apogee* (2015); "Rooted," *Pleiades* (2012); "Meeting the Monster" (as "The Day the Detectives Came"), *The Southampton Review* (2017).

The Library of Congress has catalogued the Riverhead hardcover edition as follows

Names: Yanique, Tiphanie, author.
Title: Monster in the middle / Tiphanie Yanique.
Description: First ed. | New York : Riverhead Books, 2021.
Identifiers: LCCN 2021006556 (print) | LCCN 2021006557 (ebook) |
ISBN 9781594633607 (hardcover) | ISBN 9780698183896 (ebook)
Subjects: GSAFD: Love stories.
Classification: LCC PS3625.A679 M66 2021 (print) |
LCC PS3625.A679 (ebook) | DDC 813/.6—dc23
LC record available at https://lccn.loc.gov/2021006556
LC ebook record available at https://lccn.loc.gov/2021006557

First Riverhead hardcover edition: October 2021
First Riverhead trade paperback edition: October 2022
Riverhead trade paperback ISBN: 9780593332252

Printed in the United States of America
1st Printing

Book design and map by Meighan Cavanaugh

for Mosiah, Irie, and Nazareth,

my beloved monsters

Put romantic love at the center of a novel today, and who could be persuaded that in its pursuit the characters are going to get to something large?

—Vivian Gornick, *The End of the Novel of Love*

CONTENTS

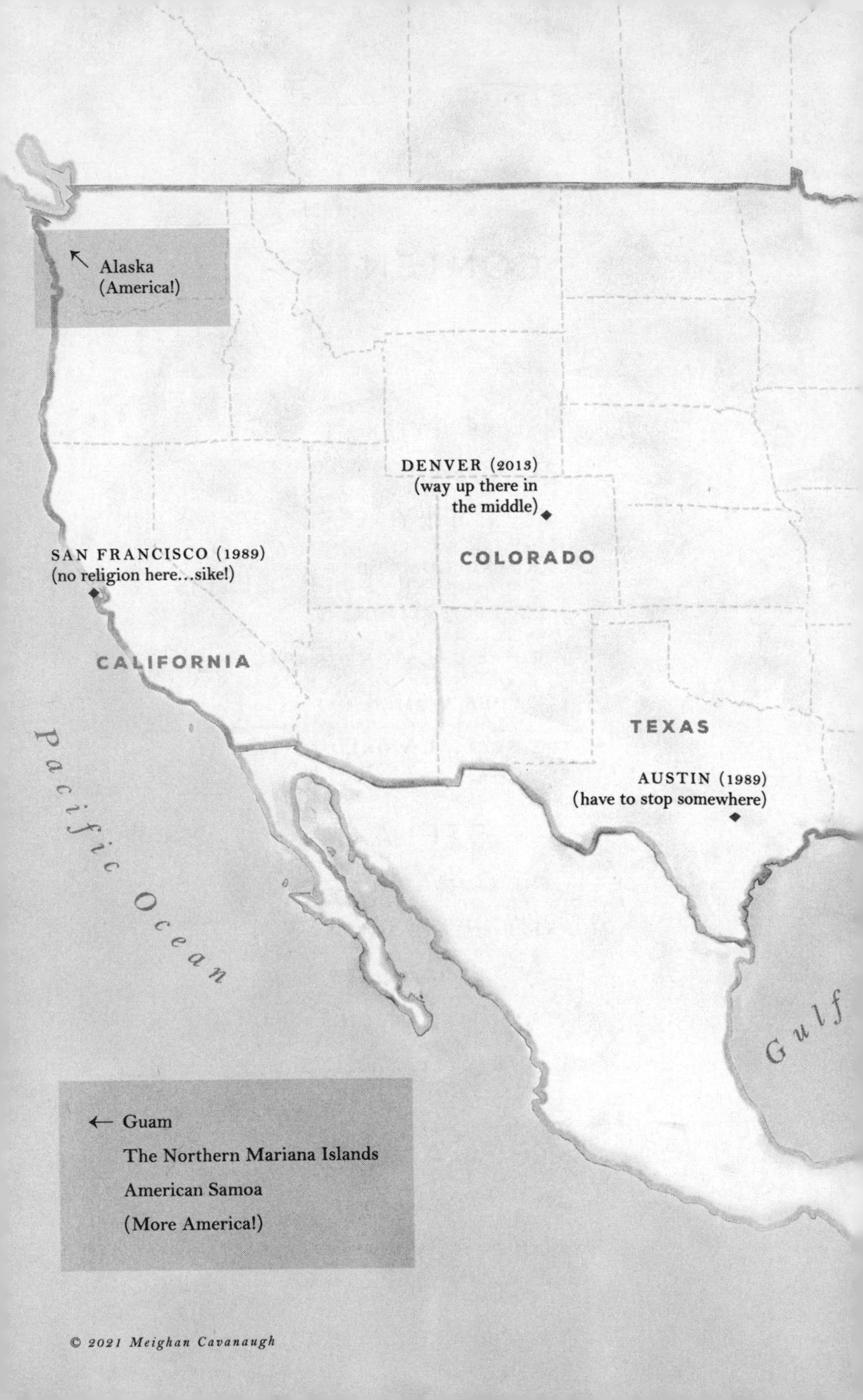
Alaska
(America!)
DENVER (2013)
(way up there in
the middle)
SAN FRANCISCO (1989)
(no religion here…sike!)
COLORADO
CALIFORNIA
TEXAS
AUSTIN (1989)
(have to stop somewhere)
Pacific Ocean
Gulf
← Guam
The Northern Mariana Islands
American Samoa
(More America!)
© 2021 Meighan Cavanaugh

MAP OF AN AMERICAN LOVE STORY

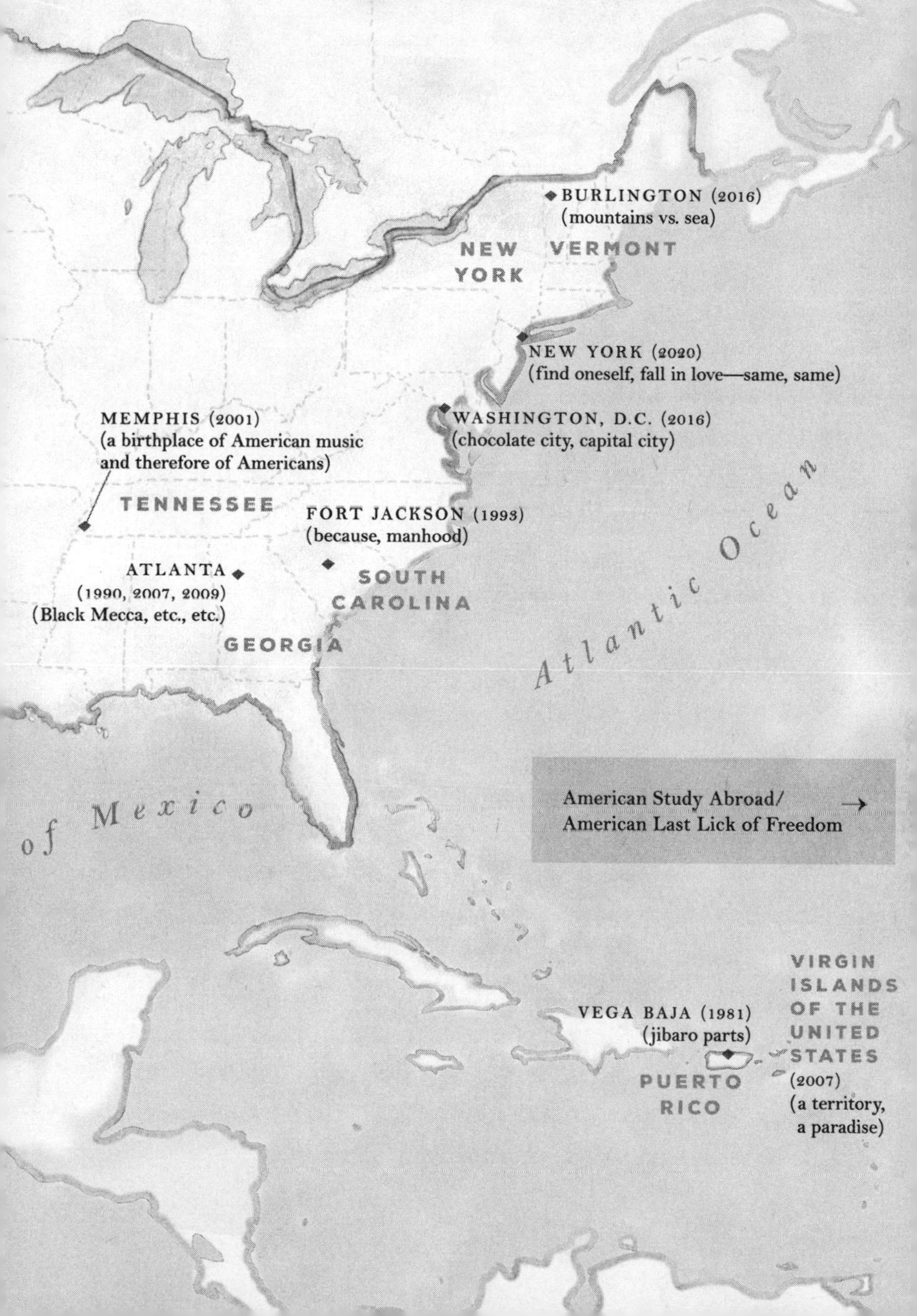

BURLINGTON (2016)
(mountains vs. sea)

NEW YORK

VERMONT

NEW YORK (2020)
(find oneself, fall in love—same, same)

MEMPHIS (2001)
(a birthplace of American music
and therefore of Americans)

WASHINGTON, D.C. (2016)
(chocolate city, capital city)

TENNESSEE

FORT JACKSON (1993)
(because, manhood)

ATLANTA
(1990, 2007, 2009)
(Black Mecca, etc., etc.)

SOUTH CAROLINA

GEORGIA

Atlantic Ocean

of Mexico

American Study Abroad/
American Last Lick of Freedom →

VIRGIN ISLANDS OF THE UNITED STATES
(2007)
(a territory,
a paradise)

VEGA BAJA (1981)
(jibaro parts)

PUERTO RICO

MONSTER IN THE MIDDLE

LOVE LETTER

Dear Loves,

When you fall in love you will be certain that it is something special about that other person. Isn't that what the songs on the radio make us think? Or maybe you will be smart enough to know it's also something special about you. Because that is what the therapists on TV get paid to help you understand, am I right? You already know that you will bring baggage into this new love thing, because it's modern times and you've heard the term "baggage." But baggage is not the most of it, you know. We know. Because listen, sweet ones, you are not falling in love with that one person. It's that you're bringing it all. You're bringing us. It's like how them old-timey folks used to say that when two people get married it's two families coming together. Or another way to understand it is that when you meet your love, you are meeting all the people who ever loved them or who were supposed to love them but didn't love them enough or, hell, didn't love them at all. You feel where this is going, my loves? Please pay attention, knuckleheads, because it's going regardless.

Love,

Your parents

FLY

And no one pours new wine into old wineskins. Otherwise, the wine will burst the skins.

—MARK 2:22, NEW TESTAMENT

OAKLAND GOMORRAH

THE STORY OF FLY'S FATHER

San Francisco, California–Memphis, Tennessee

1989

1.

The lights said MOTEL. And there wasn't a bulb missing. Not that it would have mattered if it said OTEL. Or MOTE. Not in all that rain. Not after all they had been through. The earthquake, the road, each other. They had avoided crossing the bay altogether. The Bay Bridge had collapsed, but they didn't know that for sure then. They drove south, down into the righteous belly, the holy thighs. Saint Mateo, Saint José, Saint Luis, Saint Maria, Saint Barbara, Saint Clarita. All the good men and women giving their names to those sad cities. They stopped in the City of Angels. They took the 10 through San Bernardino. Drove through Cathedral City just for the name. Stopped outside Phoenix, where he dipped a wrench into the engine and made the car purr. A day later in

Las Cruces. The crosses. There they held each other in the car while Soul II Soul streamed in through the car's CD player. They stayed on the 10. Ten became a holy number. They drove across Texas almost without stopping. But then they stopped. In Saint Antonio. Drove that city until they found the Black people. Slept on a grocer's floor. Bags of rice, their pillows. Then they started back north. "We got to avoid Louisiana," Gary said to her. "And Mississippi." It had been a mission until Texas. A sacred thing, a quest.

After Saint Antonio, the road was all Eloise dreamed. The long road unstopping. They were driving into hell, it felt like. It was getting closer to winter. And yet they were getting hotter. They abandoned the 10, took I-35 to meet Saint Marcos. Avoided Dallas. Followed an off-road just to sight some water called Palestine. Then up and up, into Arkansas. The sign to a city read Hope. Eloise held on to that image. The next stop was supposed to be Charlotte. Then they would decide. North to New York or south to Miami. Either way, a boat ride to paradise. But then the rain.

2.

Back on that first night in Los Angeles they had stayed on the couch of a dark-skinned pastor. A Baptist, Eloise supposed, though it was never said.

"An orphan like me," Gary told her. "But found his way through God. Missioned on me when the voices got nasty."

The two of them slept on the pastor's couch together, like children, brother and sister. Only they weren't brother and sister. Could never pass for that. And they weren't children. Why people opened their doors to them, perfect strangers, was strange to Eloise. Perhaps they could see her special gift. Perhaps it was as Gary said—that Black people wanted to watch out for them: a white woman and a Black man in love. But she didn't love him. Not then.

"We can stay here," she'd whispered that night. His body was clothed but still she could feel the all of him. "I don't mind waiting here until the dust clears. A week or two. I can work, even. I can type, you know." Her father had bought her the instruction manuals and the word processor. "And then we can find my parents. Get back to the church." She'd looked at his eyes, sealed taut in the darkness. Was he hearing the voices now? He did that, forced the light from his eyes when the voices became too bright.

"Ellie," Gary said, his lids softening and then opening. Now looking right at her and so close. "The dust is never going to clear. Isn't that what you said? We stay in the ark until the dove flies away."

It was true. She herself had indeed said that. That night among the angels he covered his ears with the palms of his hands and whispered to himself. She was pressed against his body and heard every word. "Leave me. Leave me go." And she knew better than to say anything. Sometimes just her voice made it worse for him.

In the morning, the pastor woke them with fried ham sandwiches, and smiled at them both as though they were his generous hosts and not the other way around. The radio was on. The pastor turned the sound up. And that's when they heard it. San Francisco had been spared. His infinite mercy. The deaths were in Oakland. Eloise's parents could still be in Oakland.

3.

In San Francisco, Eloise had been a child. Her parents were in the church but she hadn't been baptized as yet. Still, at the morning services they prayed for the saving of San Francisco and Oakland, because of her, because of her vision. They prayed that the cities would move away from sin, because of what she had revealed.

Her parents went to Oakland weekly. Oakland was their special obligation. Their missionary work. There was a time when Eloise had wanted to go with them, but her mother said no. Eloise was not yet a woman then. After Eloise graduated from high school her mother had offered, requested, even beseeched. But no, Eloise didn't want to go anymore. Her parents had revealed the kind of women they missioned to. Eloise would rather work on her word processing than pray with prostitutes. But here she was on the road with a man not her kin. She was the same kind of woman as the rest. Still, she had the good gift. Hers was from God. She believed that. Gary's was not. She believed that, too.

4.

When they'd left San Francisco, she hadn't thought they would keep going. On the road still a day later, he'd reached his right hand out, to touch her, she thought. But no. He'd fiddled with the car controls and then slid a circular disc into the mouth of the dashboard. It was a smooth, slippery motion. She didn't know cars came with CD players. "I modified it myself," he said. The secular music came on. And then she knew that they were not just fleeing desecration, they were fleeing their lives. In San Bernardino, Gary explained to her why they weren't heathens despite their abandon.

"You are Noah," he said with his soft big voice. "I am the animals you saved."

"You're not an animal," she said gently, to reassure him. He wasn't an animal to her. Despite his wool hair, dark skin. She and he were at an outdoor restaurant on the outside of the city. In a tiny Black part, which was also the big Mexican part, though still different parts. She couldn't tell, exactly, how it all was laid out.

She watched him tear the fried chicken with his teeth. She would have preferred they go to the diner they'd passed miles before, but he'd told her he didn't want white people to see them together. She tried to cut the chicken with a plastic fork and knife, but she only managed to discard the skin. Gary was looking at her as though he might bite into her. It was the same look he'd given when he first told her to get in the car, right now, Ellie. Get in, he'd said.

"I'm a tiger," he said now. "I'm a lion, a jaguar. A . . ." But he couldn't think of any other cats and he laughed at himself.

"A leopard," she said. "A puma."

"All that. Now, eat this chicken. You'll be hungry later."

She ate the chicken. She was like Noah. A believer.

5.

Her visions were not a curse. But her asthma was. You get a gift, you get a curse for balance. The sickness was the sign of Satan on her body. In the Frisco public library she'd looked up great people who had been asthmatic. She wanted to be great, to spite the devil. The librarian directed her to a book about Che Guevara. He'd had asthma, too, but he'd managed to become a doctor and a revolutionary. A nonbeliever, but still a healer and a leader. What greatness, then, could Eloise not accomplish with God in her heart? Perhaps the sickness signaled something prophetic about her.

She believed it was her asthma that had driven her out of the burning city. Driven her out to the shaking ground, out of her parents' holy home. Driven her into Gary's animal arms. When he'd pulled his car up to her, like a saving grace, and said get in, she had. She could barely breathe for the buildings burning, for the smoke and the screaming.

They'd first met because he'd come to her church. He'd gone to all the churches. Catholic, Seventh-day Adventist, Jehovah's Witness, Latter-day Saints. He heard voices. From God or a demon, he didn't know. Demon, he'd been mostly told. Exorcism had been suggested; Freudian analysis, too. At Eloise's family church, he'd just walked in and stood among them. The elders bade everyone in the chapel to introduce themselves, which was done whenever someone new wandered in. Eloise had been surprised at Gary's voice, a soothing bass. At the fellowship after, everyone flocked around him—a blackbird in a pitying of doves.

"The boy has voices," her father reported during dinner one night. A night when it was just Mother, Father, and Eloise. "The elders thought it best that I counsel him, given that Eloise has the visions." Eloise had pretended she wasn't curious. Had taken over the dishes from her mother, so that the parents could talk this through.

Gary came the next evening. Drove his own car up to their house. A car he claimed to have built, even the engine, with his own hands. Parked expertly in their narrow driveway, without fretting like her father always did.

"Where are you from, son?" This was a careful thing for her father to call him.

"Paradise," Gary had responded.

"Then you're like the rest of us. Cast out."

"Yes," Gary said. "Except I plan on getting back before I die."

After that Gary came once a week. On a day when her parents didn't mission in Oakland. He came, and when he did Eloise went to bed early. Her room just up the hallway. For a month just listening to his voice through her bedroom door caused the asthma to tighten around her chest. Until she finally realized it wasn't her asthma at all.

Just herself. Until he came one night when the parents were in Oakland.

"They say you have voices, too," he spoke from the threshold.

"Visions," she corrected. And opened the door wide to let him in.

What they did that night, and for nights after, was read Proverbs. It was a perfect courtship. So perfect that she could forget he was Black. Just remember that he was a Christian. Until he told her one night that he wasn't a Christian.

"Of course you are," she said, to reassure him.

"I go to Buddhist prayers," he said.

"That doesn't seem un-Christian."

"I answer the call to prayer on Fridays."

"Prayer is Christian. Do not fear." She rested her hand on his.

"You're not listening, Ellie." His voice was firm. "I need help with my voices. I need divine help. I take it from wherever it comes."

"I can help," she said, because she *was* listening.

"I need paradise," he whispered. "And this is not paradise."

"No, this is Sodom."

He looked at her and then gave a trumpet of laughter.

"But I've seen it," she said evenly. "The destruction. I see things. God is going to destroy this place because of its wickedness."

"What you plan on doing when the destruction comes?"

"Pray. I will pray. As should you."

"I'll get out of here," Gary said. "Why stay in Sodom? I'll take you with me, if you want."

"You would save me?"

"If you wanted."

"Yes," she said. "I would like to be saved."

Could he see that she would be so happy without her burden of belief?

6.

They were driving through Cathedral City when Gary told her what he needed. "You're going to have to give yourself over to us, Ellie." He turned to look at her. His face was showing his fear of her answer, clear enough even for her to see. But why be afraid? Hadn't she already given herself? Wasn't she here on this road with him? Did he mean give him her virginity? "Your whole self, Ellie. You can't be a white girl. You just have to be Ellie." He said this firmly. Like he'd been thinking about it for miles. She'd been thinking about her father. About her mother. About them on Fourteenth Street in Fruitvale during the earthquake. Trapped with the strippers.

"But I am just Ellie. I am a white girl named Eloise." She wanted to say white *woman*. But she couldn't.

"It can't be like that. If it's like that, then . . . Well. It won't work. It won't work at all, Ellie."

"Then you will have to rescind Blackness."

"You don't see, Ellie. I can't help being Black. There's nothing I can do about that."

They hadn't found a cathedral, though that had been his charge. They didn't make love that night, even though she had supposed. Instead, they danced. They drove themselves to a dirt road. Dusk. They parked on the bend, beneath the dry trees. He played an instrumental CD, and when he opened the door for her he kept it open. The music reaching out. He started to sing, then kept on singing. Hymns, she hoped, but no. She listened, and that's when she knew she was in love with him.

"Come on, Ellie."

And his was like the voice of God. And so she went to him. Stiff as cement, that's how she was. Unbending. "Unrelenting," he teased her. It sounded so like unrepenting.

But that was how it was for many nights. The dancing and singing. The slow flow of their bodies. Or rather, his body. She, not sure if she should follow his lead or her own. But then he would take her. Take over. And spin her and sing to her and she would laugh and laugh. Afterward, he would sit her down on the sidewalk or on the side of the road, and she would feel winded even though she hadn't been doing much. He'd been doing most of the work.

"You like listening to me sing?" he finally asked her.

"Yes, I do," she said, smiling back at him.

"Why?" He laughed. "'Cause I'm so good at it?"

"Because it comes so easy to you."

He stopped and looked at her with a squinted eye.

There was a sharpening in her upper back, where she knew her lungs to be.

"How?" he asked. "'Cause I make singing seem simple?"

"No," she said, not sure what it was he wanted, but hearing that maybe he was angry. "No, it's just that you sound natural and free." Was this okay to say to a Black man in America in 1989? That he sounded free? Was it okay to even discuss freedom? "It's just, I never sang before I sang with you."

"Babies sing," he said, looking at her, seeing her.

"Not babies in our church."

"Not true. It's natural for all babies. We all do it naturally." Then he opened his mouth in an O and let the breath out, shivering his head as though he alone was an instrument.

And it *was* so simple. That little burst of relief in her chest. Of course singing was simple and good. Here was an unknowing of what she had known her whole life. Was this God's true love? Or was she now an unbeliever?

"Someday," Gary said, slipping another of his CDs into the player, "we'll go hear a proper Negro gospel choir. Then you'll know God meant for us all to sing." The music started, disembodied, but still. This time, soul music. He'd said it was actually called that. Soul.

She puckered her lips, a sign for him to kiss her. She was always doing that. And he always saw and always knew what to do in response.

But she didn't know how not to be white.

7.

He had been raised in a series of foster homes. Back in San Francisco, on their second night of Proverbs, Eloise had asked about it.

"They all did the best they knew," he said. "But the pictures in their houses of their white family. Grouped together, the bunch of them. And smiling. Then, pictures of the foster kids. Each of us alone in our frames." He shook his head. "I'd try. Always helpful. Fix the standing fan so the blades whirled faster. But the voices would chase me down. The fan, maybe, would whirl loose. Smack somebody in the back. And then I'd be made to leave. That was it. Again and again, that was it."

"This is a parasite place," she said to him, and she meant the world, but he didn't hear that.

"I'm from a paradise place," he said. "I've seen pictures of where I was born. The islands. Like Eden." He pulled the picture he carried and showed it to her. "The West Indies," he said. "It's on the other side of the country."

She squinted at it. "It looks like Hawaii," she said.

He looked at the picture. "Black people don't come from Hawaii."

"Are you sure?"

But he wasn't sure. She could hear that.

"The voices told me," he said.

"They told you what?"

"That I will journey back to paradise," he said.

"Did they say you would have a companion?"

"What if they did."

8.

Her horrifying visions had come a few years before, when she was still in high school. They'd started one night after an elder meeting held in her parents' living room. While she was wiping the table and carrying the mugs of tea to the kitchen, an elder had asked her father if she, Eloise, had her eye on anyone. And her father had said that he did not think so. "But one never knows. Girls can be devious."

"Marry early and stay married," the elder had said. "That is the path to God."

"Amen," her father said, as if the elder had prayed.

It scared Eloise, what her father said. She wasn't devious. She wasn't eyeing anyone. She desired, that was true. She'd let a boy from their church school have his way. Touch her breasts. Put his fingers in her underwear. Mouth her nipples. But he wouldn't take her virginity. He was like a boyfriend, almost. Except that he was someone else's boyfriend. Eloise knew that, even then. Knew even then that she was his practice. That boy, two years ahead, had eventually married the real girlfriend. Ungodly, the both of them. And there Eloise was in high school, her eye on no one.

That very night Eloise imagined the old elder touching her. Imagined him pushing himself into her. Going in. But then his hips squeezing in. Then his legs. She hoped for his whole body inside her. It was never enough. It was horrifying and monstrous and when she tried to stop imagining she realized she was dreaming, sleeping. One couldn't control one's dreams. So the elder kept at her, everything from the waist down, slicking and sliding, until she moaned like the schoolboy had told her she was supposed to. She awoke with her face in the pillow, as though a suicide.

Then before the next church service that elder was in a car accident. Real—not imagined, not dreamed. Paralyzed from the waist down. And that's when Eloise knew her gift. After that she dreamed her first dream of the bay burning. That's when she told her parents.

9.

In Phoenix, they slept a few hours in the car. Parked along a stretch of desert, near a patch of cacti low as penitents. They rolled the windows up and locked the doors. It was warm in the car and would get warmer as the day steamed on. She was curled in the back seat. He'd leaned the driver's back. His head was at her feet.

"I think you hate white people," she said, not looking at him.

"You say crazy things," he said, and turned to look at the underside of her feet.

"It's because of slavery. You are afraid of white people. You're afraid that we'll lynch you or put you in jail or—"

He opened his hand and swung it sharply on her calf. Not really a smack, but a welt spread quickly anyway. "I'm not afraid of you," he said. "Jesse Jackson is going to be president. Black people go to Berkeley. Miscegenation couples get married." His hand was still on her leg. And then he was on her. There in the tight space of the back seat, made smaller because the driver's seat was in the way. It was like fighting. It was like a struggle. Even though they were on the same side. Fighting the clothes, fighting the confines of the car, fighting all that was beyond the confines.

"How could I hate this?" he said, with his eyes tight on her face, his palm gripping on her hip. "How could I hate any part of this?"

Her father had never hit her. Had never hit her mother. Even though the Bible did allow. The welt did not linger on Eloise's calf. Instead, they lay awhile in the car. The after smell of them thick as the air. She thought it was just his smell, but then when he unfolded himself from her, she knew it was her, too. Now they were in the labyrinth together.

Outside the world was alive and awake. Trucks and trailers went by. The lovers opened the car doors on the side that faced the desert. He pulled his pants to his waist and walked into the land without saying a word. Left her right there sitting, her own garments askew on her body. She stared after his back and didn't let him leave her sight. Watched as he reached into the one tall tree—fig—tugged the branches, and then walked back with the fallen fruit. "Gary Lovett," she said, voicing his full name for no one but herself.

10.

This driving to paradise might be a kind of mission work, a winding penance like the early pilgrims in corn mazes. Pastor had preached on that once. Traveling now with Gary might be missioning. Of course. After Phoenix, Eloise tried not to think of her father, who had been a real missionary. He was the one who always reminded her about chastity. Her mother's duty was to get her ready for womanhood. Her father's duty was to protect her from it. Right now her father would be thinking himself a failure. Right now he would have a broken heart.

Gary and Eloise spent their Las Cruces night in the car. But they danced again on the side of the road. Made love in the car like cats. Played the Soul II Soul CD to cover their sounds. There really were crosses in the city. In the yards, on top of the churches, on the sides of the road.

"I was conceived in Africa," she whispered, when she saw the first white crosses. "My parents had sex in Africa to make me."

"Where in Africa?" Gary asked, and took his eyes off the road to look at her.

"Somewhere. Ghana, I think," she said, spotting another cross.

Gary wasn't as dark as an African. But still, he was Africa to her—in a way.

Being in Africa hadn't been missionary work for Eloise's mother. For her mother it had been a spiritual quest. Her mother's faith had wavered when she couldn't conceive. So Mother didn't work like Father did. She prayed. She prayed a lot. Then she was pregnant.

"They were going to move from Africa, Ghana, to the islands," Eloise said. "Continue their missionary work closer to the US."

"Which islands?"

"I don't know. Hawaii?" She wasn't sure.

"What do you know?" He was annoyed with her. But she was annoyed, too. And she had an authority now. They had *known* each other. She could demand things of him. Like a wife might. And he would have to listen.

"I know I want to sleep in a bed," she said.

"We're almost to Texas already," he warned. "We can't stop in Texas."

"I can stop."

"No, we can't."

"I can." She didn't look at him; perhaps she was the only one who heard her solitary pronoun. Perhaps she would call her parents. Have them come for her. If they could. I'm alive, she would tell them. Are you?

"I'm not hearing it, Ellie," he said tightly, but he looked at her when he said it.

Still, that was the night they curved into San Antonio. He found gas for the car. They did have money, his, but not enough to make it to anybody's paradise if they paid for a bed. They drove by the city canals and when he finally saw a Black person he screeched his car to the curb.

"Brother," he said to the man. "Where do we live?" And the man, glancing at Eloise only once, directed them to the Black area. Small stand-alone homes with clean yards. It was quiet, like it was a secret. A hideout.

"We won't get a room here," he said.

"Can't we ask?"

They parked on the outskirts of the neighborhood, even though everyone had already seen them driving through. The Texans were nice enough. Nodding their heads as the couple walked past. But Gary didn't ask. And Eloise didn't know how.

"We need fuel," he said, and he meant them, not the car. At a grocer's they bought soft drinks, bread, cheese. Gary leaned in and spoke quietly to the other Black man behind the counter.

That night Gary and Eloise slept in the closed grocery. Two huge bags of rice as their pillows. A blanket for them to spread into the aisle. In her dreams Eloise saw the walls of canned goods and white flour shivering above them, but holding. She woke once and didn't feel him snaked around her, as she'd hoped. But she heard his voice from above, whispering something urgently. It was dark and though she was scared, she felt the familiar tightness in her chest and had to sit up. Give her lungs the space. "You good. You so good." She heard him chanting the bush grammar he only used on the voices. His voice was coming from above her, and then his face came into focus. He was standing, or else he was floating there. "Yes," she said, and went back down.

In the morning, the grocer grilled them eggs and bacon and they washed it all away with coffee and milk. A feast. "Free," the grocer said, before ushering them out, out of the neighborhood and back to the car. The damn car.

"Our ark," Gary said when they were back in.

After that they drove. Hours and hours. They stopped once for coffee, which they hadn't stopped for before, but he had the taste now. They drank their cups, sitting on the ground beside the car.

"You dream about the cities anymore?" Gary asked, which was unusual. He didn't much ask her anything.

"No."

"You miss the dreaming?"

She didn't think so, but then again, she didn't think she missed her parents either.

11.

The end of San Francisco and Oakland had come to Eloise many, many times. It was her most consistent vision. The one that God wanted to make sure she would pass on. Even the church had taken it up. She'd told Gary one night in her home. She was missioning to him, she'd thought then.

"I see San Francisco as Sodom, falling. I see Oakland—Gomorrah—crashing. I see people swinging into the sea. I hate to watch, but I can't stop seeing, and when I see the bridge collapse, it's always then that I wake up with a coughing attack. My chest hot and tight as a turnover." She hadn't looked at him, but she felt his body stiffen.

"My voices," he began, "come to me when I'm awake. Wide awake. They come for me." But then her lips had quaked and he'd seen. He stopped his own story, put his mouth on hers. The boy from the church school hadn't given her that. Her first kiss. She thought then that she would have to tell her father now. She and Gary had crossed a line and perhaps they would marry. Or he would be driven out. Either way it could not continue in such a fashion.

But after Gary left that evening, the cities shook. Eloise rushed out, not to see, but to be seen. The smoke was there and she couldn't help the coughing. Her chest began to knot and she wanted to scream, for Gary, not even for her parents. And then there he was. He told her what to do. "Get in the car, right now, Ellie."

12.

In Arkansas they drove through that city called Hope. "Please," she said. "Let's stay here." The motel sign was big and red and missing the first letter. She didn't like the sign, that was true. But maybe there'd be a phone and she'd call her parents. Maybe the quest was over. Or maybe hope was destination enough.

The sign went by without him turning off the highway.

"I want to go home," she said, though she hadn't meant to say that exactly. Oh, it was awful the way she sounded. Truth was, she didn't want to go home. She just didn't want to stay in the car another night. This was hellish. And just then. Just at that thought, she heard the rain.

"Rain," Gary said, seeing.

Eloise began to cry. "You don't listen! You have kidnapped me." She unbuckled her seat belt—and fast, he put his hand out across her chest to protect her. The car swerved. She screamed.

"Stop," he said, stern. "It's raining. Stop."

Scared, she clicked her seat belt back into place.

Gary put his hands back to steer, but flashed a look at her. "Don't you dare get all white girl on me," he said. "Calling me a thief. I didn't steal you from your parents. I value myself, no less than I value you. You love on me easy and giving. Like I'm your man and nothing but your man."

"How dare you bring up our private intimacy—"

"Nobody in this car but us. This our private intimacy." The car swerved. She noted another hotel sign coming up. Big and bright, despite the rain. This one missing the *L*.

"You are an animal."

"Stop with that voice."

"It's not because you're Black. It's because you are you."

"You crazy," he whispered. "Left me."

"I am not crazy," she shouted, which was the first time she'd ever raised her voice to him.

"I'm not talking to you." He turned to her now, glaring for too long. She willed him in her mind to please look back toward the windshield, back to the rain-hidden road. She wondered how long he had been speaking to the demons—usually she could tell from the lilt in his voice, but sometimes not. Now he looked forward just as another hotel sign loomed above them, then behind them. She waited for him. He eased an instrumental CD into the player. She waited. Waited an hour, then more, while the music filled the car. The rain stayed with them. Waiting, too.

"You want to go back?" he finally asked without a whisper. "Yes, I'm talking to you now," he said, and took his eyes again off the clouded road. "You going to go and point your finger and call me a kidnapper?"

"I just want a bed."

"A bed with me?"

She didn't speak and he went back to watching the road, even though there was little to see.

"Ellie. You think you're a prophet. But what did you predict? Destruction. If you're a prophet, then so am I."

"I predict God's destruction," she said shrilly.

"For what good, Ellie? Did you stop it? Did you save anyone but yourself?"

"How could I save anyone? I'm just a girl."

"You're a grown woman. And I notice that you got yourself out of there."

"*You* got me out of there," she said plaintively and then heard herself say it.

Another motel sign came. This one a steady red light. The rain beat over it, but the red was hot and burned through. They could barely see in front of them, but she knew he could see the sign. He drove on past. Kept on driving and driving.

Who was Noah here? Gary was the one shepherding the car. Eloise would have to be the white dove. She would fly out of the car, the ark, and never return.

"I'll teach you how to drive," he said as if he had heard her thoughts. "That way you can leave anytime." But still, he would always keep her. Because he'd taken her chastity. Taken her belief, even. She was bound to him. And the rain was so loud.

"I don't want to be a prophet," she said. "I just want to be a good person."

"Life is so simple for white people," he said.

He slowed the car, turned—maybe as apology for what he'd said. But then everything in front was gray. Gray, gray. And dark.

And there was a bridge ahead of them. Eloise inhaled sharply when she, so late, saw it.

Her bridge in San Francisco right then had a trapdoor at its center that led straight to the drowning water. A man and a woman had driven their car right down, unknowing. The bridge they were now heading toward was all lost in the rain. No one behind them would be able to see their car veer, careening into the river. Eloise, her chest was so tight.

Waiting for the embrace of a railing, of another vehicle. She couldn't swim. The bridge rose up around them. They were on it, at least, though they could not see. The rain roared so loudly it was the absence of noise. Eloise could pray and type, but neither one of these things was called up in her just now. Instead: What would her parents think if her body was discovered in this car with him? Kidnapped, is what they would know. She calmed at the thought.

The tires ran over something. An embankment, but Gary and Eloise were okay. In a city now or a town. Either way, off the highway and off the bridge. She hoped. The prayer finally came—please, Lord, deliver us, Lord—and prayer did feel useful. There in front of them the faint lights said MOTEL. There wasn't a letter missing. Gary slid the car slowly over. Heading toward the big sign, she knew. They eased into the parking lot. So slowly, in case they hit something, she thought, or someone. He turned the car off.

He faced her and saw her, like he always could. She looked through the windshield at all the rain.

"I'll go in, Ellie," he said. "I'll go in and get you a room." Did that mean he was leaving? Would he leave her here at this motel and continue on without her? She wouldn't be able to sight him in the storm. He might not even go into the motel. He might just keep on walking.

He opened the door and the rain slammed in. He stepped out to it and shut the door behind. His driver's seat was in puddles. She opened her door to the howling and ran toward the way she hoped he'd gone, her arms out like the blind.

Inside, it was freezing, and though they had parked right outside, they were completely wet. The attendant, a white man, was behind the desk watching TV. He looked stunned to see them. "You in from the storm," the attendant said. It was okay that he was white, Eloise told herself, but she wanted him to be a woman, at least. A woman would sympathize with their miscegenation. Might.

"How much for a room?" Gary asked the attendant. Eloise stepped forward. Stood by her Gary.

"I'm afraid you won't be able to get a room here," the attendant said.

"We have the money," Gary said. She heard him using the "we," always the we.

"Sure," the man said. "It's just that . . . Well, I'm sorry to say that we don't have rooms for renting. Not anymore."

Eloise understood. They would not get a room because they were a mixed-race couple. Because this white man, like her father, would never allow a Black man in bed with her. She stepped forward. "Please. You wouldn't send me back to the storm." She used the singular, hoping her man didn't hear.

"I don't understand what you're after," the other man said, eyeing them suspiciously.

"Yes, you do," Gary growled. "The woman needs a room. Money is money. Segregation is over. Long time."

The attendant widened his eyes at them. "No, no. We don't have rooms. Not for sleeping."

Gary put his palms over his ears and pressed them there, his face grimacing to keep something in and keep something out. The attendant stood up. Stepped back. Was he afraid of Gary? Eloise stood closer to her man. Close, close. She felt her lungs, they were close now, too—so aflame and so small. Where was God's grace? Her coughing came. Coughing, coughing.

"In Jesus's name," the receptionist began. "It's not like that. Look at where you are." He showed them the sign above his head. "The Lorraine Motel," the man said, as if they couldn't read. "Lorraine Motel," he said again and more slowly. "The Doctor King," he said. And for less than a moment Eloise wondered if this stranger was referring to Che Guevara: Healer. Leader. Maybe the attendant could just look at her, the asthma cinching, and believe there was something of that in her, too. Doctor. King. But just then she understood.

Eloise's lungs released, grace, like a window broken. Her coughing cleared. Her lungs released. Her heart. MLK had died the year Gary was born—he'd told her that like it meant something. "Oh," she said now. "Oh, my dear God."

Gary's hands were over his ears, but he looked to her.

"The Lorraine," she mouthed to him. "The Reverend Doctor."

Eloise caved her arms around Gary, but he wrenched himself from her. He swung himself around and around. Like a dancing. Then slowed. "You can't carry me," he shouted once and then again. "Carry me," he said more quietly.

"It's not a motel. It's a museum," she whispered through Gary's palms. She looked to the attendant. The attendant nodded, calmed, relieved.

"Is he touched?" the white man asked, his voice and face softening.

"Gifted," Eloise whispered. "But it will pass."

EXTERMINATION

THE STORY OF FLY'S MOM

Ellenwood, Georgia

1990

Truth be told, I wouldn't speak the whole of this to you or to anyone—not even God. That would be a giving up of power, and I'm not going back to being the kind of woman who gives up any power, no matter how small. See, the biggest thing that ever happened to me happened to someone else. You know that story, Earl. About how I was there in 1986. How it was so loud, that field where we stood. How I saw the shuttle go up and up. How there was a blast and we all cheered. Dumb as we were. Because that was the astronauts dying, though it would take us a whole four minutes to realize. I was thirteen, and there were a bunch of oriental kids and a bunch of the schoolteacher's kids. But I was there for Dr. Ronald McNair. Sure, he was the second Afro American in space, but the first had been a *Challenger* man, too. And Pop did like the name of the shuttle. Liked that the work of it all, challenge, was there in the name. My pop, he believed in things being hard. He made that known to us, me and Jenelle. Jenelle, my wild streak of a sister, who was gone by the time I got back from Florida. Like she and the space shuttle disappeared the same.

The worst thing that ever happened to me, proper, was when I was an adult. And that worst thing was your father. See, my name is Ellenora, but you and everyone from Memphis to Atlanta know that I lived with my husband's first Ellie from the beginning. The same year he parted from the other Ellie? Nineteen ninety. Same year I met Gary, married him, got in the family way, started quilting the marriage quilt. Had you not a year later. Gary never said much about that other Ellie. Some schizo white girl your father once drove across the country with. But for most of our marriage, Gary kept a picture of that one on the mantel. The bony girlfriend standing in front of their beat-up car. Family folks might think a mother-in-law is bad, but there is no way to compete with the only woman who ever loved your husband before he married you. Wife isn't power, you see. Wife is work. A marriage is a wife's challenge. Which is to say that I was a wife who felt very married.

It wasn't like that for my parents, I don't believe. The hard thing for Pop and Mama was us girls. Which is why I thank God I never had one, a girl. Instead I had only you. Though it wasn't me who was so difficult. It was my sister. True, I am loyal to Jenelle something fierce, I am. But I am her sister and so that's my place. Doesn't mean she deserves it.

We all used to watch *Star Trek*. Lieutenant Uhura, young and sharp faced. Mama would be quilting and the rest of us would be sitting with our dinner plates warm in our laps. "Jennie. Ellie. Take a look at that Nichelle Nichols," Pop would say. "Now, ain't she fine." Mama would stay quiet, stay on her quilting. But when she put us to bed she would say, "Uhura isn't just fine." Though she never would say what else.

During my marriage to Gary, we watched a world's worth of TV, but never *Star Trek.* The telly set was better company than having visitors, if I am being honest. Which I always am, honest. Visitors might see the picture of that other Ellie and have pity on me. I wanted to cut that cracker woman out. Cut her. But she'd already cut herself out. Your father taught her how to drive, then she drove away without him in a car he built with his own hands. Never giving him a good reason. He used to say he needed the picture of her to remind himself to hold on tight to me. To remind himself that I might leave him, too. I never said what I felt, which was "Why aren't *I* enough to remind you?"

It's true I put a square of a spaceship in the quilt I myself started when Gary and me married. The spaceship was just a symbol. I didn't need you to be an astronaut, son. You could be whatever you wanted to be. But a vehicle marks a boy's manhood in America, it does. Any vehicle might do—mustang or rocket. And also, your father had loved to build things that would vroom around. He said it was bikes when he was a boy, cars later. When I put my mind to marry him, I envisioned guiding him to being an airplane mechanic, a space shuttle engineer. Not exactly leaving me for wonderful, special space. No. But having a role in the great thing. I had a story like that in mind.

That being said, this here is also a story, and this story here is my truth. You see, the character of the mother always has power. A mother *is* power. All the TV shows you can ever watch make that plain.

A wife, I figured out, is something different, something powerless but never plain. When I started that quilt, my plan was to pass along your manhood from my hand to your wife's. Proper. Different from what your father had. Like my mother quilted for wealthier people, for their daughters' weddings. When I married, Mama told me she'd taught me the skill. So it would be on me to quilt for my own family. "Done enough for you girls what with all the doing I'm doing for your sister," she said.

The first patch of the quilt I did up for you was the square with you inside. That patch is still there even now, at the center. I used brown felt to make you, and I cut carefully, I did. Made you like a boiled peanut. Sweet and soft as you were from the start. Though it wasn't soft nor sweet, my marriage. Not for me. But my story of my learning to be a mother begins, I believe, years before you and Gary even showed up in my life.

That day in '86, I was thirteen and I was there. See, when Jenelle and I were wee things Pop had written to NASA to make sure the first shuttle was named after the *Star Trek* one, Uhura's ship. And so it was. Space Shuttle *Enterprise.* That name was a great success of my father's. But there was no Uhura on the real *Enterprise.* Then came the *Challenger* with Dr. Bluford, and then after him, Dr. McNair. Not fine as Uhura, but brown as her. We knew about those men in our home. And so I knew all about the *Challenger.* I had even written an essay. Pop had made me. I wrote how the very first *Challenger,* the one from the olden days, was a sea shuttle. Sailed around South Africa. I made that connection, yes, I did. With how the first *Challenger* and our *Challenger* were both important for uplifting the Black race. Got a good grade, an A, as I've told you many times. Got sent to Florida for the launch. That's how I got to my first tragedy. By being a good daughter. Obedient daughter.

Of course I wound up being a patient and kind wife to your father. At night in bed beside me Gary would whisper to the voices in his head and I would kindly and patiently hold back my tears, hold in my screaming. His speak-back voice didn't sound like his normal voice. It had a foreignness to it. It was frightening, to be true. In the mornings, I would play Al Green on the stereo, so Gary might know I was trying.

I wasn't boastful and I wasn't proud. I wasn't proud at all, actually. I was mostly ashamed. I was all that stuff the Bible required, even when it was clear Gary didn't give the Bible any primacy. I would play wild Ike and Tina, once I knew Gary liked a little wildness. I meant them as love songs for him. But he would always make me turn them down, off, when he wanted to play the Moslem music or the Jew tunes.

It was cold that day at the NASA launch. Real cold. Too cold for the South. And it was windy. We kids were right there. Waving little American flags that had been handed to us. I remember that. That year there had been a launch every few months, it seemed. Failed. Aborted. But so many successes before, so no one can blame any of us for believing. There was that teacher making news as the first teacher in space, and there was our Dr. McNair.

Still, anyone from back then will remember that there were all kinds of planes blowing up, planes being hijacked, planes falling out of the air. People just dying up there in the heavens. I'd never been on a plane, so it all seemed like space to me. That was the worst thing on TV, and it was every other night, it seemed. The best thing on TV then was "We Are the World." That was Michael Jackson and Cyndi Lauper and a bunch of others singing hard and harmonizing sweet. Like you know they must have back when they were all kids in the youth choir. The song was about saving their own American lives and some African lives, too.

Though I didn't have a full knowing yet, there it was on TV—that flight connection and that African connection. The *Challenger* right there in the worst and the best. Jenelle had a cassette of "We Are the World" and played it like it was God's own voice. I caught Mama singing along a few times, I can swear by that. Papa only said, "Song's too long. And it's not gonna save anybody's life." And then some short time after, I was there watching all those astronauts die. Couldn't rightfully tell they were dead, not from my vantage point. For weeks, it seemed like they were still on their way to the moon. I can't see what the point of death is. Death doesn't seem to make anything really go away. And that is the truth.

Take my life, for example. What is a dead first love up against a living marriage? Turns out, it's everything. Better I was a co-wife, like it's said they have in South Africa. Better me and that Ellie could stand and compete. Better we were both there in the marriage kitchen—me outcooking her, outsexing her. In the picture Gary held on to, the girlfriend has yellow hair that I could tell, even from the picture, hadn't been washed in weeks. *I* wash regularly. More classy, I am. And yet, the problem was that in the few pictures he has from his youth my husband looks as unkempt as that white woman does. He has never worn sloppy clothes like that with me. We never went for cross-country drives. He never suggested anything freaky in the bedroom, though I learned, I sure did, that he wanted a little freak. As though it was not really him with that woman. Or not really him with me. Which is to say I did fail on one of those biblical commandments, because I sure was envious of that other Ellie.

Just a picture, I tried to convince myself. Just a picture of her on the mantel. But gone people have power. Even people who have never lived at all have power. Because it started with that TV character Lieutenant Uhura. I can see that now. Now that I am looking back from the middle of this mess.

For the Halloween before, when Jenelle was fourteen and I was twelve, she dressed up as Uhura. She wore only a wig for the hair, because Jennie already had Uhura's skin and bones. I was pretty, to be sure, but not in that way. "I don't approve of you setting out alone like that," my father said that night when Jenelle left our bedroom. I wasn't going out with her. Too young for the parties, but too old for trick-or-treating. My mother had come from outside to see my sister off. But now Mama turned and went back to the garden.

"Thanks, Pop," Jenelle said, and flounced out, as though he'd said the opposite of what I knew he'd said. I'd thought, My, so that's how it works.

I wouldn't say that Jenelle came back late that night. I was still awake, after all. I heard her in the kitchen fixing something to eat. Which meant she'd been dancing. We lived in Memphis, and most everything was a dance party. Live music to start. And when the band tired, then Chaka Khan blasting from someone's car radio. I didn't sneak out to the kitchen. Sneaking wasn't allowed in our house. "Sneaking is lying," Mama would say. "Commandment number nine." Pop would whip us for sneaking. So I just walked out to my sister. Tried to be loud, so she knew I was coming.

But Jenelle was standing there with a pan in her hands like how that Arthur Ashe used to hold his tennis racket. And Pop was standing there, too. "Nichelle is pretty but she ain't a lady—kissing on that cracker," he said. Pop's right hand leaning on his cane, his left hand up like he was making a big statement. "No girl child of mine will be doing that." Honest, Jenelle and I had never watched that specific episode, the one where the captain kisses Uhura. I still won't watch it. "Don't take one step closer to me," Jenelle said to our father, "or I'll burn your face off."

It hadn't dawned on me until just then that the pan Jenelle had at the ready was filled with hot oil. And I wondered then if she would do it, burn up our father. I wanted her to, to be honest. I can't say why. Childish thinking, I suppose. "Go on and do it, then," our father said.

You have to try and see it. Jenelle was Uhura, lieutenant of the Starship *Enterprise.* Our father was just a pop in pajamas leaning on a cane. They stood that way for a long, long time. The pan must have gotten heavy because Jenelle finally put it down, turning her back to him like there was a force field around her. But Pop was already raising the cane. I left the kitchen and went back to Jenelle's and my bedroom. I can't say they ever saw me there, because they never looked my way. But back in my bed I heard them. Her screaming. Him yelling. How Mama slept through that racket, I can't say. Next day Jenelle's pretty face was fine, but she stayed in bed, the blanket wrapped around her like some space-age healing cocoon. She didn't go back to school until the bruising on her back went to normal. Took time, it did.

Some things just take time. Take, for instance, that it wasn't until after the break-in that I found out about that filthy videotape my husband kept. That's when I did a square of Gary and that other Ellie. I did. I drew them in my own hand, which was crude. You were a young man already and I was hoping you'd marry early, as I had. I pictured you and a nice young Christian Afro American girl laying up under that quilt working on grandkids for me. I'd quilted in a square of a cross from the day you were baptized. A square with some islands felted onto it, representing the paradise your father felt he was from. And a square with the letters MEMPHIS on it, so that you might know where I was from. A square of Jenelle's boy, your cousin, Brent, in his peewee uniform. Your family.

I quilted that other Ellie and your father as the final square to fit. Put them in decent clothes, not like what they ever owned when they knew each other. In the picture he had on our mantel she is wearing a hippie skirt to her ankles, and he looks to be in rags. Like the paradise they were headed to would receive them naked as the day they were born. But a red minidress for her, and a proper blue dress shirt for him, I did. Like Uhura and Spock. Why I did that, I can't rightly say. Maybe a penance for having that Ellie shunned. Maybe a way to overcome my own ungodly envy. I colored in her hair with a cloth marker. Her yellow hair. I wasn't good at it, the drawing. Still, I did it as carefully as I could. I worked on it for days that week after the break-in. What I'm telling you is that I worked hard, so hard, on my marriage. I worked it for you.

I can't really blame Gary Lovett, my husband and your father, for not letting that Ellie go in his heart. I say my husband because he's been my only one and I can't see myself doing that again. It's true I'm not much of a Christian woman these days, but I still abide by what Paul said about marriage. That it's forever. So you know why I can't fully blame the man. See, he and that Ellie, they had their first love together. I suppose that meant they were crazy together, too. The girlfriend was eighteen when they ran away to get married, though they never did manage God's blessing. I married Gary in my eighteenth year, as well—not even a year after that other Ellie drove off. But I lasted longer. I'll give myself that. I was a real something. Not like a TV show. Marriage is a real something, even if it's no good. Remember that.

My pop and mama. I can't say they had a good marriage. Can't say good was what they were after. They worked hard. They watched TV after they worked. In fact, even after that incident with Jenelle we kept watching *Star Trek* and Papa kept saying how pretty Nichelle was. But Mama didn't tuck us in to tell us that Uhuru was more than fine. We kept watching *Star Trek* until Dr. Bluford and then Dr. McNair gave us the real thing.

One thing we knew, what Pop was always going on about, was that Dr. McNair had picked cotton when he was a boy. Pop had done that, too. Still did, when we were having a hard go of it. "Gonna get you girls down there," he would say whenever we watched some news about the *Challenger*. My sister thought he meant get her down to NASA, and in our room she would ask me what I thought it would be like. "But Jennie," I would say, "you sure he didn't mean down to pick cotton on the farms?" I know for a fact that is what Pop meant.

But Jenelle didn't want any part of that. Me neither, to be honest. Which is why it was all too easy for me when Gary Lovett came singing along. No, my pop wasn't the kind of man I wanted for myself.

Gary was my get-out. Though when you were finally born a year later, 1991, I didn't drop you off with your gram and pop, like Jennie did Brent. A summer here or there with your grandparents was the most I ever allowed. Though Pop never did worry my mother as Gary worried me. The space stuff was the only thing made Pop different from other men in Memphis. See, most people in America weren't paying attention to the *Challenger* as early as 1983. But we were. Had been giving that ship our undivided attention for years. On our TV, our family watched the starship wheeled down a runway getting ready for its early missions. We watched Dr. McNair. His big smile. His big voice. His newfangled religion, even. And he was a musician. Not singing, but a sax. Still, you see how it went for me.

Gary. He had that big smile, and that big voice, and those strange religions. And he knew all about all kinds of music. The music he sang for that other Ellie had saved her, so he said. I'd believed him—in the beginning. But it became hard to know what was his crazy and what was his truth. Either way. When that Ellie left him, he stopped working on cars. Fixing things was what he'd loved as a boy and what he felt he'd failed at. It wasn't his fault. That other Ellie, she took his gift for working on cars. By the time it was Gary and me, he'd send our car to the mechanic for every doggone little thing.

And do I remember that time at the gas station. You were still a tiny thing. My breasts hard as two bags of rocks, because you never could get the feeding right. It was a too hot day and I just didn't want to pump the doggone gas, I tell you. Not with my husband in the car like that. Shaming me. So I went inside and I asked the cashier if he would do the favor. He said, "Sorry, ma'am, but I am not to leave my register." I told him that my husband was sick and could he pretty please. Where I got the gall, I can't say. The cashier was a young white boy, face prickled with pimples. Still, he came out, nodded at Gary, and pumped. On cue, Gary covered his ears, started in on the voices. Have mercy. There Gary was, asking them to left him, in that foreign accent that would take over. I watched the gas make the air look swimmy. You were in the back seat—in a fancy child chair you were always squirreling out of. But you hadn't budged since we parked. Instead you started to cry. Gary kept chanting to the voices. I kept staring at the thick sweet air swirling. Made believe I was a girl again, and there I was at the launch, watching Dr. McNair and his saxophone and his Bahá'í or what have you prayers fall from the sky to the earth.

And that white boy didn't even charge us for the gas. When Gary finally started the car and drove us away, he seemed calm. You calmed, too. It dawned on me then that maybe Gary wasn't all crazy. Maybe the voices weren't all demon. Maybe sometimes he was talking to her—that Ellie. Maybe it made him feel powerful to demand she leave him again and again. But I tried to let that go, I did. Instead, I had it in mind that maybe you might grow up and become a proper car mechanic with the certification to make it true—doing the thing your father hadn't quite managed.

That night, I tucked you in and told you how your life was good. Despite your crazy father. I told you about Dr. McNair and all that he overcame. You won't remember that, Earl. Still, I didn't tell you then about all the astronauts dying. It was a bedtime story. I told you about how Dr. McNair played that saxophone on the space shuttle as it tumbled down, a lullaby.

One day not long after I had finished the quilt I was watching the Christian channel. Not that I was really listening. Sometimes, my eyes would be on the TV but my mind would be there in Florida. Watching the *Challenger* go up and up and then explode. But there was a TV pastor asking, "Where is your marriage physically located?" I stared at the TV and focused. And I knew. My marriage wasn't in space or back in Memphis or on the mantel. My marriage was in the quilt. I held your brown boiled-peanut body in my hand, the felt cutout I'd made of you, that is, and I just knew. I turned the TV off and went and looked at the picture of the other Ellie but couldn't think of what to say to her. I searched around and found one of Gary's work shirts and cut out the pocket where his badge was. I found one of his rags that had an advertisement for bee repellent on it. Before I left the office, I turned back to that picture. "Leave us!" I said to that white girl. "Leave us alone!" Which felt like the most right thing I'd ever said, though I was saying it to a no-life picture. Then I went into our bedroom and found a clean short-sleeve that I myself had bought Gary. Something he might grill in or cut the lawn in—though it's true he never grilled a thing. The grilling was just a wish of mine, something other husbands did. I stitched all those things of the now Gary, the Gary who was *now* your father and *now* my husband, into a new quilt. I stitched in a red square because that was then your favorite color. I would rip it out for a blue one, when you changed to that instead.

I didn't play "NutBush" or any wild nonsense. Played saxophone music all through the house, like what Dr. McNair played. To give me a new inspiration for the quilt. And Gary didn't deny me that. This time, I didn't do a dignified patchwork like my mother always did. See, I'd been to the museums by then. Seen how the fancy quilts could look, how creative the quilters could be. I planned to make a great quilt of the present and the future. One that was most definitely better than my mother's. In the new one you are still there, a little boiled peanut, at the center. Your father's shirt pocket, and all that now stuff, encircling you. You see, I stitched a crazy quilt the second time around. A jazz design, like the sax I listened to. Like the thing was a maze to make your way through. Like manhood.

In that new quilt, I let everything dead go. It's true I used to imagine Gary was Dr. McNair. Before that I used to imagine Dr. McNair was Pop. No more of that, I told myself. Besides, it wasn't me, so much as my sister again, who was moved by all that space. Jenelle had gotten it into her head that she was gonna be the first Black woman astronaut. She wanted to get away from Pop. I suppose space seemed far enough.

And it did seem Pop mellowed after Jennie left. Never raised his voice or that cane again. Not far as I know. If he ever put a hand on you? Well. I made a patch of a cane in the new quilt, then drew an X over it. Then I cut out the X. Let the cane go altogether. The kind of woman's magic Mama did for us to watch and learn.

Your father had his problems, but he wasn't a man of impulsive passions, like my pop. Gary was a calm man—except for the voices. He spoke hard to the voices sometimes. Other times, though, he would sing to them. He's a singing man, my husband. Ex-husband. Sang all around our house; that is true. Hymns, chants, gospels, azans—the whole cat and cradle. He was always singing to God, Gary was. Always a different god, as he could never settle. I gather he sang love songs to that other Ellie. He never sang love for me. But you, Earl, you managed to love music, despite. I quilted in a guitar when you took lessons for a few months. Quilted in three African drums in all. Tried to make them look close to ones you had me buy you for high school graduation. Beautiful strange things. Cost me a pretty penny. By then I didn't want you to be a mechanic or even an astronaut. A musician, that is what I knew you were made for. Gary and me, we made you for that.

There is no Bible and no crosses in the crazy quilt. No pills. Nothing handicapping like that. There was a musical note, for the music that always played. There was the name of that shop where you got your first after-school job. There was your name, the one I gave you: Earl. There was you, boiled peanut, at the center. It's true, I quilted in the letters of the shuttle, but I did leave out the last one. I wanted you to have a challenge, but not one that would rise up from the past and blow you up. I never put myself in the quilt. Though of course, my hand was in the whole thing.

But you had to leave, like sons do. Not to the moon. College. I even quilted in that ugly mascot. You were close enough to drive back to me easy. I wouldn't have allowed it any other way. A long road and a white woman had ruined your father. A road and a woman can do that. Ruin the life of a man. Gary had to go and become an exterminator, getting rid of pesky things that got in the way. Rats, mice, roaches. Then me, eventually. Two years after I started my new quilt, he was packing up everything, picture of that other Ellie included. You were well into your first year of college by then.

He left me. Imagine that. And he was the crazy one. Certifiable. Took the pills to prove it. The Good Pills, I called them. Like the Good Book that we both ignored eventually. The pills made it so we couldn't have another child. The pills took that particular possibility from me. But we lived by those pills, we did. I did, anyway.

Here's something that I would say, out loud, because I want it to be known now. When I stitched that quilt to a close Gary had just left the house, but it was okay. I knew that the quilt could be done now. My marriage was done, after all. And I was sure you were on your way to a good wife. Well, even the best of us make mistakes. Look at NASA. All those smart people and look how they messed up the *Challenger.*

You know the story I've told you about the shuttle. Stories are how I made you. But here's the truth, which has nothing to do with you at all. Shuttle day found my family and me around the breakfast table, and Pop asking Jenelle to stand up. It had been some time since that incident on Halloween. There'd been a kind of peace. Though, it's true that on this morning of which I am speaking, Jenelle hadn't eaten her food. Nor had she eaten the morning before. "Stand up," Pop said. "Oh, mister," Mom said, standing up herself, "just let them go to school. Today is launch day." But, "Take off your dress," Pop said to Jenelle. Jenelle stood. And Mom started to cry and pray. "Please, God," she cried. Jenelle lifted her dress.

And there was Jenelle's belly, which I'd paid no mind to at all before. Too innocent, I was. It was tight and round, and then, right then, a little bulge punched out, like there was a space creature inside her. Pop stood up, raised his cane, and knocked my sister to the ground. Broke her collarbone. And other things, too, I guess.

Which is to say, I wasn't at the *Challenger* launch. Not really. Couldn't have been. I was in Memphis. I was on the way to the hospital with my sister. Mama driving us, though up until that day, I can't say I even knew Mama could drive. You see, a mother always has her secrets.

We waited in the waiting room for Jenelle. And that's when we saw it. Everyone crowded around the TV. The star shuttle *Challenger* gone. Rerun, rerun, rerun. Which is to say, being at the launch wasn't ever really the worst thing to happen to me, because I wasn't there at the launch at all. I've lied about that my whole life, but I won't let it go. It's my true story now, and I'm staying it through. I'm nothing if not committed. Though truth is, I didn't even watch it live on cable TV, like the kids at my school did. Still, I saw. The lines of smoke curling to the earth. Like arms stretching out to hold a person. I saw. Dr. McNair dead. Him and his saxophone and his *Challenger*. Never to be seen again.

My sister didn't come out either. She was alive. But she stayed in there. Two nights. Something about the baby. And then she didn't come back home. We didn't see her for months. I don't think Pop has ever seen her again. "Raising your sister was a challenge," Mom would say. Pop never said a thing. I always think of Jenelle pretty in that little red Uhura dress. She was something fine to look at, my sister.

Can't say the same for Gary's white chicken-leg girl. Didn't look like much in the one picture I ever saw of her. I have to guess her story is that she married religious, had babies and babies for God. Did all that nastiness with Gary and then left me with his degradation. I didn't get the chance to marry a good Christian man, thanks to her. And I didn't get a chance to have babies and babies for God. Just you. And I can't rightly say that we raised you for God. Honest to goodness? I raised you for me.

GOD'S CARAVAN

THE STORY OF HOW FLY BECAME FLY

Soulsville, Tennessee

2001

The boys were crouched in the dirt, the marbles pinging between them. Earl Lovett's biggie oily marble was blue and white, like the earth seen from the heavens. He'd already won twenty marbles by the time he noticed the music. Back home in Ellenwood, there was always singing or music playing. All day, every day. Music was a constant for Earl; it pressed onto him like a straitjacket, focused his mind. So his marbles smashed straight while the other boys' jigged. Even Earl's cousin, Brent, who had taught him to pitch that summer, couldn't keep up with Earl's streak. He'd gotten so good, he wondered if he could grow up to be a marble player. Earl's father was always going on about finding a trade.

Then the music arrived and the boys stood to receive it. Except for Earl, who stayed crouched over his catch, watching the van cruise in.

He'd been feeling the music, using it, but he registered it a bit after the others: "I've come from Alabama with a banjo on my knee." The electric megaphones were tied to the roof of the van, as if the van itself were singing.

Earl carefully placed his trophies, smooth as globes, in his pockets. Brent was older than Earl, but Earl was taller. Earl was teased for his height—"long string bean," Brent called him in front of the others. But now, when Earl stood, Brent nodded at him, as though he were finally proud to be Earl's kin. The two boys waited as the van drove into the dusty lot. On the side of the van the boys could see the words GOD'S CARAVAN painted in red letters. "Blood of Jesus" red, they would later learn.

The van parked beside the ice cream truck. The tinkling of that sweets truck suddenly sounded insignificant. And now this van, God's Caravan, reversed so that its back faced the boys. On the door was written TO HEAVEN OR BUST—also in Jesus bloodred. The electric mouths sputtered, and a man's voice came out. "When I say 'Ride or die,'" the voice announced, "you say 'Amen.'"

Now. This was the South. Memphis, Tennessee, to be specific. Soulsville, the Black part, to be exact. The marble-playing boys all understood call-and-response. "Ride or die," the electric mouths shouted. "Amen," the mouths of the boys shouted back. Earl, big-city boy but shy, rolled his loot of marbles around in his pockets. This fondling would have looked indecent if anyone had been watching. But everyone was watching the Dodge Caravan. The door, To Heaven or Bust, opened like the eye of God. And there was the pastor. Dressed in black judge's robes. There was no banjo on his knee. There was a microphone in his left hand and a Bible in his right.

The marbles in Earl's pockets grew moist from his sweaty palms, but he kept jostling them, gripping and releasing their slippery curves, knocking them into each other. "Young men," said the pastor, "welcome to God's Caravan." Earl stepped in a little closer. "Welcome," the pastor said again, and this time looked right at Earl.

Back in Ellenwood, Earl's parents used their music like music was a weapon. Mom would put on her soul music first thing Sunday morning. Dad would wake up late and blast his gospel-choir hymns, or chant his Hindu meditations at a shout. Mom would always surrender first, say it was because of Dad's voices. Schizophrenia: Gary Lovett's official diagnosis, though Earl's dad never used the word. Either way, Earl always did love his father's voice, the big brass of it singing out the Muslim call to prayer in melodic Arabic.

Pastor John introduced himself as the driver of God's Caravan. He had one of those voices, but with a confidence that had never alighted on Earl's father. The other marble boys tilted their heads back, looked at this newcomer the way they'd looked at Earl on his first day there that summer, as if a stranger might be a lit match.

"I've got sweets for your heart," the pastor said, waving his hand dismissively in the direction of the cherry-pop truck. The truck tinkled. The ice cream man, Mr. Dick, he called himself, opened his driver's-side door so that the tinkling stopped. Earl saw this, saw it as a sign, and again stepped a little closer to God's Caravan. In his pockets, the marbles were glass worlds, a constellation quaking furiously against his thighs.

Earl wasn't a bold boy. He couldn't sing as well as his father, couldn't dance as well as his mother. Didn't have siblings to show him that failure was routine, that a child could never outrun a parent. Siblings, his mother sometimes said pitifully, were the ones you sharpened yourself against. In fact, this was why Earl had been sent to Soulsville that summer—his mom said he was getting too soft. Which Earl wasn't sure meant soft in body or soft in the head. His father, potbellied and crazy brained, was both. Earl figured he'd been sent to live with his grandparents and cousin for the summer so that he didn't turn into his dad. But Earl was bony of body, and the only voices he ever heard unbidden in his mind were those of the singers on the records his parents were always playing.

Earl's cousin was the performative one. Older, better at masking his typical insecurities. Teaching Earl how to dance, Brent had told his cousin to imitate him, jerking his waist back and forth and singing "El, take my wood" in a moan. Earl from Ellenwood was still too young; didn't understand the reference to wood, but he did understand that the moaning was about sex, somehow. Which meant that it was bad, and worse, because Earl's mother's name was Ellenora: Ellie to his dad, but El to her family. Aunt El to Brent. Still, Earl, knowing his inadequacy, mimed the movements and the words until his cousin squatted into hiccupping laughter. So, of course, punk as any ten-year-old, Earl had ratted this cousin out. Demonstrating for their grandparents the moans and shakes, the made-up lyrics, even. His grandfather had smacked him, Earl, over the head. Told him to stop being such a snitch. Earl had cowered and cried, cold-hated his grandfather for a full two days. Was determined to hate Pop and Brent forever. Called his mom and begged her to come get him. "Did Pop hit you?" she asked in the same voice she asked his father if he'd taken his pills. Earl had lied, said no—that snitch accusation had gotten to him. "Then don't be crazy," his mother had said. Earl would serve the summer out.

But then Pop had brought home a video of "Thriller" and played it for the boys—all the horror and the girlfriend-boyfriend touchy stuff. And Earl could see that his cousin's moves, the moaning, even, were straight from MJ. Which made it better, somehow. Earl practiced the moonwalk in private. Though it never felt smooth, always felt forced. He could never figure out what to do with his hands, his face.

But that day in Soulsville, the music wasn't Michael Jackson. It wasn't even "Oh! Susanna," as the singing van had suggested. "Susanna" was Pastor John's signature. His entrance and exit music. But once the pastor burst out from the back of the van, he'd preach a new song. They called it "music ministry" at Grace Baptist, Gram and Pop's church. Pastor John's music was coon, not hymn, though Earl didn't know that terminology yet.

"You are not the future," Pastor hummed to the children, looking around the group, but always landing on Earl—so it seemed to Earl, anyway. "No, suh! You are spirits from the past, yes, come to save us from the present, oh yes." Then he began singing a song. The lyrics were strange but easy: *Coon on the moon, oh yes, we on the moon.* The boys laughed, slapped one another demonstratively on the back, but they sang along. All except Earl, now urgently self-conscious. How did he look? Was he standing strongly? Did he look as soft as he felt? He clutched the marbles until their hardness hurt his fingers. He didn't sing. He stared.

No one even heard Mr. Dick steer the Softee ice cream truck down the street and away.

◆ ◆ ◆

Pastor John hummed stories. Biblical, he said, though no one had ever read any of them in the New King James Version. Boy Jesus withering the hand of a child who'd stolen his favorite toy. The toy, a carving of a boat that Joseph had made for him. The thief boy had cried and cried, Pastor John said. Who wouldn't, with those frozen fingers? But spiteful kid Jesus had pouted, refused to make the hand well again.

"And guess who that little thief grew up to be?" Pastor asked. Earl was already standing apart. He felt the pastor asking him. Him, specifically. Earl had never stolen anything. His father lectured him often about stealing. Dad had said kidnapping was a form of stealing: stealing a person. If Earl ever stole, well—karma, he'd get stolen, too. Sure, Dad was always saying weird things to Earl. But now Earl really wanted to answer the pastor's question the right way. Maybe it was a trick question.

Maybe his cousin, who stole Now and Laters, was the thief? Wasn't that how this all worked, applying the Scripture to your own life? None of the boys answered.

Pastor John shook his head, disappointed in them—or maybe just in Earl. "Saint John," the pastor said. "The thief was the beloved apostle Saint John." Now the pastor's voice rose, a lifting, courageous thing all by itself. "Oh, yes! Jesus's best friend! He was the thief! The one who would rest his wizened hand on Jesus's bosom. You see . . ." He paused to look at the boys. "You see, Jesus loved even his enemy. He even put his own mother in John's care. You hear?" Earl heard.

In fact, he'd only recently heard about the beloved apostle at all. When his parents had brought him to Soulsville for the summer, Gram and Pop had made them all, parents included, go to Grace Baptist as one big family. During the reading about the beloved apostle, Earl's father had said, "Sounds like Jesus is a faggot." Loud enough for people to turn around. "Gary," Ellenora had said through her teeth. She shot her own parents a look, hugged her one and only son closer to her. Away from his father. Brent had cracked up so hard that Pop had to drag him out of the sanctuary.

So now Earl heard. Heard Pastor John speak about the apostle John. Earl looked over at his cousin and smiled a forced smile. He hoped it looked forgiving. Earl, for sure, had wanted to shrivel Brent's arms and nose when Brent had beaten him at marbles the Sunday before, and before that, when Brent had laughed at Earl's father in church. Once, Earl had wished leprosy on a kid from school who teased him for being a dope, even though Earl was older and taller and, according to his mother, more handsome and more smart. "Those kids are just jealous of you," his mother had said. Though who could be jealous of a boy with no brothers and a lunatic dad? Earl had prayed for an African famine to visit his entire school. And then there'd been a food shortage for a week, hot dogs with a drop of ketchup every single day. Which, as far as Earl was concerned, could mean only one thing—he had Bible-like powers. Some kids at his school dreamed of being Spider-Man—but Earl dreamed of being the Messiah.

That day God's Caravan left with the sun. Shouted "Oh! Susanna" into the sunset. Brent turned to Earl. "That sure was better than church," he said. Earl nodded, feeling a compulsion coming over him. His hands were still in his pockets, now squeezing and releasing the gathering of globes. The other boys were looking at him—maybe wondering what his hands were doing. One by one, Earl took each cloudy world out of his pockets and returned to each boy what he had won from him. Then Brent and Earl walked toward home, singing, "Coon on the moon, oh yes, we on the moon." Like that was a completely peachy thing for Black boys to be singing in the birthplace of Stax Records and the deathplace of Martin Luther King Jr. They just walked into their grandparents' house in Soulsville singing that. The bass-beating nineties were over. The president was a fun-loving cowboy. The hit song was performed by a multiracial group of women. It was summer 2001. There was nothing in America to worry about. Nothing at all.

And yet there was something a little bit strange about Pastor John and his Caravan. What was it? At Grace Baptist Church people were always catching the spirit. To Earl, who knew best the foreign faiths that his father brought home, this very American thing of catching the spirit looked like getting sexy with Jesus. Which was why Gram always covered Earl's eyes when a woman at Grace Baptist went into ecstasy. As if it was pornographic. But "You have so much potential," Earl's mother was always saying. Up till now, Earl had been certain that having potential was just another way of being a disappointment. But that day, with God's Caravan, he was sure he'd felt the spirit. Felt better than potential for sure.

When Earl and Brent finally got home, Gram was in her chair in the sitting room working on a quilt. She sat, as she always did, right beneath a photo of a grinning President Clinton. The first Black president, people were always saying, confusing Earl. Now Gram looked up at the president and then straight at her grandboys. "I know," she said, as if Clinton had told her. "I know already, so you might as well fess up."

Over supper, Earl spilled everything about Pastor John the Baptist. It was the first time he didn't feel self-conscious at dinner. Didn't worry even once whether he should eat the chicken with fork or fingers. Earl was too busy pontificating. Because he'd been special, hadn't he? Had stood a little apart. Pop chewed slowly, fighting a smile or a snicker. But Earl was sure, sure that the Caravan was a sign of something about himself. A sign for him—Earl.

Earl's father was always seeing signs. Dad said that Jesus was a white man's God, and so would never be enough for them as Black men in America. He'd met Earl's mother just months after he arrived in Memphis. Mom's older sister had been kicked out of the house, and Mom was rebellious (her own word), was skipping out on church. She hadn't minded Gary's Buddhism, and then his Jainism and then his Orisha-ism. Though these days? Well, it seemed to Earl that Mom minded quite a bit. But Dad never stopped being a believer. It was his beliefs that kept changing. Dad's only enduring belief was that spraying the house with DEET could keep his son and wife safe from every harm.

Though Gary took the pills, and Earl could see that the pills were something to be ashamed of—his mother certainly was ashamed of them—Gary was still Earl's father, and Earl still learned from him about signs and metaphors. So Earl was a believer, too. Though sometimes he couldn't help being plenty ashamed of his belief. But this with Pastor John the Baptist was different. This was good old American Jesus Christ that the pastor was talking about. And Gram didn't think it was crazy. Gram was smiling.

"I always knew you boys would find the Lord some way or other," she said, not a drop of doubt in there. But Gram wasn't looking at Earl, she was looking at Pop—daring him to disagree. Pop cleared his throat, looked at Earl and then at Brent. But he didn't say a thing. He went back to his plate, which was already scraped clean. He scraped it some more. Put the bare fork to his mouth, chewed the air.

Pop went with the boys the next Sunday. He walked with his cane, even though the whole of Soulsville knew that Pop didn't need that cane for walking. Brent and Earl dressed in church slacks and button-downs—Gram had insisted that nobody change into what she called their "pitch clothes." Pop wore his hat with the stingy brim. Earl carried his own two cloudy marbles in his pocket. Gripped them the way his father gripped his own fists when the voices came on. Earl kept imagining that there were two entire worlds in his pocket. He wondered how many saviors these worlds might need.

They walked in a row, the grandfather and the grandsons. Pop in the middle. Back in Ellenwood, Earl rarely walked around with his own dad like this. Couldn't actually remember if he ever had. They drove around, mostly. Dad liked cars, had built one, so he said, with his own hands. Though Earl had never seen any evidence of such a skill.

In fact, Earl didn't much know his father besides the weird stuff. Didn't think his father much knew him, either. Did he and his father even like each other? Hadn't Earl wished his father dead more than once? Just last month, to be true. Wished he would just leave Earl and Mom to their own simple joys—no voices, no chanting back at the voices in his island accent, no clenched fists, no long drives where Earl and Mom sat in the car quietly, Earl agonizing over whether the voices would tell Dad to drive the car over a cliff. Dad always wanted Earl and Mom to come on these drives. "Leave," Earl wanted to say to his father. Just leave us. A premonition? Perhaps.

Dad did always seem to like Earl better when they were apart from each other. The same way he sometimes seemed to like his long-gone girlfriend better than he liked Mom, who was his longtime wife. Dad had a picture of the girlfriend, pale skinned with flat hair, on the fireplace in the living room. Right there beside the big family portrait of Mom, Earl, and Dad together. The family one was done professionally, in a photography studio. The one of the girlfriend was taken by Dad. And there she was, up on the mantel with them, like she was family, too. Sometimes Earl wondered what he would be like if that girl had been his mother. He would look almost white, more like Jesus, maybe.

Last night Earl and Dad had talked on the phone for almost thirty minutes while Dad was driving to a job. They had never spoken that long in person. And on Dad's cell phone, for goodness' sake. Mom hated the cellular. Dad was the only person in Ellenwood, in all of Atlanta, who had a little Nokia phone, or so it seemed. That shiny thing with the creepy blue light made him look like he had a huge night beetle against his head. Appropriate, given his line of work. Which was also what he insisted he needed it for: emergency bug infestations. Earl was embarrassed by the phone. Embarrassed by his father in general. But still, on the phone they'd talked and talked about marbles and music and being a man. Dad's voice had sounded like tin, but Earl tried not to let that bother him. He liked the curly wire of Gram and Pop's corded phone—he'd wound his finger around and around inside it until the finger turned blue.

Now Earl and Brent and Pop walked toward the ice cream truck, Pop's cane smacking the ground like a warning. Dad would never carry a cane to beat a pastor. Earl couldn't figure out if that meant he finally had a reason to be proud of his dad, or if this was another reason to be ashamed. Earl had never been spanked or beaten, but Brent had. Displayed a long scar on his lower back like a war wound.

Mr. Dick of the Mister Softee truck took Pop's money skittishly. Served Brent and Earl their cones quickly. Mr. Dick was also waiting. Anxious as everyone else. Two of the other marble-pitching boys were there. Brothers who had come in their marble-playing clothes, though they didn't squat in the dirt once they saw Pop. Three other boys came, too, each with a father or grandfather beside him.

This time, Earl felt the Caravan coming. Felt the worlds jangle in his pocket. He didn't start swaying like the other boys did. But he could feel the music. Could hear the time before he heard the song. When God's Caravan came into fuller sight and sound, Mr. Dick turned down the Softee jingle, letting Pastor John the Baptist's singing take over the street: *The buckwheat cake was in her mouth, the tear was in her eye.* Pop was moving his own head side to side in a tiny switch. As the van came crawling, everyone could see now that Pastor himself was driving.

Pastor reversed the van until it was again in the abandoned lot, with its back bumper facing the boys. They'd all seen this time that in the driver's seat he was wearing a simple white cassock. But when the back door opened, he was wearing his black preacher's robe—the judge's robes—his mic in one hand and his Bible in the other, and he was sweating as though he'd been preaching for an hour already. And now, "Welcome," he sang. "Welcome, children and brethren." He nodded to the fathers and grandfathers. And to Mr. Dick. "Welcome, oh welcome, to God's Caravan."

The song he sang was "Catch a Nigger by the Toe." Then he told the story of Jesus racing a Roman chariot from Jerusalem to Jericho. The men and the boys listened to the story as if they were sitting by the radio, listening to an announcer shout the Preakness.

"You just might be the new Jesus riders!" Pastor John the Baptist exclaimed in his finale. He patted the Bible to his head, like a handkerchief. "And you"—he pointed the Bible at Earl—"you ain't blinked since I started singing last week." Earl blinked for him. "Ahh," the pastor said. "You won't ride at all, will you, son? You fly."

Earl felt the words, the attention, go through his eyes and through his ears and right into his brain and down to his what? Synopses? He was only going into fifth grade, so he didn't know the science or the story of it. But it would be safe to say that he felt the pastor's words, "You fly," down wherever his self was. A little push in a new direction of who Earl might be. He'd won two pocketfuls of marbles last week, and he'd done the honorable thing and returned them all. And now here was the pastor, signaling him out special. So Earl walked right up to the van. He was close enough that had the door shut, he might have ended up inside.

"I don't know how to fly," he said quietly, his toes curling in his shoes. Earl was scared of the pastor's sweaty face, and of Brent thinking he was a punk, and of the marble-playing boys not wanting to play marbles with him anymore. But he was also brave. This was maybe the first time in his life he'd really thought this. In his shoes his feet were so clenched they felt like fists.

The pastor, for his part, hadn't stopped looking at Earl. "You don't need to know how to fly," Pastor said seriously and loudly, looking down on Earl with his swarthy, dripping face. "I said you Fly." Which Earl understood.

On the phone later, his parents on the landline together now, Earl asked them to call him Fly. He'd never really felt like the Earl his mother had named him. But he'd sure felt more like flight than fight his whole life. Dad obliged, switched up right there on the phone. "Sure thing, Fly," Gary said, and never went back.

Pop was serious at dinner. Gram rattled off her day. The blue quilt was coming along. But Sister Loretta at church wanted one for her grandbaby, and that one had to be pink. Every quilt the family slept beneath had been made by Gram's own hands. The eggplant in the garden was growing big and purple. Gram wanted to put sweet potato in the ground, but knew well the wrath of sweet potato. They were eating food that'd come from "the family garden," as she graciously called it. Gram went on. Finally, she asked what the men had gotten themselves into. As if it weren't she herself who had sent Pop with the boys to meet Pastor John. Earl had never been called a man before.

"The pastor didn't even collect money," Pop began. "He only shouted ragtime songs and then told some Jesus stories. Strange as a steak in a shrimp catch, but good stories."

"Mister," which is what Gram always called Pop. "Mister, what on God's good earth are you talking about?"

"I'm talking about that pastor singing songs that made me feel bad, honestly. Though they felt good in the music. And then telling stories about Jesus feeling bad, having greed and being competitive in nature—but also still being the Christ. Stories, I must admit, that I was willing to stand in the sun and dirt to hear. Never felt that staying feeling at Grace Baptist."

This, for sure, was the gift John the Baptist had. There was something to his stories, something in his author-ness, his authority. After the men and boys had all walked away from the van, Pastor had called after them: "Even Jesus wept!" That night, after supper, with Gram quilting and Pop watching TV on low, Fly heard his grandparents begin to argue in their quiet, passive way: Was the pastor a charlatan or a genuine man of God?

Fly was in the bed he shared with his cousin. He knew the answer, so he forced himself to tears. Brent was deciphering a Rubik's Cube beside him, and was pretending not to hear his grandparents arguing or his cousin crying. After he locked the cube into place, fast enough to make Fly stop his weeping, Brent dug his hand beneath their mattress. Pulled out a shoe polish container, but inside were Life Savers Gummies—which Fly had seen advertised on TV but his parents had never bought for him. "These here are magic Life Savers," said Brent. Fly ate four. "Slow down," Brent said, and snatched the tin back. He passed Fly the colorful cube and Fly began to twist it and turn it and twist. The turning alone became a dance, an elegant movement. The smooth clicking of the tiles sounded like fingers snapping. "This is the best toy I have ever played with ever," Fly said.

"It's not the Rubik's," said Brent. "It's the gummies. They have drugs in them. Not superbad ones. Just a little bad one. So don't go ratting us out. Just tiny bad. Like kissing a girl, but not like fingering her." Fly had no idea what Brent was talking about. But he knew he wanted to cry again. But this time he wanted to cry because the world was strange and scary but he now knew he was brave and stranger. So he cried some more. Brent chewed two and then two more of the life-saving gummies. Then he cried, too. Then they laughed at each other crying. And laughed more. Then they fell asleep because they needed a rest from all that laughing.

◆ ◆ ◆

The next Sunday, Gram came to the pitch. And so did other mothers, and more fathers and brothers and some uncles and aunts. Even a girl showed up. When God's Caravan came up the street, Pastor John the Baptist sang his usual "Oh! Susanna," and someone's uncle fell to his knees. "Oh, sugar, that's my song," the man shouted, making Fly wonder if the man was a little crazy, like Dad. But no one else seemed to think so. "That's my godforsaken song!" the man said. The sun beat down, but the man did not get up. Not even during the story sermon.

Pastor told the parable of the ten brides who all fell asleep and missed their wedding day. The brides had been so busy getting ready that they were exhausted, missed their own party. The guests danced and drank without them. Their husbands married each other instead. "This was not meant for you!" Pastor said. "You are not meant to sleep meekly and wait. Earth is not for you to inherit when you die. The earth will die someday, don't you know. Hear me! What you want is to inherit everlasting life!" The song they sang then was "No Such Thing as a Good Nigger." And then Fly understood, for the first time, that there were actual people who'd think he was weak because they thought he was a nigger. He was ten years old, a Black kid from the South, but he'd never thought about that before.

The kneeling uncle looked around with his palms up to the sky. Something got into Fly. Like with the marbles. An impulse from his deep self. Or maybe it was the handful of Life Savers he and his cousin had shared before leaving the house. Or maybe it was the Holy Spirit. Or maybe it was all the same. Fly just walked up to that man and placed his hand on that man's shoulder. "Not meek," Fly said.

The man looked to the sky as if the clouds had spoken. He stood, just like that. Fly gave that man his manhood. This wasn't potential, this was achievement. The Jesus kind.

Gram wept on the walk back to the house. At supper, she asked Fly, though she called him Earl, to say the blessing over the food. While Fly prayed, his knees stopped bouncing, his shoulders loosened, his hands stayed still, pressed to each other. He kept praying, giving grace and more grace, all the grace feeling so good in his body to say and give, until Brent kicked him in the shins—twice. After the meal, Fly went to the bedroom he shared with his cousin. He kneeled on the bed and punched their one pillow rhythmically, as if he were training for something.

On the fourth Sunday, Pastor John the Baptist sang "Every People Has a Flag but the Coon," and then he shared Communion. He used a loaf of rich bakery bread. He gave Fly the basket to pass around. Fly carried it and watched the basket feed everyone. Like the loaves and fishes. Pastor passed around the wine. Real wine, not like the grape juice at Grace Baptist. Pastor had one large bottle, and he let everyone take a sip. Children, too. Fly let the wine touch his lips, felt it warm and tasted it bitter, even burning. "Like real drugs," Brent said.

"No body hungry," the pastor hummed. "No body thirsty. No famine. No war."

It wasn't a new church. No one stopped going to Grace Baptist. Pastor John didn't ask that of them. God's Caravan was a complementary church, a little extra on the side.

On the fifth Sunday, Gram brought one of her quilts. After everyone sang "Every Coon Looks Alike," she presented it to Pastor John. Giving away a quilt was something Fly's own mother had never done—she'd been working on the same quilt as long as Fly could recall. Now John the Baptist unfurled Gram's quilt with an expert flourish. "The doors of God's Caravan are open," he said. The flag of quilt shivered in front of him. "Somebody today loves his wife like she is mortal instead of loving her like she is divine. No, no, no," he said, singing. "Somebody here today has wondered why on earth she was put on this earth. She doesn't know she herself made this earth." Now he shook the quilt as if the people, his parishioners, were bulls. "Some child here wonders if he was meant to be banker or thief or the first real Black president of the United States. Oh, you have all got to come to Jesus!" And then he held the quilt in one swaying hand and stretched the other to the sky.

With his open arms, it was clear that "come to Jesus" and "come to me" could be the same thing. Which meant that the pastor was, in a way, Jesus just then. Fly, of course, walked to him. As he passed, his grandmother patted the air with her palms out and her fingers down. Pushing him along by magic.

But what, really, was Fly thinking? That he would be saved? That the spirit would come over him and he would know how to dance? Really dance, like the un-wifed women at Grace Baptist? That all his dreams of being cool and socially adept would come true? When Fly climbed into the back of God's Caravan, he expected the pastor to anoint him in front of the others. Press his oiled fingers into Fly's forehead. Declare Fly blessed and bless-ed. But what Fly thought might happen and what really happened were two different things. As he stepped up into the van and stooped to face the crowd, the Dodge door closed like a jaw. *Bam.* Just like that, he and the pastor were alone together in darkness.

"What the hell are you doing, kid?" Pastor whispered in a worried-sounding tone. His voice revealed a new set of sounds, an accent like Fly's father's when the voices came on.

Fly couldn't see the pastor at all, it was so dark, but still he whispered back. "You told me to come." The darkness seemed so dark it sparkled.

"I did, did I." Fly couldn't tell if this was a question or a statement, so he thrummed his fingers on the sides of his thighs, and waited. Pastor said, "Now. What will *you* do?"

"I will . . ."

"Exactly!" Pastor commanded. "Will is all we have. What's your name?"

Fly was sure Pastor knew—he'd given him the name, after all—but this was a test. "Fly," Fly said.

"Fly, Fly. Will is all we have."

Fly was crouched in the van so his head wouldn't hit the ceiling. His brains felt swimmy, as if he could see his and Pastor's voices. He figured maybe this was what Dad felt sometimes. He didn't know what to say, so he kept waiting, he began to count out the taps of his fingers on his legs until, "Take my hand," John the Baptist said. So Fly put his hands out in the dark until he felt them gripped. The pastor's hands were cool and moist, as if he'd been cradling ice cubes. Fly felt every groove in the man's palms.

"Let's figure out who you really are."

Fly breathed. He was ready. Ready to find out that he could really dance and sing "Beat It" as well as Brent. But instead Pastor began to pray. He prayed for Fly's safety. He prayed for Fly to make positive friendships. For Fly to grow up and marry a good woman. For Fly to be a stand-up father someday. For Fly to know his destiny and pursue its perfection until his dying day. Fly's head rocked pleasantly, until the rocking felt like too much pleasantry and he wanted to throw up.

"You know," Pastor said. "You know, dear Lord, you should not even be alive now." But Fly couldn't tell if Pastor was talking to him and calling him Lord or if he was still praying to God and saying that God should be dead.

The door eased open again and Fly squinted. Pop was there, like he was getting ready to charge in. Gram was standing with her hands flat on either side of her face, like she was in shock. The rest of the crowd stood still, as if they were on the verge of a major action.

"They told you," Pastor announced to the crowd, "that you wanted to be white. And after a while you began to believe it." He turned to Fly now. Pastor was not singing. He was not humming. "Do you renounce the thing in you that makes you renounce yourself?"

Fly alone answered, "I do."

"Will you strive to use your gifts no matter how they manifest?"

Fly didn't stumble or stutter. "I will."

"Ride or die."

"Amen."

◆ ◆ ◆

Back at Gram and Pop's house, Fly called his mother in Ellenwood. "Was I not supposed to be alive? Was I almost not born?"

There was silence on the other end of the line.

"Mom?"

"Sorry, I'm sure I misheard you."

He had to ask the question two more times. And then she finally answered with: "What have those grandparents been telling you?" As if they weren't her own parents.

"A pastor told me."

She sighed. "There was a pregnancy before you. It's what made me and your father marry so fast. But then all of a sudden I wasn't pregnant. I don't know why I'm telling you this. This isn't the kind of thing I would tell. But here you go. When I was pregnant the second time, your crazy father said it had also been you the first time, that you didn't want to be in the world. Like you'd committed suicide in my belly the first time. The miscarriage. Can you imagine a father saying that? I mean, have mercy. But who knows, maybe he was right in a way. He's like that. Crazy, but right. Because when you were born you weren't breathing. I'm sure you've heard this part before. Even the nurse started screaming that you were dead. What a fool, that woman. Your father held you and told you square in the face that it was time to stop this nonsense. Right now, he told you. And you came to. Just like that."

Then Fly heard his mother start to cry. He remembered that Jesus wept, too, and so he cried with her until his father came on the line and asked what was going on. "Fly," he said. "Do not have your mother crying."

◆ ◆ ◆

The next Sunday, Fly showed up early and alone. When Pastor John the Baptist came into view, Fly walked to the edge of the road to meet his Caravan.

This time Pastor turned on a little lamp, so there was light as they searched together for the basket. The back of the van was filthy. One fluffy chair with its soft guts bursting out, dust on the floor so thick that Fly felt his shoes slipping in it. He let them slip a little, let himself slide a little. Fly was high again. The near-blue chair looked like the sky, the fluff was clouds. Anyone who sat in that chair would be God. But Fly was also confused by the mess, because it was a mess—and wasn't cleanliness next to godliness?

"Pastor, why did you come here?"

"For you," he said.

"Why me?" Fly asked, unsurprised, but unsure.

"Why you what?"

It took Fly a minute to think about this. The ice cream truck wasn't there yet. The marble-playing boys and their families were gathering in the yard, but for now it was just Pastor and Fly. The question felt to Fly like a riddle. Like the kind of thing Jesus would ask the disciples and hardheaded Peter would always get wrong. Fly and Brent were getting Life Saver high every Sunday before church now, like a regular sacrament. It made Fly feel smart, so now he could sense the angle here. A kind of aim he had to take.

"Why am I here?" Fly asked, keeping all the words flat the way Pastor did, so the meaning couldn't be obscured.

"Oh, that's easy, acolyte."

Pastor bent to touch each of Fly's eyelids, and to Fly it was as if Pastor's finger contained the brightness of a wand. "Love," Pastor said.

"That is your purpose." And Fly, for the first time, felt that particular possibility swell in him. Love was his calling.

"But now it's time for another purpose," Pastor said.

And that day the money collection began. Fly stretched the basket out, and people just started filling it with bills. As if they'd been waiting, ready to unburden themselves. The basket could never hold enough, kept overflowing no matter how many times Fly emptied it. Like a mirror to the one that had carried the loaves.

◆ ◆ ◆

Pastor John the Baptist saved souls and souls that summer. He sang his coon songs and told his Jesus stories that no one could ever quite find in the Bible. "Your mind," he sang one Sunday when summer was almost over, "is your spiritual organ. That's where God is." Fly's mind felt sane and filled with God. Whenever Pastor left singing "Oh! Susanna," Fly was sure that Susanna was the name of the girl he would love. He wanted to sing that song for a pretty girl the way Pastor sang it to God. Working on a bit of Life Saver stuck in his back teeth, Fly allowed himself to think something grand: perhaps his father's mind simply held more God than most.

But then one Sunday Pastor didn't show. And then he didn't show the next. And then Mr. Dick stopped lowering his ice cream music. And then summer came to an end and Fly flew back to Atlanta. Later, Brent called to tell Fly the rumors that Pastor had first come from New Orleans. Not Alabama. There God's Caravan had been the Cathedral Cruiser and *Father* John had performed High Catholic Mass from the back. He'd placed a dark curtain in his driver's window. People would just line up at the car and whisper their confessions through a hole in the cloth. After Memphis, Reverend John moved north—so Brent said. Became the Jehovah Motor.

As Fly listened to this story, his fingers pressing the phone to his ear, Brent's voice sounded distracted, as if he were solving a Rubik's Cube, or something even more complex like algebra or the Fibonacci sequence. And Fly felt like a fool. The most foolish. His fingers on the receiver were grasping so tight they hurt. But he couldn't hang up on his cousin, who was killing Fly's greatest possibilities just by telling the truth.

Fly brought his marbles home from Memphis that summer. But he never played again. Never really learned to dance. And yet Fly could never say that he stopped believing. Could never renounce the man, not his father, who had saved him that summer.

OTHER WOMEN

FLY'S COMING-OF-AGE STORY

Ellenwood, Georgia

2007

Okay. So. My mom had adult blockers on our internet. She'd searched "Black women," getting all, you know, inspired by Michelle Obama. But instead of Mrs. Obama—some skanky images of Black women giving head to white dudes. That's what came up. Mom freaked. So, me? No internet porn. No internet, if it wasn't for school. Which was fully okay with me. Because I was pretty much against anything with a cord or battery. Analog and believing in Jesus—those were my rebellions. My sex ed was mostly magazines. Two of them my dad had given me on the low. Not because he's analog. No. My dad is into all the tech crap. He thinks it gives him an edge over other people. That matters to him because he's so messed up, you know? I mean, I respect him, he's my dad and I love him and all. But, well. Anyway, he had magazines only because he was old. And back when he was young and sex was a thing for him, magazines was all there was. But the magazines he gave me were so hard-core they made me feel sort of bad—for me, for him, for all the women in the world. He'd left them under my pillow, like a horny tooth fairy or something. But no one ever knew I had the video. I barely could admit it to myself.

I was about sixteen when it all went, for real, to hell. Dad sensed something was wrong before we entered the house. Put his hand up, calling for quiet. I responded instinctively and hushed. If Dad was hearing voices he couldn't take anybody else speaking. But my mom used the opportunity to get a word in to me. "You could have played harder, Earl. Why do you think the coach kept you on the bench? When you're on the court you look like you don't care. I wouldn't want you on my team either."

"Ellie, shut up." Which was enough to quiet my mother. Because, yo, Dad never spoke to her like that. He spoke to the voices that way. But not to Mom.

We were entering the house from the garage, which was lined with all his state-of-the-art flytraps, glue traps, and live-catch traps. He opened the door slowly. We all peered in. Was Dad seeing things now? Oh, man. I used to get nightmares like that. That his craziness would get crazier, you know? That he'd start speaking in tongues, jerking his body without control, seeing things that weren't there or start calling Mom by his first girlfriend's name. They had way too similar names—Eloise for the white girl, Ellenora for my mom. But now looking in the door, even I could see that our familiar house was, like, super strange. I couldn't tell, at first, why. Dad walked in ahead of us and we followed quietly.

Okay. So I haven't mentioned that there were also my pictures. My first day of life. My kindergarten graduation. Me at ten—a round number that my mother felt called for a portrait. Me, a couple of years before on my first day of high school. The picture of Dad and my mother in front of the house the day they moved in. Sweet, like. Me in her belly. The photos weren't scattered around like on the floor or anything, but there was something, you know, off about them.

There was also, weirdest of all, the picture of my dad's old girlfriend, who just, like, up and left him. That pic was real tiny, because my mom wouldn't allow a bigger one. But Dad insisted on a picture. "To remind me to hold on tight to you," he would tell Mom. And, yo, that line worked for years. But when I came in the house that day and looked at that pic, I for real knew it was off. It wasn't in its usual place far off to the left. It was closer to my high school picture. Like my dad's old girlfriend and me were siblings or something.

And there was also my dad's plump chair. Just where I'd left it, pulled up closer to the TV than he liked. But there was now a plate beside the chair. A half-eaten plate of my mother's meatloaf she'd told me to save for dinner. And I'd obeyed. Because that was the kind of kid I mostly was. It wasn't me who'd eaten it. I looked at that plate and then I looked at the pics and I could see that someone had turned all the pictures on the mantel to face the chair, like my parents and me and that ex-girlfriend were part of the view.

But then, real whoa. All of Dad's old VHS cassettes and DVDs were off the shelves. Piled up in, like, a pile. Like someone had watched each of them, but just not bothered to put them back.

"God, Ellie," Dad said. "Ellie, God damn it. We've been robbed."

"Don't be crazy," she said. She made to rake past my father. "That doesn't even make sense." But he, for real, grabbed and, like, kinda pushed her.

Then Mom and Dad sort of struggled, which was, like, wow. Mom was always kinda, like, chill, and momlike, with Dad. Her aggression always passive. Afraid to set Dad off into voices. And Dad always saved his loud voice for the voices, you know. Would drive, drive for, like, half a day, before he raged at either of us. But now Mom was pulling away from Dad and looking to run off into the house. And I'd never seen them do anything like that before. But I'd seen enough made-for-TV movies to know that it was my job as the son to intervene. "Stop, Dad. Stop." Which I said in a calm, commanding way, just as I'd seen on a Saturday special about Ike and Tina Turner my mom and I had watched together.

But then my dad did something I can't even quite imagine him doing. You know? But I saw it with my own eyes, so I can testify. He grabbed my mother by the neck. Yup. And then he dragged her like that from the threshold. "The robber could still be in there, Ellie. Could have a gun. Won't care for your value. Now, get you both back in the car." Which, yo, we did. I was sixteen, but I wanted to straight cry. I'd never seen my father so sure of himself. So in control. He backed the car out to the curb. In the back seat my knee just started bouncing up and down. Usually when I caught my body doing weird stuff like that, I would force myself to stop. I would clench my leg muscles, try to be strong enough to halt the momentum. But now my other knee just started bouncing, too. I looked down at my knees and said the Our Father. Said it twice, and then my knees stilled.

From the car, Mom and I watched the house stare us down silently. My dad stood in the street to call the police on his cell phone. His new cell was a tiny thing that looked like pretend in his hand. By those days, it was cool to have a dad with a cell phone. But not to me, okay? Dad showed it off all the time, like how the worst dads were always showing off their pistols. Straight embarrassing. Speaking of which—our neighbor, a white man whose kid hated me for no reason, came out to his porch and raised his hand to us like a salute. Mom and I stayed in the car and just, like, nodded back. Those neighbors had a huge pool with a slide and a diving board. The only one like it in all of Ellenwood. I'm just guessing.

When my father got off the phone, my mother rubbed the back of her neck dramatically. "You didn't have to do that," she said. "You could have just *said*. You could have just *communicated*. I'm a real person, you know." Now, I didn't know whose side to take. Even before they got divorced, I'd always felt like their bridge and their water.

When the police came, it was three of them and they were white. We had Black cops in Atlanta, even in Ellenwood, even back then. But that day white is what we got. My dad stepped out of the car. My mother applied lipstick and followed. I looked to get out, too. But "Stay, Earl," she said to me. So instead of climbing back into the back seat, I stepped into the driver's. I already had my license, but I rarely got to drive. My mother was always saying that I was spacey and might drive right through a stop sign and kill myself. Which I've never done. I mean, I may have driven through a stop sign, but I never killed myself. Just saying. I sat there until my father finally called me by the name my mother never used. "Fly," he said. "Come on, now." He said this in his normal voice. A big bass that is real easy to admire.

In the house, my father went to his office. That's where he kept his books on rats, roaches, and the contraptions used to kill them. I could see he was relieved when he had to pull out his key to open the door. A cop led me to my room and asked what was missing. I went to my jar of marbles to see if any were stolen, though the one cop scolded me: "Marbles ain't worth nothing, son." But I studied my jar anyway, because they are pretty, those marbles, and who knows, maybe they were worth something. Someday. But whatever. Nothing of mine was gone. Like I was straight unworthy. I had zero things of value. Down the hall my mother was lamenting in the kitchen. The robber'd eaten half her meatloaf and taken off with all the forks from our silverware. Which wasn't even silver. "Can you believe it?" she kept asking. Kept repeating and repeating. Until one of the cops finally said, "It must have been good meatloaf, ma'am." Then Mom smiled.

"Fly, get some water for these officers," my father said absently. My mother looked at me. She was slipping a square of loaf into Tupperware for the complimenting officer. She gave me a brief coy smile. I stood to get the glasses.

At the fridge, I noticed that the Obama-for-president magnet was gone. My mother was voting for the woman to be chief. But Dad, always that early adopter, was into the Black man. Sure, Mom liked Michelle, but Mom didn't have much feeling for the husband. Well, anyway. The magnet was Dad's and now it was gone. I was glad, actually—given the friction that magnet had caused. Though, honest, there was always friction between my folks.

I opened the fridge door. There was practically nothing at all inside, though we'd shopped big yesterday. Meatloaf was always the first thing Mom made after a big shop. Then it would be lasagna. Then a casserole. Then a stew. She liked to make food that would last for weeks. For Thanksgiving my mother always cooked up two turkeys even though it was always just us three. The point I'm trying to make is that our thief had been single-minded. Thieved only things food- and fridge-related.

When the cops left that night, my father put his hands palms-up on the breakfast table. "I need some coffee, Ellie."

"But it's eleven p.m. and you have exterminations in the morning."

"Ellenora, please. Coffee. And my pills." He turned to me and I saw his hands curl just a little, getting ready to make a fist against the voices. "You. Bed. School tomorrow."

I kissed my mother. She winked at me as she started loading the coffee maker. I walked up the hall and felt just fine about the whole thing. For real, just fine. The toaster was gone. Mom's vase that held limes, and the limes, too—gone. That fridge magnet—gone. Most of our food was gone. But my dad's VHS tapes and scratched-up DVDs seemed to be all there. Just needing to be put in order and reshelved, you know. Even all the pictures on the mantel were there.

Up the hallway the coffee smelled nice, comforting like. I made a conscious decision not to brush my teeth. To sleep in my favorite flannel pajamas. But digging through my drawer I couldn't find the bottoms. Yo, the robber had stolen something from me after all! I felt good about that. Of worth, you know? I started down the hallway to make my report, but hearing my parents speaking, I slowed.

". . . damn jivers stole one of my videos," my dad was saying.

"Calm down. You misplaced it, I'm sure."

"This is a prized possession of mine, Ellenora. This is my most important video—I cannot be calm."

"It's not that important," my mother said.

Dad must have said something quietly. I heard my mother next; she spoke coolly and carefully: "Now, what on earth would be your justification for owning such a thing? For even making such a thing? And 'prized possession.' Is that what you just called that filth?"

So, I knew which video. I mean, dang, did I know. I moonwalked back to my room and closed the door quietly. I'd asked for a lock on my door but my mother hadn't allowed it. Now I put the chair from my desk up against the knob. I'd seen that done on TV to trap people. I went into my closet and pulled down the shoeboxes that towered in the dark corner. My heart was in my stomach and pounding away.

I mean, here's the thing. I was a religious kid, okay? The only one in my natal family with a constant faith. Mom had run fast and hard from Gram and Pop's Baptist church. She claimed a general respect for God, but no trust in Him. Kind of like how people in Rome used to think about Zeus—he's for sure there, but he mostly causes trouble. That's my take on Mom, anyway. Dad, sure, was super into religions. But he was all over the place. Buddhist, Baha'i, Black Jew. Whatever would make the voices chill. But neither his super interest or Mom's, like, opposite of interest helped me with the big questions. You know? At sixteen my big question was: What is up with sex?

Sex was supposed to be the true expression of love, or something. A thing that could even make a baby. Right? On the other hand, sex seemed like something that was totally outside of love. Something you didn't do if you really respected a girl. Something I wasn't supposed to even imagine my parents doing. Something I did by myself, lonely like.

It had been my great shameful pastime for years. Okay? It got so I couldn't sleep if I didn't do it. I would go to my shoeboxes, eat a gummy or two. Go to the bottom one. Bring a girlie mag with me to bed. My hand pulsing up and down like a ghost under the sheet. Afterward I would feel euphoric for a few seconds. And then I'd feel real bummed for a long while—especially if I'd used a white girl. Never, ever again, I would tell myself and Jesus. Every night, I told myself and Jesus that same lie. As a teenage rebellion, Christianity sort of sucked.

So, the video. The decoy box was toward the bottom. Releasing that cover to let out a waft of sweet skunk smell. Edibles, to be exact. Little round gummies that a senior sold for, like, two million dollars and I used every bit of my allowance to score. If Mom or Dad found this box they would halt, thinking they'd found the thing worth punishing me for—too many sweets. Or maybe they would figure out what it really was—I guessed my dad might know, since he seemed to know all kinds of wicked-like things. But so what? Maybe they'd send me to rehab, like what happened to the rich white kids at my school. Fine. Not a bad idea, if I'm being honest. The senior who sold the gummies had been to rehab and he seemed to be doing much better. But the real secret was in the shoebox at the bottom of the stack, below the decoy.

In this box there were the two magazines my father had given me with the bubble-booty Black girls on the cover. This was in case my father managed to find the box. Enough to make him close it again and know that I was horny. But, you know, horny in the right direction. Beneath those girls were the swollen-breasted *white* girls. The real freaky magazines that the boys on the team talked about. Penetration in every possible place. Sometimes made me sad to look at them. But beneath the white girls? A Bible. It was the Bible my grandmother had given me when I first got saved that one summer in Soulsville. The Bible was also a decoy. A final effort. If I ever wanted to annoy my mother, I would pray out loud to Jesus saying how much I trusted Him to intercede with grace and love into my life. Mom? She could not stand that. So, I figured the gummies, the porny mags, and the Good Book all together were fortress more than enough. Because beneath the Bible? Yup. The video; the filth that had my mom freaking out.

I almost wished the thief had taken the video. Why had I kept the damn thing anyway? Would I have to return it? I mean, my mother was the only Black woman I knew who didn't work outside the house. She was always quilting or some other old-school thing, right in front of the TV. For reals. Our floors were carpeted only so she could sneak up on me and *know*.

I could have taken the video to school. But the thought of handing it off to a teammate or the principal finding it in the trash was a very wrong thought. So now I put the video back under the white girls. I put the white girls back under the Black girls. I put it all under the Word of God. Then I put that shoebox under the other shoeboxes that actually contained shoes. I lay down on my bed, trying to decide what to do. My father thought the video was stolen, but it was me who was the thief. I mean, I was sickening. I turned onto my belly, thinking maybe I should cry. I saw my pajama bottoms sticking out from beneath the pillow. I couldn't remember if I'd put them there or if my mother had. The robber hadn't stolen them after all.

I went to my shoeboxes. I had actual basketball shoes in there, some real nice ones. I opened them each up. I wanted to make sure they were all there. They were. Robber hadn't stolen a thing from me. No value.

So not so hard, not a thing at all, to go to the boxes at the bottom. The gummies? I had a tin full of them. Still there. I popped one into my mouth. It tasted like radish. I checked the cover and it said strawberry flavor, but whatev. I popped another. I pulled the other box out. There were the Black girls. I knew them pretty well by now. Went straight to my favorite, the page crimped and crumpled. A brown-skinned girl with a lot of hair on her head and none on her, well, you know. I brought her to bed with me, until the ghost bobbed under the sheet. Then I slept.

Next day I couldn't just fake sick, stay home, secretly dispose of the video. Nah. See, if I was sick Mom would take it as, like, an affront to her mothering. She would give me deep massages if I had the flu. So deep it would hurt, but she would never let up. Getting my mother to leave the house was even more impossible. As far as I could tell she only left with my father or with me. And I couldn't wait for her to go visit a friend. I had no clue if she even had any friends. We were all weird about bringing people by the house. Me because I was always afraid Dad might start talking back to his voices. Mom because of the picture of Dad's ex on the mantel. And my dad because he just didn't know how to relate, really, to people. Not unless he was spraying their house for termites or something. And then it was the termites he was trying to relate to. So that he could kill them, I mean. Not that we were loners. I was never alone at home. I didn't even like being home alone. I got into stupid stuff.

Real talk? That's how I'd found the video in the first place.

See, like, years before the break-in, my parents had left me home by myself—rare. The video was just there in my father's collection. In an unmarked white plastic case. Innocent like. My father and me, we'd watched every kung fu movie on VHS and DVD that he owned. He had tons with no-joke monks who could pray and still kick butt. But our favorite was *The Last Dragon*. He loved it because the main character was a Black man with a calm demeanor and a fighting spirit. The kind of man he thought he was. I loved it because my mother said the main character looked like me. Which was sort of true, actually.

But back to the white plastic case. I can't imagine why the video was just right there. True, Dad still used the VHS player, despite the DVD player stacked on top of it. He believed in all technology. He still had records, even. Before it was cool to have records again. But he was also the first person I knew to stream a video online. The very first. Me? Like I'm always saying, I tend to stay away from anything with an off-and-on switch. Which is what I should have done that day. Stay away. But I didn't.

Why did Dad keep that video? I mean, just out in the open? Maybe he had forgotten the curiosity of teenage boys. He'd been, like, an orphan, right? Adult real quick. Maybe he'd had to skip being a teenager.

I'd told my parents that while they were out I'd watch the sports channel. Study some basketball games or whatever. I'd just made the team on my first try, but nothing about the team felt good. The other guys seemed so easy with each other. After the last practice a teammate had come at me with his fist forward. "Terrorist fist jab?" he'd said. Calm and kind, like he was offering me cake. I went in for the bump. Smiled. What else could I do? Then he started laughing. Everyone in the locker room started laughing too. They each clapped my shoulder as they strode by. I made a mental note that none of the guys on the team were my friends.

Instead, I reminded myself that I was Black. Black as LaCroix and Dwayne, the only other Black ballplayers at my school. Because my school was a fancy one all the way in Buckhead. I had to write a long application to get in—well, my mom wrote it, but still, it was my application. "You need a good school, so you can know things. So no one can pull the wool over your eyes," she would say, like school was the answer to all life's mysteries. But it was a superwhite school. And LaCroix and Dwayne were so Black that they were being recruited by colleges for balling and for being broke. Me? I was there for my grades and for being middle class. Not cool at all. So now I was thinking I just needed to focus. Watch some video of game play. Research. Get good quick. Then terrorist-fist-jab them all.

But then that night, home alone, I had a change of heart. I mean, really. I was never going to be great at basketball. Why try? Right then, the only thing I was excellent at was secretly getting high on tiny teddy bears and annoying my parents by saying grace before every single meal. Was that so bad? So, instead of basketball, I kneeled to the library of videos and DVDs. Found one I hadn't yet seen.

I popped two servings of extra-butter popcorn in a pot. I try not to microwave—that is some scary technology, you know. I pulled my dad's chair up close to the TV. I inched the video to the lip of the VHS machine until it was sucked in.

There were no opening credits. Just the text "On the way to the Promised Land: Detour to the Martin Luther King Museum." The words written on a piece of paper and held up to the camera. Worse than a high school film project. I could hear giggles and then a woman saying, "Look at me." Oh, man. And when the sign came down, there was my father's first girlfriend. Buck naked.

She was laid on the bed with her legs spread open. She was young, as young, maybe, as I was. A teenager. She had flat yellow hair on her head but a brown afro between her legs. She was thin. Skinnier than

I'd realized from her picture on the mantel. But she sure didn't seem like the religious freak Mom always said she was. The girl bit her bottom lip and then her top lip. She looked up at the ceiling and then laughed; finally, Jesus, looking into the camera. "I'm ready," she said, though she sang it. Like, whoa. She made it a melody. "Are you looking at me?" All singing. Then she put all her fingers into her wide laughing mouth. Then put the wet hand between her wider legs.

I wish I could say that I gnarled the video out of the machine. Or even that I threw my popcorn in the air and ran from the room. I wish. But there was only the sensation that the woman was very pretty. And sexy. And that my dick was stiff as stone. Maybe desire is an instinctive thing. I don't know. I was just fourteen or something, okay? I sat in the chair, leaning forward. Devouring popcorn like I was on a timer or like there was no such thing as time at all. If I got to the end of the popcorn, then I would switch off the video. Something like that.

But I just kept eating the popcorn. I was shoveling entire fistfuls into my mouth. Straight from the pot. I don't know why, but I just needed to finish that pot of popcorn. But I also felt like I was betraying my father. Looking at his old girlfriend this way. Like she was still his girl. And worse, I felt like I was betraying my mom by watching this girl. By wanting her the way my father had wanted her. I hadn't yet had sex with an actual girl then.

Then there was her voice directed at the camera: "See? It's just me. It's just Eloise." Then there was my dad. Older than her by seven years, I knew because Mom used to go on about that. How Dad only wanted too-young girls. Gross. But Dad was still young, too, in the video. Lean and tall. Like me, a little older, but kind of like me. His own afro like a devil's halo around his head. He climbed on top of her. Just like that. Her pale scrawny thighs cradling his hips. His chest leaning down to meet her little pink tits. Oh. Man.

In the video now, she climbed on top of my father. From the camera's view, I could see his whole self slipping, sliding in. Then they started getting wild. Like just her taking over made it crazy. *Jesus.* The noises they made. Grunting and heaving. Like it was manual labor. Then smacking each other and pushing. Heads snapping like they both wanted out. But even then, "Please say it," she screamed. And he straight sang it to her: "I love you, I love you, I love you." His eyes were on her. Her eyes were up to God.

When the pot was down to kernels, I set it down. Now both of them on the screen were facing away from me at a side angle. Not watching me. She was on her hands and knees. And I could see his backside tensing and relaxing. I forced my penis through the zipper in my pants. I know. Okay? I know. I can't stand myself sometimes. Most times.

But her voice was calm again. "Soon?" she asked. "I'll be sore." From the profile, I could see her face bunched up. His hands had left prints all over her body. Like she'd been in a car accident or something. I felt so tender for her, protective, even. I thought he should stop. *I* would stop if I were him. See, I was hot for her, but I wasn't a jerk. But then she turned her head to look at the camera. She looked at me. I came, just like that, into my fist.

Then my father's voice. "Now, you know, I don't like being rushed, Ellie."

The exact same pet name he used on my mother. Like, what? But then he released himself from the girlfriend, and I was just straight relieved it was all finally over. Until he turned toward the camera, his face no different than mine. Kneeled her down between his legs. He held the back of her head just like I'd seen in the magazines he'd bought for me. Just like I'd imagined.

When I heard the garage door open, I knew I didn't have a second of time. My mother usually got out of the car first. Made her way fast to the door. She hated the pesticide funk of the garage. "Man smell," my father always said, slapping me on the back. Though I hated the smell, too. Now I leaped at the VHS player. And finally, Lord, finally, I had the appropriate feeling of nausea. How much time had passed? I had no idea.

But now the tape took its gentle time ejecting. Stupid technology, for real. Before it was properly ejected I just grabbed it and its plastic white case. The slick from my hands spreading all over. I ran to my room, my zipper still down. Slammed my door. Spun widely around.

I was panicking. Feeling truly crazy. Like I was my father. Someone who could just lose my mind. You know? Someone who might hear voices. Or maybe someone who might hang themselves from a showerhead. A kid in my school had done that. Everyone had been real sad. Seemed to me, though, like the kid was just real brave. I mean, I know how that sounds. But it's just how it seemed to me.

So. I stuffed the video under my pillow. Then I took a long shower in the en suite bath. En suite, my mother's fancy term. I fretted and freaked the whole time in the shower. Thinking, thinking. Wondering if the showerhead could hold me. I know God would not have approved.

When I stepped out of the shower, I looked down at my feet. I stared at them until my favorite psalm came to me. The twenty-third. Walk through the valley of the shadow of death. Then I knew what I had to do. Walk. Shoes. Shoeboxes. The idea like from God, though I guess that can't be true. But still. I slid the video from under my pillow and walked it to my closet. There was my fortress of shoeboxes. My magazines were already there at the bottom. I hadn't even thought that the video was porn. Not like the magazines were. But then I knew that the video was the same. I hid it, just like I said.

And yup, I still had the video the night of the break-in. Right there. Shoeboxes in my closet.

That night I woke up at, like, three a.m. or something, with the magazine on my chest and my dick in my hand. I was scared to shit, because I knew my mother sometimes came in to check on me while I slept. But I remembered that I'd barricaded the door. I put the Black girls back in the shoebox. I stayed awake until my bedroom curtains turned light from the rising sun.

So that next day, that morning after the break-in, my father stayed home from work. I got ready for school. "He had a rough night," my mother said with her face cold. Usually this meant that Dad's pills weren't working and the voices were waking him from sleep. Even then Mom always said "we," like she heard the voices, too. But today was different. She was working on that monster quilt that she never could finish. I swear, my procrastinating is entirely her bad example. Though if you were to ask Mom, she would say all my lame traits come from my father.

That morning, I picked a marble from my jar and slipped it into my pocket. I wanted something hard to touch when I faced my parents. In the kitchen, Mom presented me the usual brown bag with lunch. But I felt strange now. She knew about the video. Maybe she knew about me, you know? "I don't want it," I told her, unable to look at her face. "Well, I guess you're all grown up now," she said. A sourness in her voice. She turned and dropped the bag in the garbage. When she left the kitchen, I opened the can and plucked the bag out. I hid it inside my jacket as I headed out. I guess I was ashamed of my hunger. Or something like that.

I started the car. Today I would drive myself to school. By myself. First time. My father's four-gallon termite sprayers were heavy in the trunk. It didn't dawn on me until after I parked the car at school that I could've taken the stupid tape. Dropped it in the school dumpster. How dumb could I be? But I guess I had other things to worry about. Like I'd decided I needed to get a job. Immediately. Needed to be able to buy my own lunch, without asking for allowance. A metaphor, you know. It was either hang myself from the locker-room showerhead or get a job. But I didn't know *how* to get a job, really. I spent quality time with myself in the boys' room all through Algebra II, hearing my father's voice in my head: "I don't like being rushed." I sat in that stall, thinking, thinking. Taking my time. Ate the brown bag lunch right there on the seat.

That night, I came home late, like, after dinnertime. I'd walked into practically every establishment in greater Atlanta that didn't have a rectangle of the Confederate flag in its window. I wanted a job that would make me feel valued, but I'd rounded up a stock-boy position at a small grocery in Decatur. There was a package store on one side of it, but a church on the other side—so I figured I was okay. A white girl my own age did the supershort interview. Then yelled out to her boss that I was the best they'd get for the price. She showed me around. Offered to share an actual spliff of marijuana. I watched her roll and lick it herself. Looked like she was expert. "Do you think Sarah Palin is hot?" she asked me. I could tell she wanted me to say yes. "Yes, I do," I said. It wasn't a lie. I mean, all women were hot to me. I didn't even know who Sarah Palin was then. Then me and this girl went out the back door and smoked the spliff down to our fingertips. I got paid one ten-dollar bill after two hours. Lunch money.

At home there was a new magnet on the fridge. This one just said: YES, WE CAN. I knew it was about the election, but I looked at it for a long time. Looked at it until I felt sure it was also about me. Down the hall, my room was still untouched. The tape was there beneath the man of God Bible, which was beneath the white girls who were beneath the Black girls. I know because I checked. And, well, I did more than check. I kneeled to the boxes. This time I popped two gummies in one gulp. Then I went to the bottom box. I took out the Black girls. And there were the white girls.

I looked at the cover of that one for, well, some time. Just looking. Deciding. Then I did. I opened the page to all that yellow hair, and peach skin, and pink pussies. I found the worst of them. Cocks stuffed everywhere. And I imagined I was like one of Dad's Hindu gods, but with many dicks instead of many arms. At the end I was sure I'd made a loud noise and so I got real quiet. Listening to hear my mother. But the house just listened right back. "Pray for me," I said out loud. But I didn't pray for myself.

The next morning there was another brown bag for my lunch on the counter. This time I left it there, and climbed into the driver's seat of the car. My father climbed into the passenger's seat. Smiled at me. Like all was normal. He was like that. Still is, I guess. Dad's crazy doesn't usually make him cray-cray. It can make him super focused. That kind of craziness had him driving away from an earthquake, a white girl shotgun. By the time I was sixteen, I had pieced together that much from my father's history. "That's nothing got to do with you," he would say when I asked for more.

So. That brown bag lunch stayed on the counter for, like, days. I had two marbles in my pocket now, and Mom's bag lunch was less and less frightening each morning. After, like, four mornings or something, my father simply took it up and carried it to the dumpster down the street. Like one of the rats he regularly discovered in the perimeter around our garage. Even though, of course, he sprayed our house once a month. My mother and I did not even look at each other when the lunch was dumped. It was a bad time for me. And for her, I guess.

I played in another basketball game but this time only my mother came. My father had to stay late at work. The teachers' lounge at some elementary school had a vermin outbreak and he'd been summoned like an emergency worker. This was good for him. Being busy kept the voices at bay.

Like I said before, I was one of only three Black kids on the team. I didn't have to guess that I'd been chosen for my skin color and my height. But being Black seemed to make no difference. And my height was, real talk, a liability. My feet were huge, and on the court they felt like canoes. It's true, I didn't try hard. I mean, I didn't want it to look like I was trying hard. At practice, when the coach rallied and I felt inspired, I would push myself, but then always end up tripping and slamming to the court. My teammates teased that I should try that trick on game days—I was a natural to draw a foul. But I could never manage to even trip right when the game was on. It was better not to try, you know? It was best to pose like I didn't care at all about basketball. Even though I held hope that *I* would win a basketball scholarship, and not LaCroix or Dwayne. They were ghetto Black kids whose parents were on welfare or something. Just a guess. Probably not. Whatever. Anyway, it wasn't that I was so bad at ball, it was that I was choosing not to be good. My prerogative. Like old-school Bobby Brown. You know?

"Maybe you don't care enough about basketball, Earl," my mother said. She let me drive us home that night. Something she'd never allowed before. "I know you can do anything you put your mind to." She didn't follow this with something usual like "If your cousin Brent can get into Vanderbilt, then you can get into Emory." Which meant that she was holding her tongue. Trying to make a truce. So I nodded, truced her back.

But the thing is this. I knew my mother was dead wrong. I'd put my mind to being liked at school. I had a cool nickname—Fly. I played on the basketball team. I was tall, and I wasn't fat or pimply. I even had a mustache already. But the cheerleaders only gave me pitying looks. Like they all knew about Dad, and were waiting for the crazy to come on me. Real talk? So was I.

I mean, really. I knew for a fact that I could *not* be anything I wanted. I'd felt the, like, gleaming possibilities when I'd met the pastor of God's Caravan. His songs had saved me. Sort of. But, man, it was no use keeping the spirit up with my no-faith mother and too-many-faiths Dad. I liked having potential, sort of. Achievement would come when it would come. God's time. You know? Why worry with hope? Because false hope is really sad. "Georgia is going to go for Obama," my father said every night during dinner, the election news in the background. "I feel in my body that it's time for Georgia to set correct." Mom would shake her head when he said that. She was sure Dad—and all Black men in America—was straight hopeless.

When Mom and I got to the house after that game, I slammed the door of the car. Leaving my mother there. Across the street someone was diving into the neighbor's pool. Steady slicey splashes every few seconds. Like they were practicing. I went to our house and slammed the door loud behind me. I went to the shoeboxes. True. Facts. I went to them. I ate a fistful of gummies. I opened the Black girls, then the white girls. Then there was the Bible. Right there. Like it was part of it all. I opened it and it went right to Ezekiel. Right to the women screwing themselves with men made of gold. I don't know, okay? But I want to say that it was more Christian of me, better of me, jacking off to God's word. Because that is what I did. But maybe it was worse. Like, the worst thing ever. "I am a precious metal," I told myself. I heard it in my head, like it was a voice. Like it wasn't my own voice. Though, it was.

I quit basketball after that. I had a job now anyhow. Stacking shelves with bags of rice, smoking up with that girl after. Got the number to her connect, even, so I could have my own stash, which I could properly pay for now. Because, the job. I called my cousin on the house phone and spoke in a code I knew my mother couldn't figure.

Me: "I learned how to roll by myself."

Brent: "Yo, little cuz. I'm laying low on that these days. Trying to go pre-dentist track here. Can't slip." Which sounded so sad to me.

Like college meant you couldn't have fun anymore? Adulthood was dumb.

Brent: "And my girl isn't into anything unless it's those minty clove things. So, you know. Gotta keep her happy so she keeps me happy. You know what I'm saying?"

Me: "Yeah. I know. I got a girl, too. She's cool."

Which is to say I was smoking by then. The gummies were just to take the edge off. I started going to church here and there by myself, too. Once I even went to the place next to the job. The pastor preached about Solomon and had an island accent, like my dad did sometimes. After the service there was a big pot of rice and beans, and I ate a plate. The ladies were nice, but none were my age. And you know, turns out the only thing I ever really believed about church was the music. And even that, well. I couldn't even dance. Though, it's true that church is where I picked up drumming. African drums at an AME in Panthersville. Hooked me. I liked the confidence of those drumming men. And yeah, they were always men. When I was drumming I didn't need marbles so much to keep my fingers busy.

Get this. I even saved up enough to buy my own very secondhand car. Dad helped some. That car revved and roared. I showed up every afternoon to my job at the general store in that new old car. One day, the spliff-smoking girl at the shop kneeled to me in the back room. She wasn't really rightfully my girlfriend, but she is who I'd had in mind when I told Brent. "We gonna get us a Black president this time," she said. "You be him. I'll be Sarah Palin." I held her head just as the tape, my dad, had taught me. Rushed it, though. Couldn't help it. But I figured that was okay with her. When we were done, she told me she was going to Agnes Scott in the fall. Which seemed impossible, because she was just a store clerk. Still, on the drive home I imagined that we would date for real—because maybe I'd get into Emory the next year, like Mom promised.

I should have dumped the tape for sure by then. But I still didn't. I never even applied to Emory. I went to those shoeboxes again and again. All junior year and senior year. Truth? I was fiending for the video. I would sit in my closest. Read Song of Songs with my dick in my hand. Read about Solomon's woman asking him to blow her. Then I would put the Bible back down on the tape, careful like, until it seemed like the Bible was the only thing keeping me from true degradation. Because I never watched the video again. But I watched over it. Like it was an idol.

Thing is, I've never gotten those sick slick images out from behind my eyes. I'm ashamed to even think it. But, real talk. I've never been able to cut my father's beautiful voice, commanding that Ellie, out of my ears.

THE SPECIAL WORLD

FLY'S FIRST LOVE STORY

Georgia State University

Fall 2009

1. THE ORDINARY WORLD

Fly was alone. When his parents had dropped him off, they hadn't come in the building like the other parents had done. He'd asked them not to, felt grown asking. Didn't need their help with his one suitcase, half his weight, or with the backpack strapped to his body. He hugged his mom at the building door. Her eyes were furiously red, like she was witnessing the end of the world. Fly shook his father's hand. His father held on and shook and shook, until Fly lurched away. His own palm sweaty and shaky. His father's hand made a fist—nonthreatening to Fly, but embarrassing all the same.

Yes, it was good to leave his folks at the door. This is what college was for. Fly walked into the dorm like he was from the place. Never looked back.

He knew his room number by heart, but he again pulled out the piece of paper that had come in the mail: 646, it still said. He took the stairs, passing other freshmen hiking with their parents—book boxes and mini-fridges between them. On the door to 646, Fly's government name was written in bubble letters on kindergarten paper. He took it off, crumpled it into a jagged ball. He wanted to eat it. Chew it down to paste and then crap it out. Instead, he let it fall to the floor, roll sadly under the extra-long twin bed.

There was only one extra-long twin bed. Sitting on that one bed in his new college home, Fly felt just like he had the night before. Nervous, and alone in that feeling. Wondering what his roommate would be like. If they would be cool with each other. Fly left the door open. Just in case. He wondered where the other guy would sleep. He guessed they'd have to roll in a cot.

Within the hour the floor got loud and then louder. The parents who had stayed were leaving. The students were losing their minds with glee. Three girls tumbled out of the room across the hall. They smiled at Fly with manic smiles—like they were laughing at him. "He was cute," he heard one say as they went, but she sounded hesitant. Like she was surprised. And maybe it wasn't even Fly she was talking about. But no, Fly was sure it was him. That was something he had. The good looks. Not that it had helped him much in high school, but college girls were different. He'd heard.

In this fashion, Fly missed orientation that afternoon. Missed convocation that evening.

His mom had packed him industrial amounts of pork rinds and beef jerky. They hadn't been Fly's favorite in years, maybe had never been his favorite. He'd packed his favorite weed gummies, the cherry ones that he was sure were sexy, too—because *cherry*. And there he was, lying on a quilt his grandmother had made for him, munching alternately on a jerky stick and a tiny red bear, staring at the ceiling. Rolling a marble between his fingers. He was imagining his body floating six stories up, imagining that there wasn't a bed or floor or six floors beneath him, because there wasn't, not really; everything was connected, which meant that nothing really was keeping him from slamming to the ground but his own awareness of the bed and the floor and the six floors below him. He felt smart thinking metaphysical things like this. His body was calm. The marble slid easily from one finger to the next.

Then a freckled guy with hair so blond it was white leaned slowly into Fly's doorway. The man floated there, at a slant, and then smiled. Fly froze, the jerky a sad flaccid meat hanging out of his mouth.

"You must be . . . ?" The man asked this with his smile and his white eyebrows slanted up.

But Fly didn't answer. The man righted himself and stepped into the threshold. His legs were short and thick, and Fly wondered if he was a dwarf.

"You got the single," the man said, and he said it so casually and happily that Fly realized that the man was young—maybe not even a *man* man. Though the guy, Fly now took in, had a full, bushy blond beard.

"So what are your allergies?" the other said. "Sorry, forgot my clipboard."

Fly felt his mouth open, but nothing came out.

"Dude. I'm your RA," the other said now, almost sternly. Cautiously.

"What's an RA?" asked Fly.

"Oh, shit!" said the RA, regaining his smile. "It means I'm your dude. I'm like your big, uh, brother, or maybe brother is the wrong word, or whatever. But anyway. Resident assistant." He high-fived the space on the door where Fly's name had been. "Your name got lost. But anyway, I'm Clive. Look, we'll figure out the allergies later. No worries. But we have a meeting downstairs, like, now." His grin went wonky for a second, but reset. He used his whole arm to wave Fly toward him.

Fly spit the jerky out and followed.

"Remind me your name?" Clive asked as they walked down the hallway.

"Fly," said Fly.

At the meeting there was an actual adult. A grown-up. A white woman who also had a hint of beard. What was up with the hair on these people? Is this what college did to white folk? She introduced all the RAs. Half of the RAs were Black—one of those was a guy who seemed girlie . . . but one was an actual girl. Dark skinned and pretty. When introduced, the girl kept her arms at her sides but waved her hand like a shiver. Fly wished he was on that girl's floor. But when she started talking there was no Blackness in her speech to speak of—nothing Southern, even. Just all "you know" and "like" and even a "yay!" at the end. Fly looked around to see if anyone else sensed her fraud. But no one met his eye.

He was not going to survive freshman year. He was going to end up back home in Ellenwood before the week was out.

But he didn't. He got registered for classes. He started classes. Intro everything: American History, World Religions, World Music. Bare minimum credits, because he still wasn't sure he would stick, so why stretch? He started having lunch with the students from Introduction to World Religions, because the class ended right around lunchtime, so why not? They would talk Judaism. Fly didn't think he'd ever met a Jew in his life—except for maybe his dad, who had identified as Black Jewish for almost a year. But now there were a bunch of actual Jews. And they were saying things like: "We're not really white," though they sure looked white to Fly. And also: "God, as a concept, is real. But God as a divine—well, that is a social construction."

Fly started really reading; before, he'd read books just for the sex scenes. But now there was still no roommate, so plenty of time. He read and smoked and ate gummies, and he felt his brains getting smarter, looser. He blew the smoke out of his sixth-floor window. He cut his weed with mint, a thing he'd learned from his cousin Brent, so the other froshers on his floor never even knew. Back at the World Religion lunches, he would be able to add things like "But for the Black man, religion is the only safe route to masculinity. The secular Black man, as a man, is too dangerous." He'd never known he thought things like this before. It was his father who first spoke these narratives—out loud during dinner, instead of dinner conversation. Now, when Fly spoke, the others would nod or shake their heads. Even the shaking heads were an agreement—like "Ain't that something."

Walking out of the dining hall, Fly would pass a whole section where the Black kids hung out. He longed for them. But how did those kids of color all know each other already in week two, week three? There were only a handful in his classes. Where were they all and how could he get in?

2. CALL TO ADVENTURE

Fly didn't actually have any allergies, but Clive kept asking. Clive would do his crazy lean in the doorway, and Fly would offer: "Strawberries?"

"Nah," Clive might say. "Can't be strawberries. They don't give a freshman his own room for that. They would just put you with someone else with a strawberry allergy."

"Peanut butter?" Fly tried again.

"Nah. Same. It's got to be epic. Like music gives you epilepsy or some shit." Clive righted himself. His short legs now in the threshold. "You epileptic?"

"I don't think so."

"Yeah, I don't think so either." Clive had his clipboard; he looked at it and sighed. "So, classes good?" he asked Fly.

"Uh, yeah."

Clive looked up from the clipboard. "I mean, *are* you allergic to strawberries?"

"No."

"Oh, fuck," said Clive, which felt like an overreaction to Fly. Cursing always felt that way. But Clive wasn't looking at Fly anymore. He was looking down the hallway. He stared at whatever it was, then looked at Fly and took a deep breath. "Okay, man," he said. "Be good."

With Clive now gone Fly could hear what was coming. His door was open, as always, and he could hear the knocking, the cheery chatting, the hesitation, the sweet rejection. He knew they were making their way down to his room. And when they did, Fly was ready for them. Had been preparing for the fifteen minutes it took the pair to make it to his doorway. They didn't do the Clive lean-in. They stood together side by side, filling Fly's threshold, like his parents might have if he'd let them come visit. Fly didn't even let these visitors get their spiel out.

"Come on in," he said, just as he'd been practicing in his head.

The girl had dark curly hair, and he'd only seen clearer skin on babies. Smooth and white as milk. A Jew, Fly figured. The boy was wearing glasses that he kept pushing back up his nose. The glasses were so thick it was hard to keep eye contact with the dude. The girl did most of the talking, anyway. The boy watched her through his slippy glasses and nodded like that was all he was ever going to do.

"And so, we hope you can come to church this Sunday. It's just off campus. Can we count on you?"

"I'm there," Fly said. The guy was Arthur; the girl went by Suzie.

3. REFUSAL OF THE CALL

Fly knew how to roll a joint, though smoking had been hard to do in high school—the smoke itself a signal to his parents that he couldn't risk. Now his know-how meant he was finally getting a social life. He went to a house party off campus with the World Religion students. At the party they all gathered on the couch like zoo animals around the one tree in the cage. The tree in this case was the marijuana. The sophomore who had brought it called it Mary Jane, like it was his girlfriend, and Fly couldn't figure out if that was cool or lame. The house was dark, but still no one was dancing, and Fly didn't make out another Black kid in the whole place. He used the table to lay out the leaves and papers. He licked loose and packed tight, made a show of it. Just like the girl at the store had taught him. He rolled one perfect joint for each of his comrades; rolled himself two, an extra as payment.

While he and the others leaned back and lit up, an actual girl got up on a table and started gyrating, like a stripper. Fly felt gross for her, about her. But he still tilted forward to look up her skirt. Her white thighs were in shadows. He sucked Mary Jane and leaned back into the conversation: "Judeo-Christianity is a way for straight men to admit their attraction to other men," someone was saying. "Like, Jesus is a man you can love without being accused of homoeroticism." Fly put on his serious thinking face and listened. Getting high with others was definitely better than getting high by himself.

The next morning, Sunday, passed with Fly in bed—sleeping. Waking up to smoke a little, then eat the last of the beef jerky sticks. Reading a homework essay by Susan McClary on musical endings, another by Velma Pollard on reggae linguistics. He used a highlighter as he read, instead of taking notes. Highlighted most all of the page.

Fly had forgotten all about the two evangelical kids. Forgotten about church, and the Church, and who needed it? Right? Who needed Jesus when you had Peter Tosh? Christianity had been stabilizing when he lived with his faith-crazy parents, but now—now, who knew, maybe he didn't even need stable. He thought on all the ways to become a man—music, maybe? He put his hand in his pants and pulled his dick out.

But then Arthur and Suzie showed up. Right as Fly was cumming, too. They came straight to his room, where his door was forever unlocked. They knocked, which gave Fly a second to stuff himself back into his pants, and then they turned his door handle. Just like that they were in his room. He jerked himself to sitting, his body tight and coiled as a glass ball. "I really missed you in church," Suzie said. Which was the first time anyone had claimed to miss Fly besides his mother, who was always claiming it. *I miss you, come visit, I'll wash your clothes, I'll cook a meatloaf.* It was nice of this girl to say she missed him. His body calmed. And then the girl kept saying more things, like, "Should I come meet you here next Sunday before service?" And, "You can walk me to church. Wouldn't that be nice?"

The boy, Arthur, nodded at her, his glasses still slipping down his nose. "I'll be alone," Suzie said, turning her body more clearly away from Arthur. "Arthur is giving a junior sermon next week, so he's got to be there before everyone else." Arthur looked down at the ground; his glasses teetered. He took them off and cleaned them on his shirt.

"Sounds like a plan," said Fly, who was still sitting on his bed in the new pajamas his mother had bought him for college. The girl was pretty, with her dark hair and big lips. Fly stood to see them out. She was an Angelina Jolie–looking white girl, but with a little bum. Which

Fly watched as Suzie and Arthur walked down the hallway. She was white-girl pretty, which always made Fly think of his father, or more specifically his father's old white-girl girlfriend. Fly shook his head to shake away the thoughts. He wished he'd said congratulations to Arthur. Must be a big deal to give a sermon, he thought, even a junior one. When he walked back into his room, he looked down and saw that his crotch was wet. But Suzie and Arthur had never taken their eyes off his face, he felt sure of that. Pretty sure. Fly felt bad about his various failures for hours.

4. TRAVERSING THE THRESHOLD

Clive leaned into the threshold. "I get it," the RA said, smiling. "I totally get it." He pulled his body back up and stood in the doorway. His still surprisingly short legs. "You're not allergic to anything, man. I mean, could it be that you . . . ?" He looked at his clipboard and shook his head. "Sorry, it's just I'm trying to find a reason."

Fly was lying on his bed, in boxers only this time. "It's okay," he said.

"Smells like mint in here," Clive said. "You sick?"

"I don't think so."

"But you have your own room, dude. I didn't get my own room until I was a junior."

Fly didn't know what to say. "Sorry?" he said.

"Thanks, man. I guess you just got lucky. Right?"

"I guess?" said Fly, feeling something musty enter the room. Though Clive never did. Never did enter.

When Fly woke up that Sunday the sun was shooting right through his jar of marbles, making the air in his room look holy. And also there was someone knocking on his door, which he'd taken to locking since he'd been caught, almost, with his pants down. He opened the door and there was the girl. Suzie. The churchy Christian Jewish girl, whatever that meant, with the milky skin and curly night-black hair—the colored light on her face like she was a saint. Fly was only in his pajama pants this time. His chest bare. Suzie pulled her breath in and then shot her eyes to his. Kept them there like her soul depended on it.

"I'm too early," she said.

"Uh, sorry. What time is church again?"

"No, I'm early. But you don't have a cell phone. I mean why don't you have a cell phone?" She smiled, though the smile seemed mean. "It's just that I'm singing in the choir, so I like to get there on time."

"Yeah," Fly said. He looked down at his crotch this time. Checked if there was a stain there from his private activities. No. He was good.

"Should I wait out here?" she asked.

"Uh, no. Go ahead. You know. I'll catch up."

She nodded, but she seemed weirded out. It was his body, he knew. His body had made her nervous. He still had that muscle, left over from basketball, that lean teenage-boy body that can hold a vestigial tautness for years. Had a girl ever seen his bare chest? He couldn't remember. His mother didn't count. Couldn't count.

"Sorry I was too early," she said. "I really hope you come."

At the elevators, she turned to look back at him, and he realized that he was, stupidly, just standing there in his own threshold. He flung himself back into the room.

No, he wasn't going to go to some white people's church with that white girl. No way. His mother would never, ever let him bring her home, anyway. No point. Instead, he closed his door, pulled his pajama pants down, and jerked off. He imagined the cum surging into Suzie's honey throat, just like his father did with that other woman. Fly imagined Suzie smiling and that Ellie smiling, their faces blending into a perfect porn-star face, the woman enjoying his pleasure through the whole thing.

He got up to go shower down the hall in the communal bathroom. He took long showers. Good way to break up the day. Shower caddy in hand, slippers on his feet, he turned out of his dorm room door, and there was Clive. Clive had a stack of papers in his hand. "Was about to slip this under your door, man," he said. He slapped one sheet of paper to Fly's chest.

Fly walked with it to the showers. Read the list through again and again. Campus cults. No matter how many times he read it, Suzie and Arthur's church was still the first one on the list.

After his shower, Fly couldn't find his one pair of Stacy Adams. Thought, Well, that's that. But then found them. Put on a collared shirt and slacks.

When he opened the doors to the church, the choir was going, and the place was packed with students clapping and smiling and shouting and dancing, and it was a real party up in there. Real gospel music, stuff Fly was familiar with. The young people at the end of the rows noticed Fly come in and smiled bigger. These strangers were so happy he'd come. He smiled back. He could hear tambourines clanging. And one of those steel pans a guest professor had lectured about in World Music. The light was way bright. And there were more Asian people in this one place than Fly knew even existed on the whole campus. Arthur was, inexplicably, climbing from behind a set of drums beside the altar, and racing toward him.

"Oh, man, so glad you made it!" Arthur looked crazed. He'd also just said the most words he'd ever said to Fly.

"You play drums?" was all Fly could say.

"All the guys play drums," Arthur squealed. And indeed, another guy was behind the drum kit already, tapping the cymbals like he'd always been there.

"Bring it in, brother!" cried Arthur. And there, for real, was a space in the pew right beside them for Arthur and Fly, both. Like everyone had been waiting for Fly. Like Fly was special.

"Did I miss you?" Fly said, feeling weird about missing Arthur's sermon, missing Arthur's drumming—and mostly weird about why he himself didn't know how to drum, not like a proper drummer on a drum kit.

"You're here now!" Arthur shouted gleefully. "You're right on time!"

Fly found his place, between Arthur and an Asian kid so tall that even tall Fly had to look up to him. This guy gave Fly a fist bump. Then the place went hushed. Everyone looked ahead to the altar. The choir was up there. Robed like a real Black choir. In fact, all the members of the choir were Black, except for Suzie, who was there now stepping forward to a single standing mic.

"Suzanna," Arthur whispered to Fly. The whisper had all the lunacy of someone shouting from a mountaintop. Arthur took his glasses off and leaned forward.

Suzanna tipped her face to the microphone and shut her eyes tight. "I," she started. And she held it. The *I*. Held it there with her eyes so tight. "I been buked, and I been scorned." There was no music at all holding her up. She opened her eyes and sang the line again a cappella. This time straight all the way through. "I've been buked, and I've been scorned." She put her arms out with her hands like she was welcoming them all. And then Fly leaned in to look more closely at her, leaned in even though she was so many pews away.

By the time Suzanna was on "trying to make this journey all alone," Fly knew. Suzanna was no white girl. Not one bit. Not a Jewish non-white girl, even. Suzanna was a girl raised in the Church, singing since she was a toddler. A Black church. This was a Negro spiritual she was singing. Suzanna was a straight-up Black girl. It was evident to Fly now that she was singing.

Of course, he could even see it in her face now that he knew. The full lips, the curly hair. The lightest-skinned Black girl Fly had ever seen, but now he could see the color rising to her face. She was getting browner by the octave. Suzie was a Black girl named Suzanna who could sing spirituals. And Fly knew she was the girl he was destined to love.

In fact, Suzanna was, right now, looking at him. Right at him. Which meant that she knew it, too. He stared back at her. Everyone around him started sitting; the song was over. But Fly stayed standing. He stayed standing, and she stayed standing. Until the pastor started talking and Suzie backed up, back into the choir. An all–African American gospel choir, though the senior pastor, it turned out, was white. Regular, actual white, with waxy yellow hair to settle it. Fly sat down. But he stayed staring at Suzie until she looked away from him. Then he looked up at the ceiling. He could feel that his back was wet. That he was sweating through his clothes. There was probably a wet spot at the back of his shirt. But he looked up at the plain white ceiling and imagined that there was no ceiling. That he was out there in the sky because he was the sky. When the pastor said amen and everyone else said it, too, Fly returned from the sky and looked over at Arthur, and Arthur was looking at him. Arthur's eyes were hooded, like he had something very serious to say. But then Fly realized that was just how Arthur's eyes were. Arthur was some kind of Asian. Clear now that he wasn't wearing his glasses.

What was this craziness? Fly thought. What did it all mean? All the people of color were camouflaged. His fingers gripped his own knees. Maybe they had been around Fly all the time, and he'd been too self-absorbed to notice. Maybe he was camouflaged, too.

After that service, Fly started to feel exhausted practically all the time. In the one extra-long twin bed, he would stare at the ceiling and think about kissing Suzie, Suzanna, her letting him touch her. Even after weeks of walking her to church and watching her from the pews, he'd never even touched her through her clothes. A few times, he'd put a handful of marbles into his mouth, rolled them around, exercising his tongue, getting ready to use it on, for, Suzanna. Once, he fell asleep with the marbles in his mouth. Woke up choking, realizing he'd swallowed one. But that was fine. Grand, even. Because he'd been dreaming about Suzie, and so the marble was her, in a way.

Fly didn't think of his father, Gary Lovett, meeting his first love at church. Of that girl winning Gary's heart over the Bible. Fly had never heard all the details of that story, only lived in its wake. His father had been hunting for paradise, still was—poor Dad, Fly thought. Clearly, paradise was to be found right there in a woman. If only Dad knew.

This new wise Fly slept a whole lot. Masturbated like it was a job. Practice, he now told himself. Then Fly slept some more. He'd heard somewhere that sleeping a lot meant you were in love. He stopped messing with marbles so much. There was already a marble, Suzie, inside him.

5. TESTS, ALLIES, AND ENEMIES

The Jewish kids from World Religions weren't camouflaging; they were doing the opposite. They were posing as people of color—when for all Fly could gather they were really just white. He couldn't be bothered with their lack of authenticity. Fly lunched now with Arthur and the other ethnically jumbled Christian kids. Arthur was from the Midwest. Didn't speak Chinese or Korean. Though he wore what Fly knew was a Buddhist bracelet around his left wrist. Fly's father had worn four or five of them on the same wrist for years. Fly never said anything about it to Arthur, but it surely meant that Arthur wasn't totally devoted to the cult; if the church was a cult. Though it turned out Fly himself was feeling less nuanced. Actually *felt* it. He felt solid, manly, sure of his faith now. Like how he'd been as a boy with Pastor John. No more experimenting intellectually around thoughts. Now Fly would have an unbending thought and then feel real good about it. Fly had been all B+s and As but his World Religions grade slouched at the midterm. He couldn't muster a nuanced thought about Bahaullah or Krishna. He was all in for Jesus these days. He smoked less. Felt good. Felt grown.

But music was still Fly and fly. The World Music class was in a lecture hall, but the teacher was some kind of famous person who had been on tour for the whole first half of the semester. Every week there had been a new lecturer, delivering what was some kind of straight genius take on the Christianity behind this newish thing called K-pop or the Christianity behind this oldish thing called Vude. Each teacher gave homework, but Fly never did it. Homework was a dumbing down that was for the actually dumb students, not for him. Instead, after each class session Fly would go to the library. Look up the guest professor. Check out the book or books they'd written. Then he and Suzanna—he only called her by her full name now—would sit in his room and read. Just read. He his music books, she the Bible or maybe an education textbook. Though maybe she was the only one reading, because it was impossible for Fly to read with her sitting at his dorm desk with her naked feet propped on his bed. Him lying in his bed, sometimes napping, sometimes not, their feet sometimes touching.

Too often Clive would lean into the doorway, smile—"Just checking on my chickadees"—and lean back out.

6. APPROACH TO THE INNERMOST CAVE, OR, THE MEETING WITH THE GODDESS

Thinking about Fly getting saved by the Lord started to make Suzanna slutty. It got so that whenever they talked about it, she would unbuckle his pants and then close the dorm-room door—there was always that awkward thrilling moment with his dick straight up and the door wide open. She would kneel to him and say something deflating like: "I really want to be sitting next to you when you receive Christ. I just want to watch Jesus come on you!" But Fly was eighteen, the horniest he was ever going to be, so he could hold the stiffness, despite. Then she would lick and suck until he said he was cumming. She would use her hands that last minute or so to get him there, and after, she would climb into his sore, sensitive lap. All her clothes still on, she would make him hold her. Then she would say something bananas like, "When you become a man of God there isn't anything I won't submit to you for." Then sometimes she would cry.

Boy, did Fly want to be a man of God. But to be honest he felt like he was already, had been since he was a child. But Suzanna needed to witness it. Women were like that, Fly figured. So he drove home one Saturday. Picked up his dark blue suit, which was newly snug around his shoulders.

"A suit," his father said. "You drove an hour just for a suit? You going weird on us, boy?" Which was ridiculous coming from his crazy father.

"Don't mind that grumpy man," his mother said, all eagerness and gratitude. She was losing it with joy at Fly's just being home. Her face was so stretched with the smile, Fly thought it looked scary. "Are you staying for dinner?" she asked. "Meatloaf?" and then she added quickly, chirpily, "My special meatloaf."

He stayed for dinner but drove back to school that night. The next morning Fly walked up to the altar when the white pastor opened his arms. Got himself saved for Suzanna, though he'd been saved before. Pastor John had saved him from the back of a van.

But this time it was a whole production. More than Fly had realized. Anyone saved was invited, beseeched, to an ice cream social after church with the "Prayer Warriors." Arthur was there, and he took over as Fly's personal warrior of prayer. Arthur's prayers were loud and urgent and he went on and on, and Fly could see how Arthur might be a pastor, a senior one, someday. Then other young men hugged Fly—sincere bear hugs that were more male affection than he'd ever received, ever. But the young women hugged Fly, too, and that was stranger than the men. Because the girls hugged and held on, seemed suddenly to find him . . . what was it? Not just cute. Sexy; they found him sexy. They hugged him, met his eyes, gripped him with their fingers. Offered to bring him ice cream—"What is your favorite flavor?"—then buzzed around him with what he could feel was a lusty adoration. "Vanilla could be my favorite," he said, testing out his theory to a white girl. She looked down at her shoes and then back up at him, took a gulp of breath, and he saw that her eyes were watering like she might cry.

Suzanna came up, held Fly's hand until the other girl blushed and ran off with the ice cream order. He felt Suzanna's middle finger loosen in his hand; this middle finger's knuckle rubbed gently across his palm, again and again. He felt his crotch tingle in anticipation. But there were more prayers and congratulations and welcomings to Christ. And then he had to eat the ice cream.

When they got back to his dorm Fly pulled Suzanna through the door. "Leave the light on," she said, even though he hadn't given light or its absence any thought. "I want you to see me." And then she took her clothes off with the drama of someone who'd been practicing, which Fly so appreciated. Her underwear dark with wetness when she finally peeled them off. Then she flung herself onto the bed, face first, raised her hips so he could see all God had given her through the soft plump lobes of her backside. When he put his hand to her there at the center, she pressed herself hard against him, and she was slick. It made him think of candy gone sticky in the sun.

"I want to submit," she said, facing the wall, away from him. "But do it so I don't lose my virginity." Fly feared she might mean in her bum, which he wasn't prepared for. He used his fingers on her, while he stroked himself, trying to figure it out. Then, oh goodness, Suzanna started singing. Humming, really, but not in a horny way. Like, actual singing. All harmony and lovely. Wow, did he love her. He twisted his fingers in her a little; she raised her voice up an octave. He pushed his fingers in more; she trilled.

"Let me know," he said. "This is my first time, too. Let me know, okay?" She didn't answer, but when he slipped in it, not her ass after all, it was so easy, smooth, wet, sticky. He remembered what she'd asked, so he held his pelvis tight and went slow, slow. She sang sweet, so sweetly. He went a little deeper. "No," she said, talk now, no music. He felt her clench tight on him like a fist. He pulled back, slowly, and she released him but even that was . . . well . . . "Jesus, this is good," he said. Her singing started again. He went in a little, but never all in. He had the idea of what she wanted now. Just a little bit of him, the tip; maybe half of him. No more. Until the too-soon end.

"Was it good?" she asked, facing him now, her arms and legs wrapped around him.

"It was you," Fly said. "It was paradise."

7. THE ORDEAL

Clive leaned into the doorway. Then he righted himself. Fly was lying alone in his bed, but a little alone time was okay these days—he was exhausted with classes and church. Clive put one hand to his chest and the other out like a stop sign. "I'm not saying you're gay," he started inexplicably. "I'm just, man. I just want you to know that it would be okay if you are. And it would make sense why you'd want your own room, you know. No temptation and no weirding anyone out. I get it. It's just. That religious cult group . . ." Clive's hands were still in the same strange position. Hand to chest, other hand out—Fly recognized the gesture. It was like: stop in the name of love, before you break my heart. "But dude," Clive went on, "they could mess you up, you know. I mean, as far as I can tell, God loves the queers as much as he loves the, um, not queers. I just want you to know that that is how I feel." He dropped his hands.

"Thanks," said Fly. Clive nodded and then turned around. He stood in the doorway for a minute with his back to Fly. Fly was trying to get some reading done; Suzanna would be over soon. And sex with her, holding back the way she needed him to, was tiring but thrilling, and afterward he would collapse and sleep like, well, like a teenager who'd just had sex. But Clive was still standing in the doorway, and now he turned back around. "Listen. Look." He looked at the chair at Fly's desk longingly, as if he wanted to sit down. "I didn't make myself clear just now." Fly felt bad for the guy; he'd made himself clear enough. "It's just . . ." Clive seemed distraught. "Dude, listen. I've seen this before." He stared at Fly pointedly until Fly realized he was supposed to ask something.

"Seen what before?"

"I've seen this group. This girl. Specifically, I've seen this girl."

Fly wanted to sit up, wanted to face Clive, punch Clive's face, face off in some way. But instead the tension gathered inside Fly's body. Quietly, it gathered. He felt the sweat trickling down his neck.

"I've seen her with other guys. Other freshmen. Gay guys, mostly. She turns them straight. Or tries to. Or something. Breaks their hearts. Because a man still has a heart. You know. Straight or"—Clive made his hand wiggle like a fish—"still a man. A human being."

◆ ◆ ◆

So Fly got the question ready for Suzanna: *Do you love me or are you missioning to me for the love of God? Is our sex lovemaking? Or is it conversion therapy? Just because I was lonely doesn't mean I was gay.* And was lonely what gay people were, anyway? Fly, again, didn't think he'd ever spoken to a gay guy. Though he was pretty sure he'd been lonely his whole life. But then Fly didn't ask Suzanna anything when she came that night. Wanted to. Really did. Couldn't.

8. ATONEMENT WITH THE FATHER

Instead, he dropped Sue off at her dorm room. Then he got in his car and drove home. Did it fast, less than thirty minutes, when it should have been forty or more. It was late, and the house was dark. He went to his bedroom, straight. He quietly opened his childhood closet, which had been his only closet until just a few months ago. He was looking for the porno video he'd had all these years. The one he'd kept and treasured, the one that had taught him what sex could be. He pulled the video out from beneath the magazines of white girls, which were stacked beneath the magazines of Black girls. He cracked the video case. Then he carefully cracked the video itself. Unspooled the film. Sliced it to pieces with a knife from his mother's kitchen drawer. Left the house with the slaughtered tape, dumped the scraps of it behind an office building. It was dead and buried before he got back to campus. Never even woke his parents.

That was a Friday. The next day, Saturday, his mother called to cry that his father was leaving her; full-on divorce. Fly drove home that day. He went to his father's little office in the house. The older man was crowded in there, and Fly could tell that he'd been sleeping there at least a few days, maybe weeks—hell, maybe since Fly had left for college. Fly scowled silently at his father boxing things up. All the ridiculous goggles and respirator masks. All the rat-repelling handbooks. Fly wanted to curse or punch, but he couldn't tell what was his right place. His father spoke up first. "She wasn't with us in the pictures," he said. "She was separate. Alone on the mantel. And that made all the difference." Which Fly didn't understand then, and never fully understood ever, though after a few slow seconds he realized the "she" was his dad's ex-girlfriend, the same Ellie from the videotape Fly had dumped the day before.

But the father didn't seem to be talking to Fly at all, hadn't looked at him yet. Gary now had a small zippered sack in his hands. It was lumpy and when he passed it to Fly, Fly knew what it was from the feel. "These aren't mine," he said. "I have my marbles at school."

"These are mine, son. Ours, I suppose. From when I taught you how to play."

Fly felt his body tighten; a hard hot anger pressed from inside his chest. "You never taught me how to play marbles. I learned on my own." Which wasn't true, not in any way, but felt true in that moment.

"No, son. I taught you. When you were little. Long before you started playing with Brent. I guess you wouldn't remember those times. But, be it as it may, all your marbles, the ones you have—these are just the rest of them." His father pressed the bag to his son's chest, the hardness of it meeting Fly's breastbone where the marble inside him rolled and pressed back.

Fly did think about smashing the bag of marbles to the ground or into his father's face. But instead, he took the gift and walked away. Walked down the hallway to his own bedroom. His mother was in the kitchen cooking fried chicken, and a sweet potato pie, and a lasagna and whatever else she could fit onto the stove and into the oven. Fly couldn't face her, was humiliated for her. Was for himself, too. Divorce was an embarrassing admission, either of failure or of a deeply consequential mistake. Either way, awful. Fly was trying to be a man about it.

He felt exhausted. He sat on his childhood bed, which had been his only bed until just recently, and prayed for strength. He started with the Psalms, avoiding the Our Father, because, well, "Father," and found his way to Exodus, "God is song." Which made him think of Suzanna.

He went back down the hallway again. His father was taping the boxes now. The tape made a loud screeching noise when pulled across the box, was ripped with a violence at its jagged cutting edge. Fly took a deep breath and started in on his father: "I mean, really. Mom put up with you. Clenching your fists every time you heard the voices. And you doing your stupid Hindu meditation chants, or praying to Allah or worshipping anything that anyone else had ever worshipped. Because you couldn't stand yourself." Fly's hands were shaking; he was still gripping the hard sack his father had given him and now he pointed it at his father. "I mean, for years Mom has been a faithful wife. The least you could do was be faithful when she got a little lonely. And I was faithful to you. I had no choice." His arms were glistening with an anxious sweat. He had never lectured anyone before, certainly not his own father.

Fly's father looked up at him. But then Fly had to turn away, head back down the hallway, because his father was crying. And so was Fly.

9. THE ROAD BACK

Fly headed back down the hallway. He had never seen his father cry before. This was a vexing thing to realize, because Fly had always thought his father was weak, the mental illness and all. But maybe his father was sort of strong, or maybe he was really weak and this crying was more evidence, or maybe Fly didn't know a thing. Was Dad off his pills? Or was he also devastated by his own leaving? Fly was too devastated himself to consider this much, so he drove back to campus, his own tears obscuring his vision. The trip back took forever—over an hour, almost two. He imagined getting pulled over, getting handcuffed unfairly by a police officer; he imagined spitting in the cop's face, getting so brave and angry he could use his own head to smash the cop's head in. He had to actually pull over because the rage seemed to be making him dizzy. The steering wheel was slick, and he realized it was his own hands sweating. He drove so slowly. All the way back to his single dorm room.

He took the sack of marbles out and poured them into his jar. The others settled on top but looked no different. A set, they were. The same.

The pain clamped onto his chest as soon as he hit the bed. It hurt so badly he was sure he'd fallen on something hard. He wondered if it was that marble he'd swallowed; maybe it wasn't benign. Maybe it had traveled to some dangerous place inside him. The pain was on the left, where his heart was—it was broken, his heart was.

The next day when Suzanna came to walk with him to church he was still in bed, sweating and in agony. Who knew divorce could feel like this? Suzanna held back at the door, looking at him in horror. "Divorce?" she said, snarling like it was contagious.

"My heart is breaking," he said. The fatigue was in Fly's bones, in his skin—his teeth felt tired. He didn't notice the exact moment when Suzanna left. Did she make it to church?

Later, Clive leaned into the threshold, but almost fell over. "Oh, shit," he said. When health services came, they came with a stretcher.

"I swallowed a marble," Fly tried to explain.

"It's not a marble. It's mono." The nurse practitioner made it clear.

"A sexually transmitted disease?" Arthur said when he and Suzie passed by Fly's dorm room that night. Fly was less sweaty now, but still beat.

"Sorry I didn't come earlier," Suzie said. "A girl got saved so I had to stay and pray for her. You don't have a cell phone, so—"

"It wasn't the marble and it wasn't my heart. It was my spleen. Swollen. But I'll be fine," Fly explained, though Suzie's eyes were so big and he was so tired.

But of course he wasn't fine. His mother had to come get him. His teachers had to get a formal letter excusing him from exams. His final grades would be the grades he'd earned so far, which was good, because he'd barely read a thing since he and Suzanna had started having sex. Fly slept until Christmas, it felt like. Didn't feel rested until New Year's. His father didn't come.

When the spring semester started, Fly was pretty much better. Suzie came to his dorm room the first day back. She came to tell him before he heard it elsewhere. "I was saving myself for the man God created for me," she said, looking Fly in the face with the authority of a grown woman. Arthur had actually given Suzanna a real engagement ring; it gleamed like a miracle on her finger.

◆ ◆ ◆

So Fly was alone, again. Another three classes this semester. An English class on the artist in literature, and an algebra for the gen-ed requirement, plus an African drumming class for his soul. The English teacher was uninspiring, assigned them stupid stuff, like Harry Potter, which Fly felt was beneath him. Apparently, Harry was a magical artist. For the midterm, they had to memorize the various stages of the hero's journey, a form the teacher professed was the basis for all great narratives. This seemed like such a stupid thing to say that Fly lost all respect for the professor immediately. He went to the campus bookstore to return the books, and saw on a shelf for a Black studies class that *Invisible Man* was assigned. The cover looked strange and the title seemed so perfect, so apt. There was a stack of used hardcovers and three stacks of paperbacks. Fly bought one paperback and one hardcover.

Critical thinking was beyond him these days; the mono had addled his brain. Or maybe it was the actual heartbreak this time. But he could do the basics (reproduce the algebraic formulas, plug them in), though he never understood the mathematical meaning. And what did it matter?

Instead of studying, Fly would walk the campus at night listening to the music coming from other dorm rooms. He would guess what the song was based on the beat, the opening. Sometimes he couldn't hear the words or even the melody, but still: Patti Labelle, 1983, he would guess. Or "Lately," the Stevie Wonder original, not the Jodeci remake. And there was never anyone to tell him he was wrong. He would imagine the people in those rooms. Alone, he would play his djembe, one his mother had bought him. He played gently, quietly, so as not to disturb anyone. But he left his door open wide, just in case there was someone.

In the English class there was only one book by a Black person on the syllabus, and it was *Invisible Man*. A sign. Not about the class, but about the book. The main character in that one was, apparently, a musician. Fly put his copies of the book on his desk, right beside his full jar of marbles. He'd almost thrown the marbles away; he'd seriously considered it three times already. But he had trouble getting rid of things.

And despite his addled brain, he could still, sort of, memorize a list. So, alone in his room, lonely, Fly started charting his own life in his notebook—applying the hero's quest to the life he'd lived thus far. Something white boy, like Pearl Jam, rocking in from down the hall. But nah, it's not Pearl Jam. It's something more Jesusy, like Tyler Lyle's "I Will Follow Love All the Way Home." Fly felt proud that he figured that out. On the other hand, no matter where he started the story arc, he couldn't figure his way to a resurrection. So, he plugged his father's life into the formula, what he knew of it, the Lyle singing out its lonely love. There must be a complete narrative in Gary Lovett's life—Dad had lived long enough. But no, there was no heroic return for Fly's father. There never would be.

STELA

. . . the meeting of people and place, you and the place you are from are not a chance encounter; it is something beyond destiny . . .

—Jamaica Kincaid, *The Autobiography of My Mother*

THE LIVING SEA

THE STORY OF STELA'S MOTHER

Puerto Rico

1981

A road of sand separated the seas. Just a thin band of sand—that was the real bitch of it. The beach of death on the right was calm, encircled as it was by a wall of rocks. The beach of life, to the left, opened wild to the ocean. We went every Sunday after Mass. Those who could swim proper swam in life. But I could not fucking swim, so I always soaked in death.

Nineteen eighty-one is the year I manage to make myself a new family. But before that Vega Baja was my home for some stupid fucking years. Enough years for me to learn to swim, to curse even when it wasn't called for, and to meet a boy. Though not at all in that order, I must say. The boy, of course, was Martin. Spelled without the accent, but still pronounced Mar-tee-n. There were many of us there at the home in Vega Baja. The boundaries of the region were not as they are now.

The Caribbean waters was highways, not fucking national borders. So we children went and came. Children from Tortola, from Antigua, even from as far away as Trinidad. I came from Saint Thomas. Lost children, we was. Orphaned. Martin was from San Juan—a native. Still, he was an abandoned motherscunt, just like us rest.

Martin was not a mystery. No one was. The island was American, but Spanish was the language of public school instruction. As far as us picky heads could say, we would all be Puerto Ricans from here on, so before each child's arrival the women would offer the new one's personal history in Spanish. The woman with the private school education and gentle manners would translate the basics into English. This way all of us could be ready with our empathy—no bullying or nastiness. In truth, I still cannot believe they did that shit to us. The women. They did not understand a child's need for secrets, the child's desire to tell her own story and make herself new. When Martin finally came it seemed he was a man, not a lost child at all. But there he was. Sleeping on the boys' side of the house.

"My mother is not dead, como dijeron las mujeres," he clarified to anyone who asked anything at all. "Ella es en San Juan." But what was worse—a dead mother or a living mother who didn't want you? "Es verdad, I do not know my father. Pero él quería conocerme. It is just that my mother wanted to keep me as hers, solo."

It made no fucking sense, of course, but I believed him. He did seem like someone who had been loved most of his life, loved recently. In that way, he was different. We was all in awe of him, jealous, to be truth.

We march to Mass every Sunday without fail. Then the Vega Baja beach after, always. Like church and beach was both holy—same, same. But none of us was allowed to climb the rocks on the beach. A local boy had died jumping. He had dived safely, feet first, but still had not come back up until he was fucking floating facedown. And then before anyone could save his body, it had been swept through life and out into the ocean. Besides our chores around the farm, this was the only rule at the home. No climbing the *maricones* rocks. Easy for me. I was scared to fucking death of the water.

The women slept in one room together, despite the large farmhouse. Us children slept in the house, too, separated into the female side of the house and the male. The kitchen and parlor connecting us easy. The women had never had children of their own, and so did not remember their own childhoods, as parenthood may cause one to do. We was all at least five when we came; we could cook simple meals, wash our own clothes, iron them, even. We could communicate in complete sentences, most of us in Spanish *and* English. And so the women did not expect our innocence, our wildness, our curiosity, our fears. And of course we did not speak up to explain. We were grateful, all of us, that they had taken us in. Even Martin was fucking grateful, I know.

I was the middle girl. Thirteen years old. The elder girl, Darleen, kept a bag of what she said were her own baby teeth around her neck. She was just too fucking odd for regular school, so she did her high school classes via correspondence. The baby girl was six—besides the burns she was normal, not even coonoo with water like me. Her parents had died in a fire and she didn't yet go to school at all. I alone went to the municipal middle school along with the stupid small boys. On school mornings one of the women would braid my hair.

Martin was the only one of us who walked the hour to the high school in the morning. He was the eldest boy—fifteen. He would walk me and the small boys to the small school, then carry on. From the very first day, he held my hand—like my elder brother would have done if he hadn't drowned along with my everyone else. Besides braiding my hair, no one had taken this kind of care with me; no one had even held my damn hand in years.

It was on these walks that Martin told his crazy-ass version of how he came to us.

He had been leaving his school in Río Piedras and seen his mother at the gate. He was fourteen then, and she had stopped picking him up from school years before. Now here she was holding a board with words write on it. In English: THEY HAVE STOLEN MY SON FROM ME. I WILL KILL MYSELF. PLEASE HELP! Martin was a good student, well known by the teachers and staff for his diligence in all subjects, evidenced most by his neat penmanship. Now everyone watched as he walked up to his mother. But his mother did not behave as if she was seeing him. He stood in front of her. "Mamá. I'm right here. *Mira*, I'm right here." And he shook his face in front of hers until she met his eyes.

"Ay, Dios mío. Estás aquí. They gave you back. Now I can live."

For fucking real.

He took the sign from her, ignoring the teachers and students who looked on, unsure of whether to help this good boy or hamper his crazy-ass mother. His mother had been looking for him, so she said, for weeks, even though he had just left her that morning for school. "Mamá, everything is fine. Estoy aquí. I was at school."

The next morning she was herself again. But now Martin noticed that herself was fucking strange. Something he had never considered before. She had always been a woman who talked to herself, but he had never before asked about it.

"Yo praticando," she said now. Practicing? He didn't want to know for what. She had been practicing for this his whole life.

When he left for school that next morning, she kissed him on the mouth. Again, this was something she had always done. But he knew this was not normal. Had maybe known so for a while. She took his chin in her fingers and kissed his mouth gently. And for the first time ever he felt a tremor in his charlie, and he pulled back from her. Outside the door, he pressed the flat of his hand against the front of his pants until it calmed.

But after school there she fucking was again. At the gate, only this time she was shouting. "They have taken my son! I'm going to kill myself! Kill my whole self!" He rushed to her and grabbed her face until she stayed there in his eyes and knew him. The students and teachers tittered around.

On the third day, she was crying and she had a next sign with more crazy-ass words. The headmaster came out, but talked to Martin and not his mother. "She cannot do this again. We will call the police. Maybe you need to take some time off from school." Like Martin was a man. They spoke in English to make it officious.

◆ ◆ ◆

It turned out that one of the women of our home in Vega Baja was Martin's aunt. The Spanish-speaking bitchy one with the mustache who wore pants and boots. The one who rode the horses and never milked the cows. The women had taken him in as family, so he wasn't even a proper orphan. "Martin's mother is dead," both women had told us—a fucking falsehood, we now assumed. We began to wonder if they had told us other lies. If the baby girl was not from Trinidad but was full Taino, as she looked. If Joseph was the five years old he appeared to be and not the ten the women claimed. If Darleen would inherit the orphanage house and all the land like she was always saying, or if she was just straight *loca* like she seemed.

"Mi madre esta viva," Martin said. "Very alive."

On Sundays after Mass the women walked us to the seas; sometimes we would skip the whole way. Sometimes we would sing. All the children swam in life, except me. Even Baby Girl, who was the youngest. I stayed in the death. There, I could walk out to the mountain of rocks and still the water only came to my hips. My brother had known how to swim, but it hadn't saved him.

But on Martin's first Sunday with us he came up behind me in the shallow water. He placed his arm on my back and bent to cradle my legs. I didn't squeal as I knew strange Darleen would have—she was almost seventeen and had *novios* who were always leaving genips under our windowsill. I let Martin lift me and then gently lower me until I floated in the still water, his hands holding me up. I lay out stiff as a corpse and felt the sun above me.

I knew what my body looked like. Nothing like curvy Darleen. I was straight and flat as a board in all directions and now in the water I imagined myself to be a board. Floating, floating in the dead sea. What waves there were were gentle, and more gentle. Martin's hands below loosened. And then loosened more. I felt the coolness of the water between his hands and my body. I kept my eyes closed up tight. A board, I told myself. A mother's-cunting board. I steadied my breathing. The water beneath me warmed. I moved my arm to feel for Martin. But he wasn't fucking there, and I opened my eyes in a panic and flayed like a fucking fool. But my feet hit sand quickly.

I looked around and saw him, across the sand dune in the living sea, standing against the heavy waves and speaking with tiny Joseph, who was squatting in the water. Only Joseph's head came above the sea line; it bobbed like it was the only part of him. I looked away, scared as shit and stupid.

How long had Martin left me? How long had I floated on my own? At my feet little sparkling fish swam in circles. I laid my head back, stretched myself out, and then I just floated. I didn't think about my actual older brother. I thought and thought only of Martin.

The next Sunday Martin taught me how to kick. He crouched down and put my palms on his shoulders so that our faces were close, close. And I kicked and kicked. After a month of Sundays I could actually fucking swim. Like I had been doing it my whole life. Like no one I loved had ever drowned.

◆ ◆ ◆

The boys' side of the house was not forbidden to the girls, nor was ours to the boys. It was an arrangement, but not a rule. It was a regular thing that one of us would fall asleep in the living room, laid out on the rug. On our side the girls all shared a room and the women had the other one. On the boys' side, Martin had his own room, like he alone was equal to the women.

On the night of the day I finally swam, I left my bed as soon as the other girls slept. I walked through the kitchen and parlor, which were dark. The women always turned in early. Martin's door was locked when I jostled the knob. I stood in front of it. I just stared at the door, until it fucking opened. His room was moist and black, his windows closed and curtained. When I found his bed, he was in it. He took my chin with his fingers and kissed me on the mouth, his tongue stiff. I thought then that I was the sea, and he was a board and he would just float in me.

"Náyade," he said into my mouth. I wanted to say something back to him, but "shark" was all I could think of. And I didn't know how to say it yet in Spanish. His body was hot as he turned onto his back and took me with him. Me in my nightie and his whole naked body beneath mine. "If you love me," he said, "we will get married. But only if you really love."

I tried to look into his face, but it was so dark. "Okay," I said.

"When I am awarded my high school diploma," he said. "When I secure a job. When you have la edad suficiente."

"How old will I have to be?" I asked.

"Dieciséis?" he said like a question. Girls regularly left school at sixteen, started work. Sometimes married. There wasn't a girl over seventeen still at the orphanage. Darleen was almost like one of the women herself. "Little sister," she used to call us girls; "little brother," she called the boys. Which used to piss me off. But truth was that Darleen was the one we all told our histories to, if we told anyone. If we remembered.

"Can it be when I am fifteen?" I asked Martin. Two years was too fucking long to wait. I needed to make him my family faster than that.

"We can try," he said. And then he lifted my nightie. And it began. His wet fingers, then his wet mouth, then the tip of him already slick. There was a tightness and then a sudden relinquishing and then warmth.

"Mi madre," he said afterward, "loves me very much." I understood. My mother had loved me, too, until the water took her.

When I left his room, the women were already up and out tending the horses and cows. The other children feeding the chickens and gathering eggs. "Dormiste bien, hermanita?" Darleen asked when I rushed to the feed pail. "I'm not your sister, *puta*," I said. "And I haven't slept as yet." I didn't want to tell anyone, but I didn't think it was necessary to lie either.

The radio was on the news. Those years I was in Vega Baja all the islands down the chain was becoming sovereign: Saint Lucia, Saint Vincent and the Grenadines, Grenada. But that morning "Margreet Satcher!" the Spanish-speaking anchor kept hollering. But then Thatcher's voice itself came over the airwaves. Speaking in an English that sounded stern but sweet, like a kind mother might sound when scolding. The woman without the mustache sat me down in front of the couch to do my hair. Every morning she'd tackle my head. And every damn morning she complained about it. My hair wasn't *conquista* hair like Darleen's or coolie hair like Baby Girl's. But I always held my face stiff against crying, the woman's tight fist at my roots, the comb raking through the ends. But today the woman was too focused on the news.

"There is a woman head of England," she said. "And it is time, *negrita*, that you did your own hair." Right then it seemed to me like a woman taking over England might be the same fucking thing as Grenada getting free. Had me thinking about what that might even fucking mean, free woman. How did the woman without the mustache see that something had changed in me? Was it the woman become the boss of a bossy country, that made it clear? Or was it just clear that I was more grown, more of a damn woman myself, than I had been the morning before?

"Puedo trenzar su cabello," Martin said. "I always did my mother's hair." He sat beside the woman. I didn't see, but I felt her get up and then Martin straddled me between his legs and I felt the brush in my hair gently and the comb sliding. On TV, the woman prime minister spoke with her small lipsticked mouth and her coiffed hair. Everyone on the TV and there in our home seemed proud of her, and I felt jealous. But Martin focused on me, motherfucking me only. Took so long with my hair that the younger boys left for school without us. Martin twisted instead of braiding—so that my hair looked like gentle puffs on both sides of my head, and not the fierce plaits the woman had always forced.

And that was how it was. Me in his bed every night. Him doing my hair every morning. Us walking to school together and alone now, him holding my hand. And then on Sundays, just us in the death. He never touched me in the water, but any fucking *idiota* could see I was being touched somehow, sometime. There were my breasts suddenly. There were my hips. Getting curvy as Darleen. But in the water, underneath the sun, I would touch him. The water was perfectly clear and I liked to see my hands on him. "Náyade. Sirena," he called me as I moved my wrist. Mermaid, mermaid. Right there for everyone to see. For me to see, gazing into the clear water, watching him, watching my hands. Except no one saw but us. Only we were on the dead side.

◆ ◆ ◆

My birthday was a thing I knew, but that neither of those bitch women took notice of—it was this way for all of us. It was weeks after I had turned fourteen that Martin sat me down to twist my hair. He leaned in and whispered into my neck, "You are a woman now." It was true that blood had been on his sheets that morning. I had noticed, but that was how it was sometimes with us. Sometimes it was milk, sometimes it was blood. "No," he said into my ear. "This is your real blood." Did this mean we would marry now? That he could be my family?

On the walk to school he explained, "We cannot continue. You will become pregnant. I will be seventeen in just over a year, but you are not close to fully grown." I didn't remind him that we were getting married. It was the first time I felt he could abandon me. I let my hand go limp in his, but he squeezed hard.

That night I did not go to him. I wanted to, but I was fucking refusing him and myself. I lay in bed and wondered what I would do if he left me. I would stay here at the home. I would be like the women, sleeping with other women and working the farm. Perhaps raising other people's children because I didn't have any who belonged to me. The other two girls slept as they usually did. In her sleep Darleen always gripped her pouch of teeth, like it was precious. But after not a minute Darleen sat up. She looked at me as though she was quite awake. "No le vas?" she asked. And I realized that everyone must have known. "She got her period," Baby Girl said, even though that little burnt bitch had also seemed well asleep. "Muy malo para ti," Darleen said, lying back down, clutching the pouch again. "Little sister, now all the fun in your life is over."

So my life was over. Again, it was mother's-cunting over. But then the knob rustled and Martin opened the door. Our room was more lit than his, the girls' windows always open with the large moon shining in. "Sirena," Martin called in a whisper. And I got off the bed and went to him.

Instead of going to his room, we walked to the beach with the tide-pulling moon above. It was a school night, so Mass, and beach after Mass, were still days away. It was the wrong day and it was also too late at night, but still we walked into the water. We went to the living side, which we never did. Which I had never done before. And we did what we'd always done in the death—only now when I touched him he had to hold me with both his hands, so our bodies would not be taken by the waves. Afterward we sat in the sand and watched the big moon and he said, "We can still marry, mermaid." I leaned my head on his shoulder and he put his arm around me. But he had more. "My mother is getting out of the hospital." He said this with his gaze on the two lobes of life and death. "Volveré a San Juan. I will go back to being a boy with a mother," he said. "I am not a man. Realmente no."

"You are seventeen." I managed to say this, though I was scared as shit.

"No. I still have almost a year," he said. "And my mother is still my mother. And now that she is better, yo soy de ella."

I began to cry. I hated my baby-ass self for crying. Martin held me until I wrenched from him. I walked through the familiar dead water, stepped onto the road of sand, and then began to climb the forbidden rocks. And if you know anything about how stories work, you know I was heading to those fucking rocks all along.

I did it like I'd gone to Martin's room that first night; I did it without thinking. One finger of blood was crawling down my thighs because I'd left the cloth the women had given me. The rocks were sharp and hurt my feet and I couldn't always see. I stepped on something slimy—I slipped. I felt blood come to my leg, a different blood. But still, I climbed until I saw the other side. Really, I could hear it more than see it. I could hear the spitting spray and I could hear the wind wheezing. And all I could see was the white frothing of the waves, gleaming like teeth in the moonshine. It meant something, to have climbed that rock. It meant something that there, just there, was the true swallowing ocean. But, fuck, I didn't have the words for the meaning. I was a woman now, but I was still, mostly, a girl. A baby mermaid.

I stood there for a damn long time. Then I turned back to the shore, to sight Martin. But he wasn't there. I looked into the waters of life and death, and he wasn't there either. And I looked down the rocks and didn't see him climbing after me.

Don't forget that it was the middle of the fucking night. It was a half-hour walk, at best, from the women and the other children. My mother and father and brother had all died by drowning four years before. And now I was high up on the rocks at the beach. I mean. I was only fourteen fucking years old.

I opened my eyes wide and tried to see. Was that another person on the rocks now? A bad person coming to steal me? A wild dog coming to bite me? No, it was just a casha bush shivering in the wind. What was that in the water below? A hungry chupacabra swimming? A shark surfacing? I knew the word for shark by now—*tiburón*. Like someone's last name.

Maybe that would be me, Sirena Tiburón. Mermaid Shark. But not fucking really. Maybe I was a mermaid, but I would never be a shark. My disposition was too warm, especially given my hot mouth. I sat on the summit of the rocks and I cursed louder than the sea. I wanted anything living or dead to know that I could scream. I thought of all the bad words I knew: fuck, shit, bitch, motherscunt, *maricón*, *puta*, *cabrón*, *pendejo*. I shouted them, but the tears also came. I did all that until I was tired. Then I waited. Not for Martin. I waited for the sun.

The sun, at least, would return, and then I would be able to see and climb down and then I would wade through death. And then I would go back to the home and go be a little orphan girl again. A girl who didn't belong to anyone.

I waited for hours. My throat was burning from the tears I swallowed.

I saw him, my *tiburón*, just when the sun started to rise. He was walking along the beach, calm and cool and his body sloping. It was then that I really noticed that something was not normal about him. That he was not a normal boy. He had, maybe, what his mother had. He didn't resemble a grown-up at all. The woman with the mustache was more man than he.

We hadn't known then that I would be taller than him by the time I stopped growing. We hadn't known then that I would call him Papito, for his small size. But Martin was sick, that would become certain, and I would love him because he was all I had until I had you. A mermaid love for my shark man. Even when the sickness began to spin him into frenzy, even when he was the frenzy. But that day, simply by returning for me, Martin had done everything I would ever need. Made you possible. Made this whole fucking future possible.

He stood at the shore until I climbed down and waded out. He had packed his things. He had packed my things. They were in the same one bag he carried. In the bag also was the comb and brush used to do my hair, which meant he'd gone into the women's room as they slept. Fucking stolen them. And finally, there was Darleen's tiny bag of baby teeth, which he alone knew I coveted. The motherfucker had to have taken it right off of Darleen's neck.

"Can you be in San Juan?" he asked, as if he wasn't sure I could exist anywhere else but there between life and death. I nodded. I could be wherever he was.

◆ ◆ ◆

And that is what we did. We went to San Juan and retrieved his mother. But we weren't like before. We were brother and sister now, neither of us orphans. He slept on the couch and I in his old room. Sometimes at night he and his small mother, smaller even than he was, would sleep on the couch together. Sometimes I would walk out and see them. They would be embraced, maybe like a mother cradled her baby, only this baby could carry her. Hateful bitch, I would think of her but never say. We never spoke of her sickness. We never spoke of my odd arrival—a sudden sister, a sudden daughter. He and I barely spoke at all. He was steely and quiet. Like he was waiting, like a shark waiting. It was like I had always been there, but that I had always been the less loved child. I did my own damn hair now, with the stolen brush and comb. It made me feel close to Martin, remembering he'd taken it for me, despite his quiet distance. We went to Mass, as always, but there was no more beach.

Martin would do his mathematics and literature into the night. And sometimes in the morning he would still be there at the table, erasing and redoing—that perfect penmanship. On those days, I would sit him between my legs and comb *his* hair. Wavy boriqua hair, like our old ocean. I would tell him how sharp and strong his letters were, how architecturally fine his algebraic fucking equations. He would relax his cheek into my thigh, and I would know he still, somewhere inside that *coño* broken brain, still loved me. I was learning how to really love him, I suppose. The way I would always love. With care. Carefully.

But his mama, she was still sick. If we were ever alone, she would often ask me what I had said, even when I had said not a damn thing. And my Martin was also strange. Sometimes I would reach for him, as I used to. But he would turn an empty look on me and gently step away. He never called me anything but Mermaid. And so that was what Mama called me, too. They said it in English, though my Spanish was good by then. Puerto Rico was still, always, seesawing Spanish to English and back—national language versus official. But in our home it was clear. Martin and Mama were nationalist with each other—officious with me.

Some nights I lay in bed and touched myself with one hand and held the bag of baby teeth with the other. In the morning I would raise my fingers to Martin's nose and he would wrinkle it as though he didn't know the scent. "You stink," he would say. Like any older asshole brother.

I was no longer a board in the sea. I was no longer the sea with him in me. There must have been an ocean somewhere near, but nestled in our neighborhood, we never went to it. Boys at the school noticed me. I was more developed than the other girls my age. And now when we walked to school, I lurched my hand out of Martin's. I stepped away from him. I had been touched too early. Abandoned too early. There was a difficult future ahead of me.

But it motherfucking happened, again, just like Martin had told. Mama came to our school with the placard. Only this time it read: THEY HAVE STOLEN MY SON AND MY DAUGHTER! I WILL SLASH MY WRISTS! I WILL HANG MYSELF! This time the headmaster didn't wait for us to even step out of the school doors.

"Mermaid," Martin said to me as we watched the ambulance swim away. "I am graduating from high school in just a few weeks. We can go back to the dead sea. Or we can go to where you are from."

So, I took that boy back to my island, Saint Thomas, where my mother and father and brother each had a stone in the western cemetery, though their bodies had never been found. Never went back to the Vegas. Never back to those fucking seas. We took a boat. Held each other like captives all the way.

Soon after we left Vega Baja, Martin's mother hanged herself in the Ramón Marina crazy-people place. She'd braided the rope from palm leaves—an art project, the nurses had thought. What I thought was: Crazy bitch, but brilliant. That's how we women are, I guess.

Martin and I married a week after Princess Diana did. We watched the whole thing on TV like it was a fucking tutorial. We'd never seen a wedding before. On our day, other girls and boys were lined up at the cathedral like getting married was in style. No one had a dress like Diana's; mine seemed simplest of all. A white dress I'd made myself of cloth I'd stolen from a woman whose house I cleaned. That was my life then. Lots of stealing to get what we needed for love. Not like the life Dad and I have made for you and your brothers. But regardless of my plain dress and thieving ways, my Martin looked only at me, like I was a princess. I was fifteen years old. I cut a hole in one of the baby teeth. Wore it like a pendant, and I was fucking sure it looked good as mother of pearl. Every Sunday of our marriage we went to Mass and then to the beach. Our ritual. That was our formal family-making.

Together we, shark and mermaid, had you. Took us some time to get to that. Something about him, his man parts, made it hard. But it was good we managed it, you, because I knew I wouldn't have Martin for long. He would be wild for a week, wander the streets, bare his teeth if I signed a check sloppy. Then he would get contrite. Start in with his Jonah death wish. Always trying to find a reason to get himself killed. "Throw me over so you don't have to deal with me," he would joke when we took the ferry to Saint John for a day trip. Given both our histories, I would take that shit seriously, hold his body close to mine. I would have carried him inside me if I could. He even tried to join the army, but he answered their questions with more questions, kept his head low like hunting. They wrote on his paperwork that he was dimwitted. Good, I was glad of it.

You were born ten years into our marriage. By then I really was a fucking woman, and I was desperate for you. The doctor, a woman, too, had warned that I might feel sad a bit, in the postpartum time. The happy hormones leaving me all at once, when your body left. But it wasn't me who was overcome with the wave of sadness. "Save yourself and the baby. Throw me in," Martin would say. Until he climbed a mountain, of course, jumped in the water, and swam away. Or drowned. Either way.

Who is to ever fucking know if I did the right thing, marrying so young to my shark boy? We were together just more than a decade. Was he keeping himself alive just so you could come? Would he have stayed alive if you hadn't come? Well, I suppose there are entire histories that arrived before he and I even met, pushing us like currents toward each other. To now.

But I decided to live, you hear? College, I thought, and it wasn't so fucking hard then as it is these days. Didn't cost so much, and if you were smart it could cost less. So, I left Saint Thomas for the States. Did well in college, finished so fast you don't even have any memories of Atlanta—though that is where you made your first steps, learned your first words. It was there that I fast found another love to love. A good man, the one who raise you—Dad. He already had his sick-and-tired old-man ways when I met him. Felt like he could be more father than brother, which was pretty much what the fuck I needed. And I can't lie, the man was patient and steady—no shark in him to speak of. He and I had the boys, your brothers. Settled into a real family fast as we could.

Yes, it's true I was vexed to not have Martin with me. Vexed that he'd finally left me and for good. That is how death fucking works. In Saint Thomas I put up a stone for Martin beside my parents and brother.

And now I am glad to have given you my story. Shit as it is. Of how I was afraid, but how love made me brave. And for me, that has been a good enough way to live.

MONSTER IN THE MIDDLE

THE STORY OF STELA'S DAD

Fort Jackson, South Carolina

1993

Listen, daughter. There is no way to know anything for sure. And thank God for that.

Thank God for that New Year's Day, 1968. That day the monster was on my back. But then again, the monster has always been coming for me. I'm a warm-blooded person. Because of where my blood comes from. Island blood. Thank God for that blood and for that island. But, sweet Stela, I had never been so cold. The monster was in the air. Maybe the monster was trying to *nyam* me, eat me. But there I was. I was the kind of boy—and I was still a boy—who would come to wear sweaters in the summers of South Carolina. Let my mother kiss my forehead that morning, then climbed aboard a plane. Nothing with me but a bag. One change of light clothes, suitable for the West Indies, a toothbrush, and a razor . . . the last because my mother had heard that there would be no one there who knew how to cut my Black boy hair. Though she hadn't thought about my needing a winter coat.

And thank God for that long plane ride where I was too excited to be scared and so watched the sky. And for that long sleepless bus ride where my sudden fear kept me from rest. Thank God for this Saint Thomas boy in a bus, me, not sleeping, but looking out the window as it became winter before my eyes. Cold monster.

Did I clarify that it was New Year's Day? That the kiss was my mother's last? She was dying of cancer. You know that part already, right, sweet girl? Breast, though no one but me and a doctor over in Puerto Rico knew. I wasn't allowed to tell a soul because sickness of the breast or the uterus or any part of the body we call private—the parts we use to love, to make life—sickness in those parts was a shameful thing. And so I boarded that plane and climbed aboard that bus, maybe heading to my own death; not sure, but feeling also that I'd likely never see my mother again. But still, thank God for the burn in my mother's breast before I left. Thank God for her kiss goodbye that let me know it was indeed goodbye.

I could tell you more about my mother. Your grandmother. I should. For even she is the monster—and her mother, too. I just want to explain how this goes. It's a journey, but you're not alone in it, my love. None of us is. You feel alone. But also you take the journey because you don't want the loneliness. Maybe people go off to war because they want to be left alone. But left alone and lonely? Different things, those. Me? I didn't want either, baby. Just don't be confused by my life. Or all these lives. It's easy, really, to understand. See, these lives are yours. Have I made it clear that I am so thankful? Thank God for my memories and thank God for the memories that made me.

We can't outrun the monster. Run, monster. And girl, did they make us run that first night! The winter air like pins in my nostrils. I had a bloody nose before a mile. But kept running. Because the drill sergeant was shouting and because everyone else was running, too. No matter that I was in short pants in air colder than I'd ever known. Thank God for the short pants. Thank God for the ash on my knees that looked like a disease. Thank you for the blood in my nose that busted out and coated my mouth and neck and shirt and scared the sergeants just enough.

That night I shivered. So loudly that a bunk mate threw his blanket on me. Thank you, mate monster. Generous monster. Thank God. That extra blanket helped. I slept. But it started again and again. Every morning the blasted running. Every night the cold. And the sweating in the cold. And the sweat freezing me. And the letter in the mail before basic was even out, telling me that my mother was dead.

The question you must have is, what is at the middle of it all? I'll tell you, even though I shouldn't. Doesn't matter. You'll still have to do the thing to know it. So what's there, at the middle? Myth and magic, both. No shame in that. We all know it takes a village to raise a child. But I can tell you honestly that it takes an ancestry to make a man or a woman. I would never have made it to my middle if it wasn't for my mother dying and for my daddy being already dead. Because then I would never have signed myself up for a war we would surely lose. A war everyone else was running from.

My father had been fighting a war his whole life. A white man, he was. From the continent. A proper American. But not *white* white. "Cajun," he always insisted. Had fought in a war or two. Seen nothing but combat. Finally, too shocked in the mind and broken in the body, and so found himself stationed in the Virgin Islands. Saint Thomas. But it wasn't sunny for him. Lived on our island but lived like he was already dead. Absent without leave in no time. Made a half-breed baby who looked nothing like him—me. Then sat down on the bench outside a rum shop praying aloud to die until he did. But even that I'm thankful for. Thank you, old monster, thank you, dear suicidal poppy. I went to the American war to out-war him. But then my mother died and it was so cold and well . . .

That wasn't my true middle. No. We are the middle. This right here is the middle. Always. Oh, and I'm thankful for that. Because though everyone was heading to die in Saigon—I was not. Not me. It wasn't that I had connections. No Rockefeller father to save my backside. No joining the air force instead of the army. We didn't even know about those ways out on the island. Army it was. My own no-choice choice. The base, cold as an ice chest. My lips frozen and my teeth knocking. No one could understand anything I said. I hadn't learned to talk Yankee yet. So I didn't have to say a thing. All I had to do was fake sick.

I'd been living with sickness for over a year. Close to it. My mother told me she'd never breastfed me. Baby formula just arriving on island when I was born. Everyone thought the powder was better, best. So Mommy scraped to provide it for newborn me. What I'm trying to say is that even as a baby I'd never seen my own mother as God created her. But then as a grown man I had to face her breast. Care for it that long hot summer of love. The nipple sinking in. The huge red blister that took over. Until my mother dived into it, the blister and the breast. I was there. Taking care of sickness. I knew it well. Thank you, God.

Black-boy bile, the officers called it. In America, I was the Black boy, despite my half-blood history. Coughing up spit. All fake, but it fooled them. Remember, sweet one, I'd bled so bad those first days. It wasn't that I was a coward. It was just that I realized I didn't want to war with the history of my old man. Not after all. I didn't want anymore to hold up my life to his and see if mine was more worthy. Not after my mother died. I never really knew the man, my father. He didn't live long enough. He was my first monster, maybe. And I knew he would follow me. Has followed me. But with a dead mom . . . well. Well, I decided I wasn't going to 'Nam. I wasn't going to be the drink-till-I'm-dead poppy, this time of half-mongoloid children. But still. His story is mine because I lived against him. That made his life as much an influence as if I'd lived beside him. I didn't get that then. But now I just thank God.

America believed me. Even though they couldn't always catch what I was saying. I'd been a good talker back home. Talked to the doctor. Talked to my aunt about what to do with my mother's things—in the event. The army officers believed I was sickly. Too sickly to shoot a gun good. Too sickly to even look like a good target. So sickly. Me? My whole life up to then I'd never even had the flu. I'd sprained my thumb once but never a wrist or an ankle. Sick wasn't my thing. Until it was. Then faking it so well made it so real. Now that's how you know me, Stela. Your poorly papa. Your hypochondriac dad.

Well, the war. For me there was no walking among tropical trees that might make me long for home. No blinding light just before the rat-a-tat of a screaming enemy. No warm sweat in my face and pits. My war stayed cold and quiet.

I was put to ironing the uniforms of those who came back dead. I ironed alone and in air-conditioning. Had to keep the clothes crisp. Ready them for their formal funerals. Easy work on the body. Hard on the mind. Because it was Vietnam times. And so you know about the many who came back dead. And so you know about the many shirts I had to iron. And so you know about the many monsters that lived with me. I never fought in that war. I ironed. And I did it well. Did it tender, like how you do your drawing, your art. So to that I say, thank God for every collar. For every sizzle of the metal when it kissed the starch. Thank you, God, for the dead who came home for me to dress them.

Because, dear one, what happens to you is on me. My fault and my parents' fault. And Vietnam's fault, too. Because when I saw you in that basket, you reached to me, and it wasn't like you wanted to be picked up. No, ma'am. It was that you wanted to embrace me, rub me on the back. Just a baby, but already assuring me that I was going to be just fine. Fine. Fine. Fine. So, you know about need. Known since you were a toonchy thing. My fault, for sure. But what I am trying to say also is that you can choose against me. Like I did my pop. It worked for me, when I turned away from instinct. Go with your gut, my mother used to say. But sweet girl. The gut isn't always good. Depends on what you been feeding it.

Because regardless, this monster is still coming for you. Is always coming for you. The undershirts hot from the drier? Yes. They came for me. And I was thankful for the heat in that cold, cold room. And that is my whole war story. No clearing of light and jungle of grenades, just a still life of stiff shirts. I was an artist in there, of a sort. Pants with creases that could cut you, my sweet, sweet girl. Being honest sickly since is the small price I pay. And I am thankful for my wife and my boys and for you—the daughter who chose me, the one who cares for me best. I do thank God. I'm only sick now because I wasn't dead before. And let me tell you, there were so many ways to die in America that 1968.

For me, it's going to be cancer. Like my mother. What else would it be? Mine in the private prostate. The story of the monster on my back, the monster on your back, is not just one of fathers and daughters but also mothers and sons and mothers and daughters and even grandparents and aunties and first loves and second and third loves and who knows what else. It's all there. Meeting you in the middle, where you are. Where you always are. This is how the whole of history works, sweet girl. And you and me and the whole of us, we aren't anything separate from history.

When the government released me there was the Servicemen's Readjustment Act—the GI Bill, they call it now. It was that or keep working heat in the cold. Pushing an iron was the only skill I'd learned in the army. I did it expert but it didn't serve me. Couldn't go back home to our island of Saint Thomas just then; there was no home there anymore—not yet, anyhow. So what did I do? I wandered. Years of that. Small jobs, medium jobs. Malcolm had been killed. King, too. By then I was American enough for that all to matter. It seemed like Black manhood was dead. Guess that was the point. Took me a while, years, to get on a good path. But I knew I didn't want to be alone or lonely. So. Eventually. I marched to Morehouse, where the Afro American boys went, like it was my duty.

Yes, this is an American love story. Because on the first day of school orientation there was a speech for Morehouse men and Spelman women. The two schools tight together. The speaker said that thing I gather now the college presidents in America always say, white or Black: "The person sitting next to you might be your future husband or wife."

And me, I was at the end of the row. I was older than most and I'd been unsure about coming to the big meeting to begin with. By then I was even a little ashamed at having been a soldier at all. Death will do that to a man. So, I'd snuck in late. On one side there was no one next to me. I stared at the empty space for a while to think about that. It had been so lonely ironing all those years. No buddies to grieve over because they were dead. Dead when they came to me.

But thank God for that New Year's Day. And for all the new years and new days. I am thankful for all of it. Every bit. Because there in the great hall with that man talking about looking to our right and left . . . who was that man? I wish I could thank him. He spoke so well and so clear. . . . I turned from the emptiness at my right. And there to my left? Your mother. Looking at me like she'd been on a long journey just to get to that selfsame spot. And when she said, "Good morning," I heard her accent. Imagine. A Virgin Islander. At her feet—a baby basket. What year was it by then? Nineteen ninety-three, must have been. Because in the basket? You. Sleeping, though I would come to know that sleeping wasn't so much a baby's style. Me? I didn't know yet how your mother could curse me like cursing could kill. How she could love like loving alone would make me live. How she could take a motherless man—me—and make a father and a husband. All I knew was that I hadn't heard those Saint Thomas sounds in so long. Sounded like my own mother.

And then you made a noise. Like about to holler. And me and your mother together looked into the basket. Your eyes open. Looking at me like you already knew I'd be your daddy. Your arms reaching out to me. Like you'd been waiting, waiting for me to find my way to you.

BELLY OF THE WHALE

STELA'S FIRST LOVE STORY

Saint Thomas, Virgin Islands

2007

1.

Today Johann shows Maristela how to hold the rope and release herself down. Her bare hands grip the rope; her bare feet slide down the soil, shifting aside the dirt of the mountain. He is in front of her on the trail but below her because they are going down. This mountain doesn't lead to a valley. It leads to the ocean. At the bottom, there is not even a beach. There is only a patch of dirt just enough for Johann and Maristela to sit on. There, he fastens the flippers to her feet and tells her to spit into the goggles. He adjusts them gently, but tightly, on her sweet face. This is Stela's first time. It is a gift he is giving her. She is fourteen and he is nineteen. It is Christmas Day.

Johann says, "The flippers are so you don't step on the sea urchins."

Stela looks into the water, which is shallow here. The black spines spear out of the urchins' round bodies, making them look like underwater porcupines. Stela is afraid of them. Johann, who loves her, can sense this. "You have to dive into the shallow water, face in and flat like a board. Keep all of your body at the surface." He says this serious but kind. "Don't put your hands down until you're in the deep. If you get pricked the blood will be bad and those stingers don't come out. Just glide like Superwoman."

Stela is certain that one of the spines will pierce her hands or face or chest. But she nods anyway. Johann smiles and then kisses her mouth.

"Follow me," he says. And she does. As far as Stela can say, she will follow Johann forever. They bend their knees and snap forward until they are gliding over the shallow area. Stela holds her breath, anticipating the needles. Her flippered feet kick like propellers. When she can no longer hold her breath, she tests with her arms and feels nothing below her but the thickness of the water. She pushes herself to air. She and Johann are there together, swimming in the open ocean.

◆ ◆ ◆

Johann was born in landlocked Johannesburg. So-far-away South Africa. His parents are American but they'd met in Europe. His mother had already decided on her order of sisters and his father was already a seminarian. Europe was just supposed to be a last lick of freedom before committing to a life of the cloth. But then they'd found their way to Catholic India, Pondicherry, and married rashly after accosting a priest. India led them to South Africa, where Johann was born—named after the city of his birth. The parents taught English in order to eat; wrapped the baby to Julie's back like a rucksack. The story they told themselves was that their love was seeded in exoticism, and needed something foreign in order to flourish. After South Africa, they'd settled in Saint Thomas. Johann had not even been one year old when his father strung the rope down the mountain.

Stela was born here on the island. Her mother's name is Mermaid—a nickname, but no one alive has ever called Mermaid anything else. Even Stela calls her that. Her father, who is not her real-real father, but he is real enough, is an army vet who gets sick if anyone sneezes. Their family goes to the beach every weekend, just like they go to church. Dad ever only wades in; a soak, he says. Even in the years since her mother taught her how to swim, Stela stays most of the beach day with her father. She lays out his lunch. Reminds him to shift so he stays in the shade as the sun moves. She never swims out with her brothers to touch the buoy and look for sharks. She has never been in the deep of the open ocean like she is now with Johann.

2.

"Whales," Johann says today, treading water. "Yesterday, we saw whales from the deck." He points up to his parents' house at the top of the mountain but Stela looks out at the ocean. She is from this island but has never seen whales. "Don't worry," he says. "They won't hurt us."

"I going hurt you," she says, smiling.

"Come and try."

He splashes away and Stela follows him. Though Mermaid taught her how to swim in the free sea and Johann learned taking private lessons in his family's private pool, he is faster than she is. He swims with his head under the water, which otherwise Stela has only seen anyone do on TV during the Olympics. But he lets her catch up. Beside him, Stela can look down and see her legs furiously kicking to keep her afloat. Beyond her legs the blue turns dark, until the black just keeps going.

"I hope we see a whale," Stela says, her Saint Thomian accent clipping into something more American, as it does whenever she is with Johann.

"Not while we're out here," he says sternly.

"But you just say they wouldn't hurt us."

"They wouldn't mean to. But they're so big. They'd just swim by. Then? The end."

"Oh, my God."

"Don't worry. I'm keeping watch."

Stela thinks if she died out here that her father would just die, too. Who would mix his tonics? Who would fill his pillbox? Johann would survive, though. Johann is strong and healthy and barely needs her at all. She swims to him, wraps her legs around him. He holds his weight and all of hers, keeping them both afloat. They are the same height, they weigh almost the same amount. Their bodies are both lean, but hard and heavy. His is just that bit harder, heavier.

He says, "You always want to hug like this in the water." His body is trembling with her weight as he treads. "We can hug on the land."

"You don't like holding me?" she asks, though she can hear that he is getting out of breath. He is holding her as though rescuing her.

"It's just that there's so much to do out here," he says. "We're doing nothing."

Being held by him is not nothing to Maristela. It is the most of everything to her. She is a teenager in love. But she is ashamed of this feeling, so she lets go of him and smacks her hands against the water, keeping herself afloat. "If we are just going to swim, we could do that in your pool." She says this all salty, to cover her shame. Truth is she would pick the sea over anything.

"This is our Christmas cathedral," he says, and lifts one arm out of the water to gesture at the entire ocean.

Stela cuts her eyes. Go have your cathedral, she thinks and feels the biting jealousy. She lies on her back and floats. Pedals her legs to stay flat and to stay calm. Then she looks up at the sky, an entire smooth blue. Johann is right, she allows herself to think. This is God's true cathedral. She will use chalks to draw the sky, maybe. This must mean her ocean period is coming to an end.

◆ ◆ ◆

Back when Stela was in middle school at their K–12 and Johann was in high school, she knew about him as one of the skateboarding Columbiners. The white kids who smoked weed behind the buildings. Everyone suspected that those American kids would set the school on fire, at the least. But Maristela and Johann were neighbors on the sparse west side of the island. Her house just off the main road, his at the end—at the cliff. Johann had his own car, and would sometimes give her a ride home from school when her parents had work meetings and couldn't pass for her on time. It was a long drive from their school to their homes, the roads empty and winding. Stela didn't feel shy with him, despite his being older, in high school. Johann didn't feel weird with her; he liked that she was kind of artsy and nerdy. Their parents knew each other; their stretch of road was a neighborhood. Johann driving Stela home was easy, meant nothing.

Then he invited her over to his house for dinner, a gesture, nothing more. "Jo seems like a nice kid," her father said when he granted permission to go. But she'd felt her specialness with Johann's parents. Maybe he'd never brought a girl home for dinner before.

When Johann left the island for college, he'd call Stela sometimes. Stela would send him letters, like he was a pen pal from the time before email. Her letters didn't have words, they had drawings. Sketches of the things from home: a sand dollar, a pile of shells, the shells in her hand, and just her own hand. And Johann kept calling. Told her about boring things, like how he went skiing for fall break in Denver with his new bright friends. Denver was close to Columbine, Stela had found herself thinking, judging him for that choice. Really, he was just a high school alum who missed the island while he was up there in the snow. Really, she was just some lowerclassman he'd known back in school.

3.

Today Stela opens her eyes to the sky, but now the sunlight is so bright. She turns her face to look at the water. She thinks of a dinosaurly large whale slowly mounding by. Lifting one large fin slightly and slapping it over her, pushing her down and down into the black blue. She looks around for Johann and finds his blond, glittering head. He is studying something on a rock that cuts through the water, the rock like a baby volcano. He is so far away that she feels panicked but she also feels that she loves him. She watches him for a while—the waves would be hard for her to get right, all those various blues; the air even harder, with its various yellows. But watercolors could maybe make it. Maybe oils—but she's never painted with oil and isn't sure; she just thinks the oils are very romantic. Johann's hair is also yellow and his swim trunks blue. This is what her boyfriend is to her—the sunshine and the ocean.

◆ ◆ ◆

Johann is a college sophomore in Virginia now. He has already declared mechanical engineering as his major. Stela is a freshman, but in high school. She draws seascapes in colored pencils, and adults question if she really drew them, if she is capable of this. The doubting makes her feel special, like her talent is so great it is unbelievable. She draws shells and sand and beach sunsets. It was her art teacher who first called this her ocean period. Stela thinks she maybe will not draw anything besides the sea.

Stela is sure Johann should be studying oceanography or marine biology. But she's not his wife yet, and so doesn't feel she has the authority to interfere. His university has seven different kinds of engineering majors, though the building where those classes were housed is still locked down. Stela isn't really sure what "engineering" even means. She pictures her Johann driving a steam engine train, a puffy hat on his head and a smile on his face.

Johann attends a university in Virginia that neither of them had heard of before, though the whole nation knows it now. Because some crazy Korean kid had shot up the campus. Not Korean, Stela's dad had pointed out; raised in America—American of Korean descent. But it didn't matter. Immigrant, either way. Johann himself had felt immigranty on the campus his first few weeks of college—a white kid born in South Africa and raised in the Caribbean. But by his first school break he'd felt less so. Felt more like one of the family in the States, one of the tribe.

4.

Today, Johann slowly turns his head and motions Stela over. She swims ten clumsy strokes to him. He is not that far away after all. At the rock, he is studying a sea cucumber that looks soft as foam but feels like hard muscle when she touches it. "Strange," she says. "Beautiful," he says.

He points up at the rocks. They have swum around to the opposite side of the mountain, the sharper side. On this side, there is a cliff. "That's where we'll jump from," he says.

"Okay," she says, trying to be brave for him. He takes her hand under the water. There is no rope here, so they free-climb up. She does not look down. She does not look back where she has come from. "Step where I step," he says. And of course she does. She watches the heels of his feet for signs. She can see that it is a long drop to the dark ocean. "Suppose," she asks, "there's a rock under the water and I smash my head when I jump? Or suppose I jump and then I keep going down and down into the water?"

"I'll jump with you." He holds her hand and they face the open air and the ocean together. "On the count of three." He starts at one. Stela sees the whale at two. At three Johann bends his body to bound off, but she tugs her hand out of his grasp. He goes over the cliff without her.

◆ ◆ ◆

The tragedy happened in Johann's freshman April. He'd called her first, before he'd even returned his parents' calls. "I know the girl!" he yelled, inexplicably, into the phone. "Her eyes, Stela. Like the sea, those eyes." He'd landed back home two days later. An extended spring break that became summer break. The truth was that he hadn't known the girl at all, the first one shot. He'd only seen her in a science class they'd both taken the semester before.

Still, Stela was strangely jealous of the pretty dead white girl. Until Johann invited Stela to his house for dinner just days after he arrived home. The shooting was still on TV every day, every night. This time, while his parents were loading the dishwasher Johann took her to his bedroom, sat her down on the bean bag, and told Maristela that he loved her. He unfurled all the sketches she had sent him as proof—he'd kept them, treasured them. And she didn't blink, because she realized that this was what the stories she'd heard her whole life had been leading to: him and her. So she knew exactly what to say: "Well, now we have to go out on a date."

Before that moment Stela had always been the one who ended up sitting behind Toy and Akil as they felt each other up in the movie theater. But now Stela had her own boyfriend. Her first. They'd been a real thing since then. And they were in love. Even with him in college, everyone at school knew who Stela really was: the girl who could draw, and the girl who was Johann's.

5.

Today Stela sees Johann, far below, hit the water. She is on the edge of the cliff and he has jumped some fifty or sixty feet. When he goes into the water, the water keeps him. Maristela watches the ocean and keeps watching. Johann has disappeared so surely there is no evidence that he has ever been. She wonders if this is how it had been for her mother, when her first father died. But no, it's Christmas Day, she reminds herself urgently. Johann can't die on Christmas Day. She watches the water. It is still, which means it might be easy to paint now. It is not Johann blue. It is a dark, dangerous kind of blue. Stela starts to pray. She keeps the words calm, pulling her beloved to air with her mind.

At first his head, then his shoulders burst through. "Why did you do that to me?" he shouts up at her.

"Why did you do that to me?" she shouts down.

"The only way to get home," he now confesses from far below, "is by jumping down, and swimming back to the side we came from. You have to jump."

She kneels on the ledge. Her hands firmly on the ground, her head down so he can hear. "I see a whale," she says. He turns briefly to look at the sea. Then he looks up at Stela for a long time, as though the whale is her.

◆ ◆ ◆

Johann had been home from the shooting for a month and they had been dating for that month, when he rented a fancy tourist hotel room for himself and Stela. He didn't want their first time naked together to be cramped in the back of his car, or sneaky in her bedroom while her parents and brothers slept. So she'd told her parents they were doing a movie, but instead they sat together on the large hotel bed and took off all their clothes. They marveled at their similar tight bellies, their similar shoulder freckles, their similar round bums. They avoided the differences—color and texture. They admired the different places that would someday allow them to lock into each other—his penis hard and curved, her vagina sticky and warm. They presented these things to each other like treasures: "So smooth," she said to his; "So sweet," he said to hers.

Mermaid had already explained to Stela all about intimacy: the intrepid magic of the clitoris, the tender mechanics of the anus. Mermaid had no judgment for Stela dating an older and possibly more experienced boy, and so Stela had no judgment for herself. Still, Stela was waiting to have full-on sex, waiting for Johann—though he was right there, of course. Waiting for marriage, to be more exact. But not out of any shame; out of a belief that it would be more holy that way. This was exactly fine with Johann. He'd always figured he'd marry early, like his parents had done.

In the resort room, he'd kissed her back, used his fingers, then swam his tongue in her—her forehead pressed against the pillow. This was her first time doing that. Afterward Johann stroked her back with his knuckles. "When we get married will you take my last name?" he asked.

"Whatever makes you happy," she said. His last name was Scott, like his father's. From then she was always Stela Scott in her mind. She fell asleep with church bells in her ears. He woke her in time to preserve the lie she'd told her parents. She took a shower and squealed when the huge showerhead made it feel like it was raining. She thought to ask him if it was okay to take the soaps, but then she just took them. She wanted to take the bathrobe, too, but didn't.

6.

Today Johann climbs back up the rocks. Standing on the ledge, she watches him make the journey more quickly than when he'd had her following. He is so healthy, so strong. He takes the little juts and clefts in the mountain as though each one has been placed divinely for him. When he ascends onto the ledge his face is set, and she has a thought as though he might push her. Sometimes his strength and health scare her. It's not how her dad is. Stela's toes grip the ground.

"You count us down," he says this time.

She starts at ten and makes her way slowly down the numbers. She can see the whale. She can see its mouth of soft plankton-eating teeth spread wider than a gate. She can see its mermaid-graceful body lifting high out of the water. So easy to draw; she's drawn hundreds of whales. At the count of one she does not jump. Instead, she feels Johann let go of her hand.

His arm comes around her back and she feels the push, like an embrace, lead her down. She can see them shooting toward the whale's mouth. The tongue of the animal lolling out. They slip down the whale's throat.

It is soft and wet inside the whale's stomach. Johann's arm does not let her body go. "Are you okay?" he asks in the darkness of the belly.

"Maybe we'll never get out," she says. Their words echo around the belly walls. When they stand, the water comes to their knees. "We don't need to get out," he says reassuringly. "There are fish in the whale's belly, which we can have for food."

But actually, when they crash she goes under. The salty water shoots into her nose and her mouth. Stela is filled with it. She flails and flails and she can't tell where Johann's hands are. She goes where she thinks is up and when her head comes above the water she is coughing and her nose is burning and they are not in the belly of the whale.

"You're okay," he says.

"Again," she says.

They jump three more times. The third time, Stela jumps by herself. Each time she cannot escape the image of the whale's mouth opening and taking them, then just her.

They swim back to the strip of land where the rope waits. Johann cups his hand into the water and makes the sign of the cross. "Up the mountain," he says.

"Like Moses," she says.

◆ ◆ ◆

This past semester Johann had flown home every month from college. This was the deal his parents made with him if he insisted on going back. He'd only been back to campus for three weeks, but when he returned home that night, he walked the mile inland to Stela's house, the ocean at his back. He knocked on her bedroom window with the rat-a-tat she recognized. She'd shushed down the hallway and onto the porch, and they'd kissed on the porch and then sat close in the dark corner of the porch, and then they'd lifted her nightie and taken down his jeans and pressed their fingers and palms and tongues to each other. They took turns, Maristela first and then again last, because they had discovered that she felt it more intensely the second time—she'd described it "like a wave crashing over me."

Over the course of his visits from college this past semester, he and Stela did everything a body in love with another body could do—except actual sex. And they did this everything everywhere they could find—in public parks at night, in alleyways at dusk, on her parents' porch in the still-dark morning, and in daylight on the deck at his house overlooking the sea. By the time they are swimming deep in this ocean they have seen each other naked so many times and in so many ways that they feel native to each other.

◆ ◆ ◆

Now has been Stela's sophomore year of high school, and she and LaToya drive around with LaToya's boyfriend, who has access to his older cousin's car. They go to the club that doesn't card, and dance to soca, and they sweat and scream when the songs tell them to scream. Stela thinks of Johann in the States, but is also glad that he doesn't see her so wild and so West Indian. The white kids on island don't often go out dancing, and she doesn't want Johann to feel their differences—it's enough that they have to know them at all.

LaToya has been fretting that her boyfriend is pressuring her to have sex. Stela nods along with her friend and listens and widens her eyes at the appropriate times. Stela is sure that the waiting she and Johann are doing is something radical and beautiful—like being an artist.

But since Johann has come home from college for Christmas, Stela hasn't gone out dancing once. True, her father's numbers have been low, and Stela has sat with him in the same doctor's office twice in two weeks. But it's also that she's been drawing more. She has been perfecting individual parts of Johann's body—she knows his hands so well that she can tell if he's been swimming or if he's been in the sun too long just by the lines.

7.

Today, back up in his parents' bathroom, Stela and Johann stand in front of the mirror. Her face still holds the impression of the goggles. His face is red with sunburn. Tomorrow it will peel or turn golden, depending. They both look at her reflection. Her skin is richer than before and not reddened. His eyes are blue and gray—ocean colors, like the pretty dead girl's. Stela looks into her own eyes, ready to see a sadness. But Johann kisses her cheek and they both watch her face rise into a smile.

"What should we do now?" he asks.

"We should get in the big tub," Stela says hopefully. This is something she's been wanting to do since first spying the huge thing in his house.

"But we've just been in the world's largest Jacuzzi," he says. "Let's take a shower instead."

Stela doesn't want him to know that she feels this difference, that his parents can afford a big tub with shoots that massage—and hers cannot. She says okay to the shower.

With the water coming down on them, Johann wants to wash her hair, but Stela avoids him, lathering it up herself and pronouncing it clean. Johann's mother has smooth blond hair that sheets down her back. Stela's hair is dark and curly, and has never been longer than her shoulder blades.

"I love your neck," Johann says to Stela, touching, then kissing it.

He asks her to touch him while he kisses her. She does. Then he asks if Stela will do his favorite thing. She does. And when he says, "I'm cumming," Stela doesn't pull away like she knows some girls do—even the upperclassmen. LaToya doesn't even believe in going down at all. But for Stela, taking all of Johann feels more truthful. "I love you so much," he says afterward, sloppy, the way he always says it after. Stela thinks that maybe they should just go ahead—make love, have sex. If they love each other so much. This thinking scares her, so she turns to the shower and rinses her mouth. She doesn't know why she loves Johann. The love she has is there to give and he is there to receive it. The giving and receiving arrived together and now they go together—always will.

Sometimes when Stela thinks of herself and Johann, she thinks of her parents. Her real ones. She is devoted to her stepfather; never thinks of him as step, calls him her dad and nothing else. But it's Mermaid and Martin who she thinks of when she thinks of real love. Like them, Johann and she also love each other over water. This means their love will begin young and then last as long as they both shall live. Water never goes away; it only keeps returning in new form. That is the science, and that is the story.

The shower becomes cool, then warm, then cool again. In Maristela's house, her mother is always cursing over the water level of their cistern. Stela's dad hasn't been able to work full time in a while, and so money is tight. During the Christmas season, it doesn't rain much and water is expensive to buy on island. Stela is Dad's favorite, and it's she who boils the water for his tea. She fills the tub only halfway for his baths. But here Stela and Johann stay in the shower until her body begins to feel raw and sore.

After, when Stela asks for lotion, they must go to his parents' room and dig through his mother's things. The lotion is in a tiny round jar marked El Mar—the Sea. The design on the cap is of tiny fish eggs. Stela spreads it thickly on her knees and elbows. They go out to his deck, their bodies naked and soft. From here they can hear if his parents drive up. So Stela bends over the deck to watch the sea, and Johann spreads her open and licks her until she shudders. This is her favorite thing.

Afterward, they dress and then lie on the couch. He holds her tightly and Stela thinks that he must smell her body but also his mother's lotion—both together. It makes her feel brave. "What if the whale had swallowed us?" she asks.

"I don't think there was a whale, Stel." And even though they are too old for make-believe, he doesn't say it with exasperation. He says it calmly, as though he has considered the possibility.

"We could have lived in its belly," Stela says. "Ate the fish it ate. Lived safe and healthy. Telling each other stories."

"No," he says, holding her a little tighter. "It would be dark in there and full of seawater. If we didn't drown, the stomach acid would kill us. Either way, we'd be dead."

"I can't die," Stela says; she wants to add "because my father needs me," but instead she asks Johann, "Tell me nice things."

"Mermaids," he begins. "Angelfish. Sea fans and sea nymphs. Turtles. Dolphins. Damselfish. Whales . . ." Stela falls asleep to him listing the ocean.

◆ ◆ ◆

Johann's parents have gone to an afternoon Christmas Mass. Their church is the one closest to the sprawled houses and open land where the other white people live. It is also the church closest to where Maristela lives, but she has never attended his church.

Maristela went to Mass that morning with her family—first thing. They always go to the cathedral, which on Christmas Day is crowded with people wearing red and white. Going to church is their family tradition, though it will stop with Stela.

On this Christmas Day there was a play, and an art show and singing and steel pan. Stela's two brothers play pan, but Stela is an artist. Always been. She'd drawn a triple portrait of Moses, Martin Luther King Jr., and Senator Obama. Drawing people isn't so much her thing, but the priest had requested this image exactly. "A trinity of deliverers," he had said in his sermon. But in the pew: "Those men ain deliver me from one fucking thing," mumbled Mermaid. "I deliver my own damn self." It was a mystery that Mermaid still went to church at all, for how sacrilegious she could be. The boys were with them, too, and now one rolled his eyes and the other pretended to gag. Dad was at home, in bed, as he tended to be. The only part of the portrait that Stela felt good about were the hands.

Johann is an only child and he had chosen entirely against church this Christmas. He had chosen to worship in the sea with Stela.

8.

Today when his parents come home Johann and Stela are dressed and clean and on the couch. Stela stands to meet them. Ms. Langley, who has a different last name than her husband, hands Stela a small box wrapped in blue paper, and shouts, "Merry Christmas, Maristela!" in a surprising and loud way. Stela knows now why his parents have taken so long at their Mass. They went into town to buy this for her. Pushed through the maze of high-season tourists to get to a fancy Indian jeweler's.

"Jesus," Stela whispers when she opens the box.

"Put it on, put it on," says Mr. Scott. Stela fumbles with the clasp but Johann takes the gold necklace and its blue sea pendant from her.

He tiptoes to lean over her, like maybe her father would if he wasn't always so sick, if his medical bills didn't make it impossible to afford this kind of thing. Johann fastens the jewelry around her throat.

"What kind of stone is it?" Stela asks.

"Larimar," Mr. Scott answers, glancing at his wife. "It's *the* Caribbean stone. You've never heard of it?"

"Maybe." Stela looks at it, then reaches out to hold Johann's hand. They had exchanged gifts as soon as she'd walked in the door—that seemed like days and days ago, but it was only this morning. She'd given him a CD of reggae music. He'd given her jeweled clips for her hair.

"I hope you like it," Julie says, looking between Stela's breasts, where the teardrop pendant is hanging.

When Stela leaves that night she will have the tiny jar of Ms. Langley's lotion, El Mar, in her own back pocket. No one will have given it to her, but she'll know they would have. If they'd considered what she really wanted, and who she really was.

9.

It is many years later that they will be in Johann's stateside apartment, which is not near his university at all, but near that mountain ski resort. Not in Virginia—Denver, despite Columbine, despite it all. Johann and Maristela will take a bath jumbled up together in his tiny tub. "Don't you miss the ocean?" Stela will ask him, one of her legs dangling over the side with his, her toe skimming the perspiring floor. "Not really," he will say. "I like the snow." There will be no fuzzy soap bubbles but they will stay in the tub, soaking like bags of tea until the water grows murky and cool.

◆ ◆ ◆

Today Mr. Scott gives Stela a glass of wine. The wine is pink like a seashell, and tastes like it came from an animal. It is Stela's first time drinking alcohol. Johann will be that for her. First glass of wine, first love, eventually first person she chooses to have sex with. Today was the first of countless trips down the mountain and into the ocean. Now she sits with his family—her in-laws, she thinks—on the terrace to look for whales.

EXPERIENTIAL STUDIES

STELA'S COMING-OF-AGE STORY

Legon, Ghana

2013

Johannesburg. Mother Africa. Africa for Africans. Stela, a sophomore in college but already engaged to be married to a white boy, Johann, who was born in Africa and named after the big city itself, though not even Afrikaans—but American. The wrong *A*. Which meant Stela needed to go. To Africa. To figure herself out, before giving herself over to him.

In the study-abroad magazines Cape Town looked like Saint Thomas, just bigger. Big mountains strewn with sand. Mountains that only just some short time ago had been under the very sea. Or maybe she would go to Joburg. Where the mountains were mine hills and were red as the setting sun. And the people lived beneath galvanized roofs, just like in Saint Thomas. Either way, it had to be South Africa. Country of revolution and resolution, of Mandela and murder, where sweet Stela might fall in love with the land and not just the boy who was born in and named after the big city. And then she and Johann might, who knows, love there and live there. And no one would think the two of them weren't right for each other. He would be as native as she, as foreign as she—and in different but complementary ways. It was always about love. Love, love. All we need. Even Stela's mother, who was always telling her brothers to date Black for their own safety ("Emmett Till!"), could get down with Johann. "An African boy," Mermaid would say and smile. Or smirk. No matter. Truth is, Mermaid herself had first married an almost-white Puerto Rican.

But South Africa said no. A sign? Likely.

South Africa was a popular place for studying abroad. Who knew? True, it was beautiful in South Africa. It was political but the politics weren't even America's fault (right?). And yet it was still African enough—even had Africa in the name! It had real Black Africans and African townships and it wasn't anywhere close to the Congo (not really). But wait, watch the complementary contradiction: the country was also white and had consistent electricity and good plumbing on the university campuses. American parents could send their children there on safari with the least of worry.

So Stela of the good (but not great) grades was not competitive. And she needed to go on scholarship; Mom and Dad didn't have the money for her to just go. (Dad was sick, again, though Stela would be clear across the globe, not close enough to care for him.) So Stela, Maristela to strangers, ended up in *West* Africa. Too far from her Johann's Johannesburg for a hop and skip over. But she was still in Africa. And farther away from home and her sickly second father than she had ever been. And what the hell was she doing here? Her college offered South Africa as a journalism program—*Witness the Revolution!* West Africa—Ghana, to be specific—was the music program: *The Origins of Hip-Hop!*

Stela was a visual artist—not a writer or a musician. This was the wrong program. Wrong region and reason.

Yes, there was a study abroad program in visual art heading to Italy. But Stela needed her study abroad to be negroid. (Because once she lifed up with Johann, life was going to be, well, less Negro.) And the only visual art program her school offered that fit her Negro requirement was the study in Haiti. And, well, you know. Haiti had been Haiti since the beginning and that program was on one year and off for another three—political upheaval here, hurricane and earthquake there, AIDS, AIDS, AIDS. The Haiti program—*Create Primitive Art!*—had been off since Stela had arrived at college. And besides, Haitians, African as they might be, were Caribbean just like her. How much more African could their Africanness be? What more could they teach her about her Blackness than Culture Man on the Saint Thomas radio waves hadn't taught her already?

No. Maristela was determined to go somewhere where the melanin was *African* African. She had to go real Black because of really white Johann. Because Johann had put a ring—silver and with a topaz, but so what—on the finger to save for marriage. She was still saving her virginity for that, too. Johann was patient, another reason her parents liked him. She and Johann would get married after she graduated from college. (Toy, Stela's best girl friend from high school, was engaged, too. But LaToya and her guy were already doing, you know, *it.*) Stela and Johann, good Caribbean Catholics, were imagining a sweet, gentle lovemaking for their first time, with her still in her white veil. After the little pain and the little blood, they would follow the sweetness with a supersexy screwfest—and then babies.

Sure, he would still be in college, at the rate he was going. Couldn't focus at V Tech, he said. Legit, she supposed. So maybe she would move to the snow country where he went to hide away, learn to ski. Be his wife and his lover—Mother Mary and Whorey Magdalene in one.

They'd find their way back home—Africa or the Caribbean eventually. They'd been planning it half a decade.

So fine, Legon. University of Ghana. Stela's father was freaking out over it. She'd be farther from him and everything she knew than she'd ever been. Dad didn't say, "And what if I have an emergency? What if this thing with my prostate turns out to be a real thing?" He didn't say because he didn't have to say. Mermaid said it more straight: "America and the Caribbean ain safe for not one fucking body. Look how that devil man keep those girls locked up for years up in the States. And he was a Caribbean man. The only thing keeping anybody safe is prayer, and even that ain barely shit. Might as well go live your life where your spirit send you."

Now two months in Stela was turning twenty years old. And her birthday was the twentieth of the month: 20/20. Auspicious. On her birthday, she would see clearly. Good. That was what she'd come for. A good metaphor. She'd been taking art classes back at her own college, but so far had not gotten into the art program. How could she not be good enough? Everyone back home had always said she was *good* good. Best. Her father's vision was failing these days—some part of him was always failing. But Stela knew there was something she still needed to get, to see. And she needed to get far away from Dad and Mermaid and all their tales to do that.

In Ghana, the American students were all science majors or music majors, and most were both. A harkening of her future, perhaps, but one Stela didn't care to consider. "Can I take painting instead?" And the vice chancellor had shrugged. "You are our guest," he said, but he smiled and bowed like he must be joking. Stela tensed; she didn't want to be a guest and she didn't want to be a joke. Growing up in a tourist trap had her hating tourists. Still, the VC found Stela a painting class. Stela registered. Easy as American pie.

There was also the required Language Class for Foreign Students of

Music Studies—which included and focused on how to say "Bottled water, please" in Twi, Ga, and Ewe. And the names of African instruments. Also, names for traditional songs. Names for types of African music—though those were strangely in English: Afrobeat. Highlife.

The other classes were full-on academic. The Modern African Novel: Achebe, Gordimer, N'Gugi. Big writers. Same as saying Hemingway, O'Connor, Updike. But angrier. The other American students from her American college were taking a musical instrument instruction of their choice (djembe, calabash, fula flute), and they also took the Origins of Hip-Hop! course around which the whole program was formed. True, in the University of Ghana course packet the class had a more sedate name: Pan African Musicology. But Stela had said no thank you. Instead of that music class, she took painting. And biology.

In Painting for Intermediate Practitioners most of the other students were white girls from England. On the first day, Stela had reported, "I'm from the Virgin Islands," with pride. Her home was a beautiful place where everyone wanted to be—if the number of tourists could be counted as evidence. One of the British girls smiled at Stela: "Is that close to Turks and Caicos?"

"Same region," Stela said. The girl had kept on smiling, but the smile turned sour, sad. This confused the hell out of our girl Stela. She smiled back, tried to think of a follow-up question. Ah, but then she remembered. Poor Turks and Caicos. Their sovereignty had recently been snatched back from the British. These girls must know all (or just a little—enough) about that. "But my islands are American," Stela said. Which she thought would make her feel better but didn't.

There was one boy in the class—he was called Edi. Edi was not really a student. He was a teaching assistant. An African boy, Ewe tribe, though he was blond and freckled, his hair shaved to bald so no one would ever know how kinky or how straight. Edi the Ewe, that's how Stela would remember him. "I was born in England. My mother was white," he told her that first day when he'd stopped her outside class. "She abandoned me here with my father's people." All this in their first conversation. Stela figured he must see something special in her. He seemed special, too. His story was the same as the president back in the US. Almost. Except with the president, the African father had done the abandoning and that had made all the difference. Apparently. In Saint Thomas there were tons of things newly named after the US president: Obama Grocery & Tings. Barack's Bakery Delights. All this assured Stela that Edi would be cool.

The other course she took was Human Biology. She needed the requirement. So in these odd classes, painting and biology, Stela was well isolated from her fellow (Americans?) college mates. In Human Biology there was only one proper American. A Black boy, deep brown skin, about six foot with a fade, whose name Stela never could remember. TBA, she called him to herself. The Black American. Which is (partly?) why she will remember this boy's face when she first meets Fly Lovett. Because that boy, TBA, tried to take care of Stela. And who knows what leads people to love who they love?

The biology class was in a big lecture hall. The teacher, ostensibly, was the lecturer. But in every class meeting at least one Ghanaian student would stand and deliver his (always male) own competing or complementary lecture on the construction of living human ears or how uterine infections could lead to insanity. Sitting in the lecture hall Stela would stare at these students, wondering how they knew so much, and why they even cared. On the first day she had raised her hand, said one small thing in response to what she'd thought was a regular old question from the professor. But by the end of that class meeting even she could see how silly, how flippant she was beside these students who wore suits to class. Carried briefcases instead of backpacks. Stela had taken care of her father her whole life, had done fine in high school biology. Had bathed her father's living body, had dipped a dead frog into brine. She understood how bodies stayed alive and how they didn't. This class seemed abstract, useless.

Stela chose to sit in the middle of the lecture hall, thinking the press of the other bodies would shield her. It was easy to sketch the heads in front of her through the more complex parts of the lecture. Once Stela put herself in one of her doodles, and that was when she realized that she was the only one without sober colors on, the only one wearing orange or yellow to class.

Then one day, two weeks or so in, The Black American stood. He wasn't wearing a suit after all, but a blazing red dashiki. He gave a ten-minute monologue on the Tuskegee syphilis experiments. Sweet Stela, still a virgin, had never even heard of syphilis.

"Dang," she said to herself when TBA finally sat down. But he didn't even look across the room at her. Just nodded, once, to all the eyes he knew were on him, and then went back to taking notes. Stela couldn't help but look for him after class, but he fled. In his shirt, he was there flicking past the others like a flame.

After the first exam, the professor announced the grades to the entire auditorium. Stela was daydreaming about the sketch she was working on, a Caribbean scene she was wondering if she could make more, you know, African. She loved daydreaming, believed her best artistic ideas came to her then. But when she heard the prof say that an American had the highest grade she snapped out of it and looked for the dashiki dude. Even she could tell that so many chests in the room were holding on to their breaths. The professor went on, "and a woman at that."

Stela scanned the room for this American woman, until she realized that she was the American. The class, all those faces and eyes, turned inward, to the center of the room where Stela was sitting. Oh, snap.

After dismissal The Black American found her like a dagger. "I want to go to medical school," he said, out of breath. "Help find a cure for Africa's diseases."

"I just want to make art," Stela said quietly. She had never felt shameful about this before. And worse, because hadn't she come to Africa for Africanness, not just for art? Was (just) wanting to draw selfish? She surprised herself with that thinking. She didn't know what to think about doing so well in biology.

Well, after that she and The Black American always sat together in class. He sought her out to study in the study hall (which was also the cafeteria that was also, on Sunday mornings, the Catholic church). She sometimes went with TBA for lunch there. So she wasn't totally isolated. The first time she went to Mass in the church cafeteria she'd gone by herself. The African student Catholics wore formal church clothes to the service, and Stela hadn't brought anything like that from home. She didn't know where to buy things like that here. She didn't know who to ask.

The only other person Stela spent time with was Edi the Ewe. The teaching assistant from the art class. Here was an African, half of one, at least. In the art class Stela wanted to do well. It was complicated. She wanted to do well because it was an art class and being an artist was what she wanted. But it was also, strangely, a class where she had something to prove. She had to be the best in this class and not for art's sake at all. (For Blackness's sake?) See, Stela was from the Virgin Islands and yes, okay, she was American. But she was also black. Or Black. The other students, the British girls, were white, from a white university, from a white country.

Stela hated those girls. On principle.

She liked Edi. Edi liked her. That seemed to be on principle, as well.

When she presented her paintings at the art class midterm (acrylics of a Saint Thomas Carnival parade in black and white), Edi's critique was that she used irony well. He pronounced *carnival* as "car-nee-vhal," and with such authority that Stela began to wonder if it was she and her whole group of islands who said it wrongly. Stela also did not get how black-and-white charcoals of Carnival were ironic. But the professor had nodded at Edi's comments and so Stela had nodded, too. After class Edi curled his finger to her. When she went to him he whispered: "You'll be famous. You'll come back here and I'll be your assistant." She didn't get it. He was older; he'd never be her assistant. But he looked set in his comment. And so Stela tried to comfort him: "We'll both be teachers." But he laughed. "I was joking," he said. And so she laughed, too, though she was confused.

But really, it was simple. Stela was good at art *and* at science. But science was not special. Not to her. Science was simple and straight and could never be as slippery as oils or watercolor. Never be as human and humane. Look at the awful science had done. Justified slavery. Justified colonialism. Had a painting ever done that? (Well, not that Stela knew.) But there she was. Biology with TBA and art with Edi the Ewe.

She wasn't choosing between the two men. She had a man: Johann. Not just a man, a full-on fiancé. And wasn't he, as a born African, more African than the African American, and at least as African as the half-caste?

Stela's 20/20 birthday was on a Sunday. She went to Mass in the cafeteria/study hall/church, wore a skirt even though she still looked more casual than the Ghanaian girls. It was Stela's birthday and the next day was another biology exam, and so she prayed for clarity, 20/20. The sermon was about Solomon—unrelated, she surmised, because where was the simile for sight? This birthday Stela was meant to see. And also, she wanted to be seen. Dancing, she announced. "I want to go dancing." There was a dance club at Labadi Beach. Beach! Of course, that is where she'd go. The white anthropologists and musicians from her program came. And TBA. And of course, Edi the Ewe.

The dance floor was right on the beach, but with a little concrete lip, so the sand wouldn't swish over the dancers' feet. It was dark, so Stela couldn't see the water, and the music was just loud enough to drown out the waves. She hadn't brought her bathing suit, thinking she'd save the swim for daytime. A mistake, maybe (definitely). She could smell the ocean, but it was different, more briny, than her sea. Still, Stela danced. Edi moved along with her. The DJ played Michael Jackson and nothing else. "Rest in Peace!" the DJ kept shouting, though (Come on, already!) it was Stela's birthday.

"You dance like an African," Edi said. And it was then, though she liked what he said, that she realized that something was not quite right. Because she wasn't an African, really. She wasn't really an American either. But whenever she said, "I'm Caribbean," even here in Africa, they wanted to know where in Jamaica she lived and if she knew the Marley boys. So she wasn't really Caribbean, not here, was she? She was the only one of her kind. But she did dance. "Not like an African," she said to Edi, a sweet Jackson 5 tune now playing. "Like a Virgin Islander." And she'd meant to make it sound strong and proud, but "Virgin," he echoed, smiling, as though they had a secret together.

"Maristela," interrupted TBA. "A moment, please." And she left Edi's arms and went to the future healer of Africa's diseases. "It's my birthday," she said, looking at him, her eyes open, open. "Yes," he said quietly. "But can you see what's going on here?" Of course. She had the 20/20. Edi came up beside her, but TBA stood like a sentry. Guarding as if to keep her safe. "But it's my birthday," she said again—she'd been drinking just a little. TBA nodded and then shook his head, whispered into her ear. "But you're, like, offering this guy something more than you mean to." Poor boy, Stela thought. He liked her. (Hadn't she mentioned her fiancé?) "I can see what I'm doing," she said.

One thing she could see was that she needed to study for their biology exam the next day. Indeed, she and TBA had agreed to study that night, despite it being her birthday. Bacterial colonies. Viral invaders. The dining halls stayed open until two a.m. for group study. Stela hadn't been so affirmed over anything in a while and it felt, well, good. Since she'd started college, her drawing had been a source of downing on herself. Her father, sick her whole life, had always said she'd make a fine nurse. He'd even suggested nursing as a degree. Which is to say that she liked taking care of him, but she didn't think she wanted to make a career out of it. It wasn't that biology was easy—it was not. It's just that she was, well, good (as if Dad had understood something intrinsic about her). And now the professor had thrown down a gauntlet. Maristela was the one to beat. Stela wanted America to lose—her islands were a colony after all—but *she* wanted to win. She wanted both these things to happen. Somehow.

But a young woman on her birthday had to eat. And Edi announced that he had cooked. "Not for anyone do I cook," he said to her. "I've invited many friends. It is not so far from campus."

The music was "Don't Stop 'til You Get Enough." But the other students were easing out—they'd had enough. Gave Stela a kiss and hug and happy birthday, and gone. Some going down to the water to dip their feet. To wade in to the hips. Sounded dangerous to Stela; swimming at night wasn't something she'd ever done. Though, truth? If she'd brought her bathing suit she would have joined them. (Twenty-twenty! She would have been able to see anything dangerous in the sea, right?) And so she felt a kind of strange dread about *not* going to the sea. And really she wasn't one for that kind of thing: dread.

But here's what she was thinking: If I go inland to dinner with Edi, I will fail the biology exam. But so what? What did Stela really give a damn about biology? She was an artist! But then again, wouldn't it be useful to boost her GPA by doing well in biology? Maybe the painting program back at her college would look at her application more favorably if her GPA were higher. (And then she'd be an artist and then she'd graduate from college and then she'd marry Johann and learn to ski and then they'd move to South Africa to have babies.) Seemed like a sturdy plan.

"I have to study," she said to Edi. The dance floor lights were starting to flicker on. (You don't have to go home but you have to get the *beep* out of here!) It was a school night. Even the clubs closed early.

"I also have to study," Edi said gravely.

And Stela didn't want to be the kind of American who turned down a birthday dinner cooked in her honor because of a bad feeling. She looked around for TBA just to give him the courtesy of a goodbye, but he'd slinked off. Stela climbed into the tro tro with Edi. But even then she felt as though she should be heading back to campus, readying her review of herpes simplex.

The tro tro was loud and crowded, even this late at night. But that was fine. That was expected. What wasn't expected was how far away Edi's place was. She couldn't talk to him in the van, because it was so loud and everyone was so close. Each time they stopped, she would mouth to Edi, "Us?" and he would shake his head once, like she was a fly in his ear.

But then finally the shouter called, "White lady!" and Stela knew, sadly, that this meant her. Edi took her hand, not a white hand, but what did it matter, it was closer to white than anyone else's hand here. He guided her off the tro tro like she was a queen.

The walk to his flat was a series of many roads with large metal gates barring her, forcing a turn there, walk and turn again. It was as though they were walking a labyrinth. At the center there would be a minotaur. They kept curving around buildings, and then around tents. Shacks. Cars passed, though there was no paved road. Despite the dark, the dirt was red as fire beneath their feet. Stela knew she would never find her way out of this alone. Whatever this was.

At the flat there were not throngs of invitees, as Stela could have sworn Edi had promised. There were three roommates. All men. Of course, Stela thought of TBA. Of how he'd tried to keep her safe, of what he'd asked her to see. But it was dark. And it was late. And it is strange what people do when they feel the decision has already been made for them.

But first there was the food. Dinner, as promised. They five ate the seafood and rice from one pot with their hands. The conversation was simplistic and laborious; everything Stela said had to be translated, as the roommates seemed to speak only basic English. After dinner, she checked her watch. Almost eleven p.m. "Time for me to go," she announced. "It's been so nice."

"No more tro tros going to campus. Not until morning." Edi said this calmly and with a smile, like she should have known. Like he suspected she did know.

So that night, in the labyrinth, Maristela drilled herself on biology. Sat in Edi's kitchen and wrote out the diseases and the treatments. Fell asleep at the table. (Intentional, even, a defense mechanism.) But still, when she woke she was in Edi's bedroom. Concrete floor. She knew because they were lying on it, a meager mattress beneath them. And she could see the moonlight through the window. She noted all this before she noted the hands. Which were taking off her clothes.

"Please," she said, pushing at him.

"No," Edi said calmly. "No." Which was her line. The woman's line. And left Stela unsure of what to say. And then she was naked. And he was pushing. And she was telling him "Stop." A new word now. But she wasn't shouting. She said it all quiet and tight. "Stop, please." She didn't want to wake his roommates. If she was quiet, she was safer, she was sure. And besides, she really was a virgin. Just like he'd joked. She couldn't lose her virginity like this—just all bodies and biology. "Stop, please," she said again.

"Don't make me stop," he responded. His words making it all seem different than it was. "I will be so thankful afterward," he said. Like he was begging for something she was hoarding.

"Mother Mary, save me." This Stela said out loud but still quietly, even though she'd only been to Mass, what, maybe two entire times since she'd been in Ghana? It wasn't the fancy church clothes that really kept her away, was it? No. Really it was when the African priest brought out the statue of Jesus for the adoration. The African students had lined up to kiss the white feet. That had made Stela feel a kind of shrill sickness. Yes. On Edi's cold concrete floor Stela could now know this about herself. She hadn't wanted to be one of the Black people kissing the white feet of Jesus. And that pride of hers must be why she, Stela, was not saved by the Virgin Mary this night.

Either way, this night, at the very moment Stela spoke those praying words, was the loss of her faith. Because right then Edi finished. Fucking, hell. It had been a fast thing and perhaps that was a kindness, a bit of grace. But it also didn't give Stela a chance, did it? A chance to find her fight. Instead, Edi collapsed beside her like they'd been balls to the wall and she'd worn him out. She felt herself a stone. She couldn't see Father, Son, or Holy Spirit. Mother Mary was definitely deaf. Oh, and fuck you, Magdalene.

How fucking silly it had been to keep sex from Johann, for them to keep it from each other. There on the floor Stela tried to picture being naked on a beach with Johann. Tried to feel the sand on her feet. The waves at her toes. Tried to think of a painting she'd done of her and Johann's hands in the surf—though she still hadn't gotten the waves right. Tried to think of beauty. But instead the smell of her own blood, a biology, rose up and repulsed her. Edi curled away, stilling into sleep. As if nothing so strange and sudden had happened.

It was a while before the moon outside Edi's window turned into a sun. But Stela waited. Waited for that sun. While she waited she called for her mother in her mind. Mermaid was the siren who could kill a man with words. But thoughts of her father came, too, and those thoughts made her feel ashamed. She would never tell him about this; he would have wanted to protect her, but he'd never been able to do that. She thought instead, if a scientist can make a living ear, maybe they can make a living prostate. Maybe they can make a new living vagina. Maybe they can make a new living soul.

Then finally, the sunrise in the window. With the sun came a voice from the common room. A woman's. (A white woman's, Stela guessed from the guttural accent, but so fucking what? Any woman might be a sister now.) Stela lay, still stone, as the voice spoke to another voice. The voices spoke in the West African pidgin. Stela didn't know all the words, but the syntax was the same as in Saint Thomas. Here now was a white woman who knew the native vernacular. The voices spoke as they made a morning meal—the smell of it rich. Where had this woman come from? Now Stela smelled the crisp of a sweet cigarette.

She was scared. Perhaps she would never be able to leave this room and this mattress. Stone as she was. She became ashamed of her own fear. The shame was worse. Keeping her stone. But then the sun kept chopping through the window. Stela saw. And she imagined what those girls trapped in that man's house must have thought all those years. (Is that a sign from God? The sun rising, is that for me?) Yes. Anything might be a sign. So Stela crawled to her clothes beneath the sun-blooming window. A bit of faith returning? Maybe. But it hadn't been soon enough for Stela.

She dressed as slowly and quietly as she could, looking at Edi to see if he moved. (He did not.) Then looking around at the room, staring at anything she could sight through the shadows. She wanted badly to take something from this spartan room. A stupid, toothless sentiment.

Besides, the sun was only in patches. And she'd been lucky to find her own clothes. But until the day she dies, this will be the greatest regret of Stela's life: Not that she went to Edi's at all. But that she didn't steal something back from him.

Out in the common room Stela recognized the white woman. She was one of a German cohort who wore cloth shoes and carried their books around campus in hemp bags. With this woman was one of the superrich Nigerian boys who strode around campus like princes. Stela had once seen the couple together roaring by the science block in a shiny red car.

"Maristela," the woman said, as if they knew each other. Though Stela didn't even know this woman's name. The woman reached for Stela and touched her hair. Something a white woman had never done in America. (White Americans seemed emphatically wary of Black girl hair. Even the Obama girls had taken some grief over their braids.) The Nigerian boyfriend stood to give Stela his seat. The two spoke to Stela in their foreign English. "I have an extra room here," he said cryptically. He offered Stela a clove cigarette and she took it, though she'd never smoked before. "My flatmate on campus is South African," the man continued. "Colored lad. Doesn't like when I bring my missus around. You know?" But Stela didn't know. She just knew that she needed to stay close to this woman. Stela sucked the cigarette into a sharp crackle. Looked at the woman.

"Can you take me the fuck home?" Stela said; the first thing she'd said. Without missing a beat, the white woman kissed her Black man and took Stela by the hand.

"Are you okay?" the woman asked when they were back out on the winding road.

"Sure," Stela said. But she never said anything else to that woman. Not even a thank-you when the other finally hailed her a tro tro and told the driver, in Twi, to take Stela to campus.

On the tro tro ride Stela thought of the beach the night before. How she should have gone to it. Even by herself. How that sea would have been safer. When Stela finally found her room on the Legon campus she wanted to take a shower, an ocean approximation. But the water in the pipes wasn't running. So she bought a bottle of orange Fanta from a stand. In the bathroom, she used the soda to wipe the blood and crust from her thighs. She scrubbed it up and in herself. It burned so badly.

It was then that Stela realized she didn't have her engagement ring. The topaz and silver ring Johann had put on her finger. Lost, stolen. Either way, it was back where she'd never go again. In Edi's room. She still wore the pendant and necklace that Johann's parents had given her. She took it off now and wound it round and round, a temp, on her wedding finger. But it couldn't fit. Never would.

It was later, weeks, that the American cohort went on a day trip to the coast. Finally, thankfully, a sea for Stela. She wore her bathing suit under her jeans and T-shirt. Packed a towel in her bag. No matter what anyone said (the coordinator had said that the water "wasn't for them," but what did that mean?), Stela was going to swim. Needed to. Needed to be baptized, dipped, dunked. Needed the Atlantic Ocean—even if it was the exact opposite side of what she had been born to.

Had she been thinking all those weeks about what had happened with Edi? Had she been curling into a ball and rocking herself to sleep every night? No and no. She'd been drawing and painting. And when she wasn't making art she'd spend every spare second with TBA. Like he was a best friend. Or a bodyguard.

But these weeks later, at the castle on the coast, the tour guide pointed to where the newly enslaved women had been kept. Made them, the college girls, stand inside the dungeon. Walked them along the winding passageway where an unlucky girl (maybe their own age, he said) would be prodded along, the last door opening, like a secret, into the floor of the white governor's. Stela felt her own crotch burn when she saw that door in the floor.

The other American women, the ones studying African music, wept like a chorus. A little too late, thought Stela, but the tour guide just deepened the details—how many pregnancies resulted, how many deaths. The boys from Stela's cohort walked away to look out at the shore. She couldn't follow the rest of the tour to the hypocritical Catholic church that stood, un-secreted, in the middle of the castle. Stela walked away with the boys. The ocean was out there, gray and silver, like something that could cut her. Which is how the soft tissue between her legs felt now. Like there were little knives there. She didn't swim. Not after all.

Instead, when she was back on campus she made an appointment at the Accra clinic. She was still the one to beat in biology. Had aced that first exam and the next. So she knew. She knew before she even met the doctor, who was fat and ringed with gold. "I'm Indian," the doctor said, as if to clarify. "Do they have jobs for doctors on the island where you're from?" All this as the doctor stuck her gloved bangled hand in and she and the nurse peered between Stela's legs. Not a baby, but another biology to carry for life. "Herpes," the doctor confirmed, holding her hands up so the nurse could peel her gloves off. "Close your legs now."

"Fucking Christ," Stela said quietly. This kind of holy cursing would be the closest she'd get to prayer for a long while. And then she finally cried and cried, right there on the examination table. The nurse came with a box of tissues. "Were you raped?" she asked. And Stela hadn't even thought to call it that. Hadn't called it anything all these weeks since. She took the sheath from the tissue box. "Me, too," the nurse said. And looked at Stela. "It can happen anywhere. To anyone." And Stela could never figure out what that nurse really meant. But she knew she was now the sickly one, maybe sicker than her dad had ever really been. Look at her. She couldn't care for her father; she couldn't even take care of herself.

That week Stela stopped going to art class (which had been a way to worship, a kind of praying, hadn't it?). She'd still been going right up until the doctor visit. Edi the Ewe had been shy or maybe not shy—aloof. Or maybe angry or maybe afraid or maybe ashamed. Stela had felt brave, superior, even, just by attending class. But truth was that all she'd wanted to draw was what had happened. And she couldn't. Because Edi was there. And because it hadn't made sense. And now neither did this. So she just stopped going to class. She went, instead, to the vice chancellor. The VC had said during orientation that they (the foreigners) should come to him for anything. But the conversation with the VC turned out to be rushed and embarrassing—sort of like what had happened with Edi. ("Are you sure?" the vice chancellor had kept asking her. "Because African men don't rape Black women. What is the need?")

So for the rest of the semester abroad, her find-herself African adventure, Stela kept her head low. TBA still sought her out for study. But now, strangely, she avoided him. But she kept up on bio. (That was a real class for real credit.) The painting class would never appear on her transcripts. It just disappeared. Like she'd never taken it. Like Edi had never happened at all.

And then Stela went back to America and then back to the Virgin Islands. Didn't go to Mass again until she married. Never told why, not to her mother or her brothers or her dad, especially not her dad. Instead, in college the next semester she took a marine biology class. Wrote a paper on the healing properties of salt water. Another on the ruining of coral reefs. Became a biology major. Excelled. Did her senior thesis on whales. Fuck painting. Fuck art. Fuck Africa. Fuck Americans. (Well, sort of.) Maybe she'd become a doctor. Save her own life and her father's and her mother's, go back in time and save her mother's drowned parents even. This is how her mind was working (not working) those days.

She herself never called it anything. Because weren't white women always accusing Black men of rape—a way to exercise their own pale power? How could Stela do the same? It all made her sure that somehow the Edi ordeal was Johann's fault. Loving Johann had confused her over Black men.

That semester just after Ghana was the semester that Stela went to visit Johann in the freeze of ski season. Up on a mountain so far from any sea. At the airport Stela had been unable to find him among all the blond heads bobbing out of winter jackets. And for too long he couldn't find her either. "I barely recognized you," he said when he finally had her. "You're so pale. You look Korean." She wanted to ask him if he was afraid of her, afraid she might fucking shoot up the airport, but she knew that was an odd thing to ask. So didn't.

Johann, still stuck as a sophomore, was on a leave of absence from Tech. He was working at that ski resort in a place colder than either of them had ever lived in or than she had ever even visited. He, too, had stopped going to church, but not in the same way as Stela. He was going through his own thing—disappointing his parents with his grades, disappointing himself with his lack of focus. He wanted a certain kind of life—marriage to Stela, children, church. But he couldn't identify the major and the career that might make it all come to be. And he didn't want to wait anymore; he wanted to have sex. And Stela was his girlfriend, his fiancée. True, he was just in a funk given his age, his gender, his race—perhaps mostly given the shooting at Tech—but still he was in the deep of it. And his girlfriend, his fiancée, being gone for three months on her study abroad program hadn't helped. He'd started obsessing over things medieval and Hellenic, cursing Catholicism whenever he could.

Stela saw Johann's books about labyrinths as soon as he opened his apartment door. (White people culture! she thought with panic.) Piles of these maze books were winding around the floor like they themselves were a labyrinth. She turned slowly around the small room. Saw his bookshelf filled with old CDs. Hopefully, she bent and scanned it closely but found only one reggae contribution. A CD she'd bought him for Christmas. Years ago. Lives ago. No soca or calypso to speak of. Like their Caribbean home didn't exist at all.

A huge aquarium took up an entire wall of Johann's living-dining space. Stela tripped through the labyrinth of books on labyrinths toward it. Hopeful for the small sea it promised. Instead, she found herself staring into a dry tank filled with dirt and weeds. Her heart sinking like a fucking ship. Johann had gone to turn on the tub, for the bath Stela had requested.

She stared into the waterless tank and thought of her best friend, LaToya, who had eloped during Stela's abroad semester—so Stela hadn't even gotten to be maid of honor. She hadn't even known that Toy was pregnant. And now what? Now this bullshit. She finally spotted the thick snake in the tank curled on itself, not even a sea-dwelling eel. The sadness folded over and over—until it was tight and hard inside her. When she heard Johann come up behind her she turned and tugged her sweater up over her head. (Get this shit over with, she figured.)

If Johann had been paying attention he would have said: "Stela? What happened? Why are you so sad? And why are you cursing so much now?" But he was too focused on his own quarter-life sinking. And besides, he was nervous and excited because of the soon-to-happen sex. He was just a boy himself, really.

So after the bath, and after the sex, when Johann finally noticed and asked, somewhat incredulously, about how she'd lost the ring he'd given her, Stela told him a lie. And he didn't know any better but to buy it. She said it right to his beautiful, awful after-sex face: "I want us to break up," as if that was the reason for the ring's loss. Either way, it was the exact opposite of the truth.

The night before she left Johann for the last time, Stela secreted his heaviest labyrinth book into her own suitcase. Inside it had an inscription in Johann's own handwriting: "To the love of all my lives," which Stela was sure meant that it was for her anyway. Or should have been. So she just stole it, because she could never really say to him what she'd seen, where she'd been, and what she'd become.

ROOTED

THE STORY OF STELA'S STARTER MARRIAGE

District of Columbia—Vermont

2016

1.

For a time, Dr. Steven and Mrs. Maristela Jones had shared the same mistress. They should have known better, really. Instead of knowing, they chose an ending. But that came later. First, the thing to know is that Steven Jones had been in love once before he married Maristela. In graduate school he had dated a woman, an Asian woman. Japanese, to be specific. Not even a good brown Filipina. She came uninvited to the BGSA meetings and would raise her little fist, white as a white woman's, if you said any word that sounded like it might mean revolution. He couldn't explain it, but despite his own white mother, this pale woman was a thing Steven was ashamed of. His private pleasure. He couldn't take her to parties. He couldn't take her to Mass. He couldn't even tell his brothers about her.

Steven and this woman made love in his graduate dorm room and he held her feet in his hands. Afterward, he would kiss those feet and rub those feet until she slept. The woman overwhelmed him, like a sea.

Once during their lovemaking he felt so filled with that woman that he started to cry. Afterward the woman held him like his mother had when he was four and they'd just brought him home from the Saint Ursula orphanage. The next morning he slapped the woman across the face for leaving her dirty underwear in the soup of their damp sheets. The problem, really, was that his dissertation was secondary. The fight for more Black faculty was secondary. The primary thing in his life was the ocean of this woman's insides. And so he slapped her. And he had no doubt that she would forgive him and that they'd be better for it. Strong, even, like his mother and father had been. But his lover's pale skin held the black bruise for days. The woman could not avoid her friends and nor could he. And so her parents, stern and small, were summoned, and she was washed away before a week was gone. He stopped going to the Black graduate student meetings and then stopped going to campus altogether. He and his adviser communicated via email. Steven was depressingly focused then, finished his dissertation fast. Got an adjunct position in no time.

And then our Maristela—with her cursing and Caribbean accent—came into Steven's life. She was a Black Catholic and he was a Black Catholic.

They had met, as people do in D.C., down in Adams Morgan. He'd pulled her waist into his own on the dance floor of a tiny dark highlife club. She'd seemed eager to make love. So they did that very night, in his cell of an apartment. Bareback, which he'd never done before, because Maristela didn't care, and he didn't ask. "You're the one" is what he said to Maristela that very night after he'd fucked her. She wasn't his student or anything so lurid, though she was basically the same age as his students. She was earning her graduate teaching certificate in the city and teaching at the same time. His words, "You're the one," arrived on her like a splash of water might for a person parched.

And before half a year, he'd asked Maristela to marry him. Stela wanted this, wanted a man, marriage, monogamy. Had wanted it since she knew it was a thing to want. And Steven checked all the boxes she had those days: Black and educated. But still, "Why?" she'd asked.

"Because you're the perfect woman for me," he said.

Which was good, but still Stela couldn't help but challenge this. She knew her flaws: First, her STD and the adjacent action that had caused it—both of which left her sullied. Second, the fact that when she visited any of D.C.'s free museums, saw a Klimt or maybe a Rodin, she still, always, thought of Johann, whom she'd loved and then dumped because she had changed and he had changed and they hadn't gone through any of those changes together. Actually, there were so many no-good things about her. Too many to count or say. Steven didn't know any of these things. His not knowing was wonderful. So, "How am I perfect?" she needed to know.

"You're a little wild but still a lady, and still, you know, sexy, but sweet. And because . . ." Steven hesitated, suddenly shy about what he thought was honorable. "You make me better. More of what I want to be."

A sweet lady. Secretly wild and sexy. That could work for Stela. She could be that. But she had also hoped he would say something brainy, like about them being in the same fields—teaching and biology. A team. Or something about her own mother having been an orphan, how she and Steven had that connection. But Stela didn't want to push her luck. This was a second chance, after all. A good man. A Black one. And educated. Her ex-boyfriend still didn't even have his bachelor's degree, but he was already engaged to someone. Someone not Stela. So Stela and Steven went to Mass together that Sunday. Her first time in years. Steven prayed for their union. Stela stared at the new, progressive Pope smiling down on them from the chapel walls.

Stela took Steven home to meet her people. Dad was besotted. Steven was strong, and handsome and nerdy enough to seem innocuous. Mermaid took Steven's face in her palms and kissed each of his cheeks—"Mine was near the sea. I remember it like I remember my own name. I left when I was fourteen." Steven's eyes welled. "Mine was with nuns. I only remember the day my parents came for me. I left when I was four."

That night Stela's brothers were shooting hoops with Steven on the neighborhood court. They said he was like President Obama: a professor who could ball. Though Steven was a PhD, Dad claimed he actually felt stronger, healthier already just knowing there would be a doctor in the family. Dad and Stela sat on the couch and looked through the window at the young, healthy men slamming into each other, getting the ball into the hoop. Stela leaned her head on her father's shoulder, and her father held her weight.

2.

But Steven was not the kind of man Maristela had imagined for herself. In high school, she and Johann had been something so true she'd assumed it would last forever. So grasping was the story of her and that boy that Stela ran from it fast. Self-protection. Ran from his sweet peach skin. Had been fucked as far as West Africa, even. Had a stupid STD to prove it. Amen to antivirals.

The few short years between the high school boyfriend and her soon-to-be husband, Stela had dated only one guy. He was a Bahamian brethren, a townie, really, who lived close to her college. He said "I" instead of "me." Said overstand, instead of under-. Called her "my queen" from day one, and Stela was never sure if he'd ever learned her name. The second time they hung out he asked her to cover her hair. She'd just stopped straightening it, so the roots were puffed, but the ends were limp and breaking. "It will look better once it's all grown out," she defended herself. "No, my queen. You should cover it because it's too beautiful. It's not for the world. It's only for you and I and Jah." Stela had been quiet, not even sure if she should consider this. But then she hadn't had to. Because the next time they hooked up he said, "We'll move to Ethiopia and have a true African family."

Um, no. She didn't have the Africa urge anymore. Sure, she still fantasized about South Africa, but only when she fantasized about Johann. Which wasn't often. Not that often.

Less often since Steven.

Stela was twenty-three when she met Steven. He was a decade ahead at thirty-three. STD-free and with a PhD. Once they moved in together, Steven blended green juice for them every morning. He ate a fist of pills every night to ward off cancer and the common cold. The herpes receded from her mind and, it seemed, from her body. She never needed to even mention it. Besides, Steven was making her healthy, making everything just right. His dreams weren't dreams, like her painting had been. His dreams were goals—they were well planned out, they were attainable. It was a smooth and simple thing, this love, Stela thought. Easy as water. "Your steadiness," she said to Steven, speaking slowly so she didn't curse. "Your attention to your health. We'll grow old together. I love all that." It's what her mother hadn't had the first time, and didn't look like she would get this time either.

True, none of Stela's D.C. friends were getting married so young, and none of them had kids. But Maristela was a West Indian woman, and hitching up early was the West Indian way. The Catholic way, too. Her best friend from high school was on baby number two and had been married three years already. And Johann. In the pictures online of his wedding reception, his wife looked like she'd been his forever. Like there'd never been a Johann and Stela at all. Stela needed a marriage. A band solid and showy as gold to hold her down. Hold her tight. Hold her safe. Her father had cancer.

But actually, no. Because there was so much Steven and Stela didn't want the other to know. If she felt even an itch down there she would claim exhaustion, fake herself to sleep in front of one screen or another. When Stela asked about Steven and his brothers, he would clarify, "Your mom was an orphan. But my brothers and I were adopted. That's totally different." Which he had never clarified before they were married. In the presidential election they were voting for each other's rival. Steven had pretended to like Obama for eight years, and now it wasn't a betrayal of Blackness or manhood to say out loud that he didn't think much of the man or his manhood. He was voting first Bernie, then maybe the carnival barker, because both were brash. Stela had loved Obama's style and what he'd done with health care—but her husband was better read, and she felt simple when she tried to defend her reasons. She was voting the woman because the woman was brash. Stela and Steven both believed—and they were right—that the other person was just voting for what they wanted to be. And then there was culture. Steven was Black but he wasn't West Indian, and, surprise, Stela hadn't realized that he would feel as foreign as if theirs were an interracial marriage. When she made Steven tea, he would complain if she put in milk. "True, it's a protein, but everything in moderation." When she made the breakfasts she'd always made for her father, Steven would only eat the dumb bread, pour olive oil over it, shake his head at the boiled bananas. It wasn't just that Steven didn't need her care, it was like he didn't want it. But then again, that wasn't really it, either.

They coexisted as though they were of a different species. They needed different things to feel fully human. He, the mountains. She, the sea.

3.

To be fair to them both, Malaika was an accident. Soon after they were married, Maristela and Steven had seen art. It was not the kind of thing they'd done during their brief courtship, and not the kind of thing they did once they were married. Stela had gone to pick him up in the SUV his father had bought them as a wedding gift. Steven wasn't waiting outside when she drove up, so she parked illegally, and walked into the building that housed the biological and social sciences.

Right there in the lobby there was a soiree underway and Stela felt pressured to take the glass of red wine a handsome undergraduate offered her on a metal tray. The walls were newly covered in paintings of brown bodies. Stela had loved most to draw sea things—coral, whales. Her tries at human forms had always been underwhelming or unintentionally ironic. She'd been good at drawing hands, but then the only hands she'd ever drawn well were Johann's. Here in the lobby, faculty snobs stood around talking to each other with plastic champagne flutes between their fingers. Stela saw her husband standing off by himself. Standing too close to a painting she couldn't make out from this distance. His arms to his sides as though in punishment.

Maristela stood watching Steven, looking at him in that way she used to look at things—like how she could paint him looking at this painting. Then Steven saw her and seemed, she thought, panicked. He came toward her with urgency. "Sorry to keep you, darling."

"Fine," she said, despite the car parked badly.

"Let's go. Let's go now." And he took her by the elbow.

On the way out, Stela saw a painting of a brown adolescent body in silhouette. A leg raised in such a way as to obscure the gender. Stela turned her head to keep looking. And there standing among the paintings was a woman.

Though Steven was fighting to get himself and his wife out, he also noticed the woman, because something in her face looked like the women in pictures his parents had shown him of Kenya. He looked away and kept going. Stela looked at the woman because she was a beautiful woman standing solo, single. She glanced at the woman's bare ring finger and then down at her own banded one.

The next day found Stela sitting in a café in Adams Morgan grading Jerome Williams's exam over and over again. Jerome Williams was a seventeen-year-old senior only a year in the United States. He wanted to be a medical doctor, he said, and so was taking two of her twelfth-grade biology classes—marine and human. During tutoring sessions he didn't need, he would put his hand on her shoulder, and say in his Jamaican accent, raw as the yard: "Help me understand, Mrs. Stela Jones." And it didn't help that Jerome, jailbait Jerome, always said her first name—elongating it like, Ste-la. Just like she'd seen Marlon Brando do in a YouTube clip. Jerome was flirting, she knew, but he was seventeen and she, frankly, was susceptible at twenty-three. Why didn't they cover this sort of thing during teacher training? She felt unprepared.

Because though Maristela was tutoring Jerome on the intelligence of whales, she was seeing in her head his young, tight body taking over hers and, fucking hell, the only thing that helped her stay on marine biology was thinking of her own Dr. Steven Jones's hairy legs gone ashy in the D.C. winter.

In the café Stela was daydreaming of her too-young student. How smart he was, how handsome, how he would be fucking great in bed, and even if he wasn't, he would be patient and let her teach him how she liked it. He would be amazed at what her body could do. He would say, "I so grateful, empress," when she told him that he had to go because her husband was coming home.

Daydreaming always worked. It had sustained her through the fruit-boxing Panamanian at the grocery store, through the Trinidadian security guard who lived in their apartment complex and strode around in his uniform, through the assistant principal of MLK K–12 Magnet, a Martinique man who held on to his French accent. All of those she'd survived. She'd gone home to Steven and made love without guilt or any reduction of passion—more passion, actually. She longed for the passion, though that wasn't why she'd married Steven. They still went to Mass every Sunday, but she didn't feel any fucking passion there. Church was a thing she did with her husband, like a Netflix night, to pass the time. They were an old married couple, not even a year in. And really, that is why she'd married Steven. She wanted to be over it. The *it* being love.

The café in Adams Morgan was so crowded that even someone like Stela, sitting alone, was sharing a table with a perfect stranger—a student-looking girl with bright chunky headphones. Then there was a slow darkening. A woman touched Stela on the shoulder—"Can I sit here?"—and she sat. Fuck off, Stela wanted to say, but instead, "Yes, of course. Let me move my bag off the back." People didn't touch so easily in stateside cities. It might be dangerous. It might be someone about to throw you to the ground. Stela eyed the woman. She looked like an adolescent boy. A boy with astonishing big eyes that shone as though they would right now break into tears or laughter. The boy-woman's skin and dreaded hair were the exact same dirt color. Her shirt read PAINTERS FOR PEACE. Stela thought she recognized the woman but could not place her. "Where are you from?" The woman got to the question first.

Stela didn't hesitate. "The Virgin Islands. Saint Thomas. And I'm Maristela." The woman was thin, yet something about her seemed firm and fixed and unmoving. "Call me Stela."

"Stela. I'm from Ethiopia."

"Really?" Mythic motherland of her Bahamian dread, a place of mystic wonder to most Caribbean people.

But Malaika was wearing that T-shirt, and ever since her abroad semester, being around actual painters made Stela stiff. But that afternoon, Malaika asked Stela so many questions that Stela settled. It seemed Malaika thought teaching science was interesting, fulfilling, honorable. They exchanged numbers after Malaika offered to give a lecture on figurative painting to Maristela's Human Biology class.

That night Maristela and Steven made love quietly, but Stela didn't think of Malaika then. She didn't think about her until Malaika came two weeks later to give the talk. And Stela watched Malaika walk across the dusty courtyard with a painting under her arm. And she watched Malaika smile when asking the custodian for directions—a conversation that seemed to go on longer than directions would require. And she watched Malaika laugh at herself when she had to go back to the man and ask again. And then Stela watched Malaika walk into the teacher's lounge, where she had turned to meet her, and then Stela felt herself hug Malaika as though they were old friends. Stela could just feel Malaika's little braless mounds, rising up like volcanoes to meet her own soft chest.

The painting Malaika had brought was the one of the brown adolescent in silhouette. It was then that Stela remembered her—the woman standing alone, watching, in the gallery. This bitch, Maristela thought.

After the lecture Jerome Williams asked Malaika question after question, and Stela let him despite the pangs of jealousy. When Malaika tired of the handsome boy, she looked past him to a quiet girl in the back and said, "And you. What thoughts do you have?" The girl shrugged. "Of course you have thoughts," Malaika insisted. "Everyone does. I can see in your face that you're curious." And the girl, whose name Maristela could never remember, began to talk. For the rest of the class period Stela just looked at Malaika's painting. Bitch, Stela thought again. But the word was all admiration.

That night Maristela opened her bath towel before the mirror. She hadn't looked at her own naked body in a while. Not since getting married, maybe not since what went down in study abroad. Of course, she clipped her toenails. She washed her own belly. But she didn't look at her whole self. The mirror went almost to the ceiling but not all the way to the floor. So Maristela stood up on top of the toilet bowl lid. She raised her arms into the air so her breasts lifted and looked extra perky. She cinched her waist with her breath. She stretched her neck long; she'd always liked her neck, liked it to be touched and kissed. There was a knock on the door. "I'm fucking busy!" Stela breathed out. And then her husband jostled the door open and asked his wife what the hell she was doing. "I'm checking for moles," she said, pulling her towel around her and climbing without grace off the toilet bowl. Steven pushed himself in.

When he came to bed that night, Stela wanted to be on top and he let her. When she moaned and collapsed into his chest, he held her and for the first time, he didn't seem to worry about finishing himself up. That day, Steven himself had gone back to the school gallery. To the painting of the Black man embracing the pale woman that Stela had caught him helpless before.

4.

Steven Jones was a good man. The worst ones always are. He brought home flowers for his wife's birthday. He added a box of chocolates to this on Valentine's. He drove them to church once a week. He voted in local elections. He looked good in a suit or in sweats. He was also the type of man who loved quietly. Needed quiet in the bedroom to cum. Needed it just so. He was neat. And this was strange for a man who grew up in a place with the endless soil and grass of Vermont. But he hadn't grown up in *that* place, really. He'd grown up in Burlington, with his parents, who were white, and his three brothers, all adopted like him, and all Black.

His parents had read all the books. They had gone to all the training sessions in New York and Detroit, and so they were good about making sure that their sons had Black action figures and picture books with Black characters. Taught them about Lumumba and Nkrumah. Put them all in basketball. Spoke rudimentary Swahili and made it the language of all dinner conversation. Drove across the city for Mass to a parish where there was an Indian priest—not Black but at least brown. The parents were sure they were the first to celebrate Kwanzaa in all of Vermont. They hung up posters of Kenyan women with clay pots on their heads; men with staffs that made them look biblical. They told the boys, "That's the motherland. That's where you are from," even though all the boys had been delivered to the same Catholic Charities in Texas and picked up at the same Saint Ursula's orphanage. The family had cable, and though they never had BET, they did have MTV when it first came on and then MTV had *Yo! MTV Raps*, which was the only show that the Joneses would let their sons stay up late to watch. The Joneses made sure their sons knew all the other Black people in Burlington—which really wasn't a hard thing to do in the 1980s.

On weekends the family sometimes rented a cabin in the mountains and then there'd be quiet and the cabin would be pristine. Even the dirt was clean. The outdoors had a purity to it. Since he was not a farm boy Steven never thought of the outdoors as laborious or smelly or bloody. He never saw those things. He thought that he was most himself when it was just him and his family and the mountains. But then Steven's mother had died. In a bloody, dirty car accident. She had been driving by herself in the middle of the day and something had made her swerve, a moose, maybe. Or a deer. Or a dusty future. At the funeral, the boys learned from an old bat of an auntie that their mother had been pregnant when she died. Everyone had always thought she was infertile. Steven, the eldest, was twelve. He hadn't yet kissed a girl.

And so, though his father actually lived in D.C. now, and though his brothers were in either Europe or Asia, Steven forever filled himself with hopes of returning to Vermont. He'd been rabid in his support of the Vermonter for president, even canvassed in D.C.'s Black neighborhoods, convincing Black people to vote for the wild white man.

"I've lived too motherfucking long without the ocean," Maristela said once when they argued—her excuse, like PMS, for losing her temper. She wanted to say, I've lived too long away from my father, but she knew that wasn't what a wife should say. But Steven was sure the mountains would be more than enough for Stela. Better than any ocean. And he was her husband, which was better than any father.

But this is not true. Hills are impermeable. Hills must be climbed over or blasted through. You cannot wade through the hill, you cannot be surrounded by the hill, you cannot float in the hill. You can only be rooted. You cannot sway. You cannot allow the hill to enter your mouth and your eyes. You cannot stick your head into the hill and see an angelfish, a whale, another world.

"Yes, you can," Steven said. "The caves and ravines are like portals to other worlds," he explained. "And in a mountain you can breathe. And the air is good, the best. And in a mountain there are trees older than we will ever be. And in a mountain there is something that resists you and that is a blessed challenge over the ease of water. You will love the mountains, Stela." He insisted and he believed.

And of course, as we know, no one can replace a father.

But all of that was months ago. And now they were in Vermont. And the presidential election was over. The Vermonter had lost, and the woman had lost. The election had gone as neither of them had predicted, though it was how Steven had voted. They were both shocked—though Steven also felt a delicious vindication that he tried to hide from his wife. But the move to Vermont was supposed to fix all that. Because Vermont wasn't like anywhere else in America. Because here in Vermont their true lives were supposed to begin. Babies. A house. They had left D.C., landlocked and missing mountains. But they had also left Malaika. Their marriage wasn't even a year old. Her father was in remission.

5.

Maristela awoke the morning after Malaika had spoken to her D.C. high school class. Maristela was in her own bed but she could not tell what time it was. Steven insisted on keeping every window in the house curtained at night. He needed complete darkness to sleep. It was natural, he'd said, when on their very first night together she'd told him to get his ass to bed, opening her legs to reveal what was waiting. He'd continued pulling the curtains all over his little apartment, and he'd closed the bedroom door before going to the bed and nestling between her sticky thighs. They hadn't yet known each other's last names. Back then she'd thought his love of darkness was something mysterious and wondrous about him. But there had been times over the months of their marriage when she'd rethought this. Thought maybe it wasn't wondrous at all. Thought maybe Steven was some kind of hobbity woodland creature.

That morning, back in D.C., Maristela had lain in bed and thought about waking up with the sun across her face before she'd married Steven. Even better, waking up to the sun as a small child and going to the beach in Saint Thomas with her family. Sitting beside her father, then swimming beside Mermaid, then napping in the sun beside her father's legs. Or swimming in the open ocean with Johann and then falling asleep in the sunshine on his parents' deck. She wished now she'd thought to tell Steven when they'd first met that this, too, was natural: waking up to the sun. But she'd missed her damn chance. If she brought it up now he would think she was nagging or he would think she was really talking about something else. . . . He always said that: "This is really about something else, isn't it?" And usually he was right. But not today. Today Stela wanted sun. She reached up and pulled the curtain an inch aside. A stick of sunlight chopped in and sliced across Steven's cheek. He shifted in his sleep. Woodland creature.

In the bathroom Maristela looked at herself again. The way the frazzled light from the window peppered her throat. "Regal," the Bahamian man had once called her neck. Maybe she should have married that one.

"What's wrong with your neck?" Steven said, his sour morning breath shooting at her from the bathroom doorway.

"Nothing. What you mean? What the fuck is wrong with it?"

He came close and inspected it. "You're staring at it. And last night you were checking for moles." He took up his electric toothbrush, added some toothpaste to the head, and then moved the contraption lazily over his teeth. It made a high-pitched noise—like something unhappy with its task.

Maristela sucked her teeth and looked at her neck. "I'm still pretty," she said, and then quickly looked over at her husband because she hadn't meant to say it out loud. He stopped moving the brush around his mouth to look at her in the mirror beside him. The whine of the brush continued. Without expression, he nodded at her reflection. Then he spat into the sink and brushed his tongue.

Steven wasn't sure what she was expecting of him, so he brushed his tongue for a long time. Until he gagged on the toothbrush. Then he rinsed out his mouth three times. Still, she was there staring at him. He couldn't tell what she wanted. He wiped his mouth on the towel there for that purpose. He thought maybe he should tell her that yes she *was* pretty. But it was early in the morning and really she was no prettier than she normally was. In fact, she would look much prettier after a shower. "You should take a shower," he said and walked out feeling fine. Of course she's pretty, he said to himself. She knows I wouldn't marry an ugly girl.

As he whisked the eggs and added the pink sea salt to their white omelets, he thought of the painting he'd been visiting again and again. It had made him feel lonely to look at it. But still, he would stare at the painting until the staring felt like a kind of infidelity.

6.

Steven met Malaika a few weeks later.

His friend Allen took him to a Baltimore sports bar that was also a strip club. Allen was huge, had played football himself as an undergrad. He always said, "I was a nerd and a jock," making sure no one thought he'd gotten into that school just 'cause he was Black. Steven felt skinny and uncool, as he often did with his friend, but he also felt that the place was demeaning, not to the women so much as to himself. But "these hoes," Allen shouted, even as he'd hooked a stripper's little shirt to peek down her chest, "have nothing on my wife!"

Steven has seen Allen's wife. Chubby and white with blond hair, stiff as straw. Everyone needs someone to love them, Steven had joked once to Maristela when describing Allen's wife. Maristela had laughed loudly and easily at the woman's expense. But Steven hadn't seen when she'd gone into the bedroom and pulled down her own hair and felt it against her face.

At the strip club, the bar was sopping wet when Steven leaned over. He was wearing long sleeves and now his elbows and forearms had dark wet patches that felt cold and thick. "Oh, that's too bad," said the woman beside him. "Now you're stuck like that." He turned to her, readying himself to smile politely at a snarl-faced stripper. But no. He knew immediately that this woman was the woman from the gallery, the painter. "Where are you from?" he asked, hoping with something he didn't understand just then that she would be West Indian—someone his wife might want to befriend.

"Where are *you* from?" she responded.

"But I asked you first," he said.

"Oh, I can guess," she said. "You're from up north. Someplace spacious and cold like Minnesota or Wyoming."

"That's incredible. Yes. I'm from Vermont."

"Oh, where that guy who wants to be president is from. Well, I'm from Kenya."

The motherland, Kenya. "No fucking way." He didn't normally curse; that was Stela's thing. But this woman didn't flinch; she only looked at him with her head to the side and said, "My name is Malaika."

"It sounds like a flower."

"It's an angel."

"Which one?"

"The one."

He could feel his underarms growing moist. He could feel his pants growing tight. None of this made sense, so he allowed it. They stared at each other.

"The fuck you doing with the drinks?" That was Allen.

"Sorry, Allen. This is Malaika. Malaika, this is Allen." Steven went in close to her so Allen couldn't hear. "I'm Steve. And it was nice to meet you." He smelled her. Here in this dank whore bar she smelled clean. Like water. She pressed her face against his, her wavy brown dreads tucked behind her ear. Her face was smooth and soft, and he wondered what the underside of her little breasts must feel like.

"Steve, the feeling is mutual." Her accent sounded British but more fluid somehow. He pulled back and followed Allen to the other side of the bar, the side where you could order chips and a lap dance all while sitting in a comfy chair. Once, only once, did Steven look back. And Malaika was there, clear to see despite the crowd, with her back turned to him. "A mountainous ass," he said out loud. But it was too noisy in the bar and Allen didn't hear.

Steven went straight home after dropping a drunk Allen off to his wife. He knew that he had to tell Maristela about the painting of the Black man and the pale woman. Talking to Maristela about it would help make the painting something that didn't feel so much like betrayal. Steven was a good man. A good Catholic man. He loved the Pope. And Jesus and Mary, too. That Japanese girl was in the past.

But at the front door of their apartment Steven fished out his keys and there in his jacket pocket was a sturdy piece of paper. Not folded.

Not to be mistaken for trash. Just resting there and still open to the writing: "Malaika," followed by a phone number. He knew then that he wouldn't tell Maristela about the painting. He turned around and went back to his car. He called the angel on his cell phone as he drove slowly, like a thief, around the block. "It's me," he said when she picked up.

"It's you."

7.

Steven and Maristela found each other out because they trusted each other. They'd married fast, fucked faster, and so the trust had been automatic, though also nonsensical—the things they didn't know about each other were their most essential parts. But they did know each other's bank codes and cell phone key locks and email passwords. It was the email that got them. They could delete the phone messages of Malaika moaning her orgasms. Of Malaika weeping out of longing. Of Malaika laughing and saying, "Yesterday. Oh, you made me see the goddess." But the email messages, those were silent joys to return to. To read again and again during one's prep period at MLK or during office hours at District Community.

Steven had been searching through his wife's account for the email address of a friend of hers who was dating a curator. He wanted to offer the contact as a little gift to Malaika. He searched "art" and Stela's emails to and from Malaika came pouring out. "Oh, Christ have mercy," he said out loud. He pushed himself from the computer as though it was a flood coming toward him. Malaika had contacted Maristela? "Oh, my God. Oh, my God." And he said it over and over again. And he didn't stop until he pressed the Open button and read the first email. And then he cried.

From: mrsjones@gomail.com
To: paintersforpeace@nubia.org

So tell me, when you think of me does a) your heart get heavy, like it's tied to stones in your belly that are pulling it down, like you can't believe you've gotten into a messy fucking love affair with a married woman? Or b) does your heart get light, as though it will break loose and float around the cavity of your chest, because you're somehow willing and willing and willing?

From: paintersforpeace@nubia.org
To: mrsjones@gomail.com

B. Yes, b, all day and night. B for my baby . . .

But Maristela had gone to Steven's email with a different purpose. She wanted to see if it was true that her husband had saved all their emails. He had once made this claim as proof that he had loved her from the start. If it was true then maybe that was enough to hold her down, peel her from the mistake of Malaika. On Steven's email dashboard there was a folder called JOY. Maristela felt her heart grow as though filling with sweet water. Like Ma Mermaid always said, even in marriage a man can fucking surprise you. Stela opened the folder and there was "paintersforpeace@nubia.org" tumbling out like hay. Maristela covered the screen and looked around her empty classroom. Oh, shit. He knows Malaika's been taking care of me, she said in her head. And it was something of a relief. Because she hadn't even known that care is what she'd been taking from Malaika. And now she knew. Stela lowered her hands and opened an email. And then she cried.

From: steven.jones7@dccmain.edu
To: paintersforpeace@nubia.org

You got me on the internet begging. . . . where are you? I'm so ready to see you, angel, that I'm going to come there and tie you to all this loving . . . I need to taste you, to be drank by you . . . I'll be firm and a man about it, conquering and controlling and tender.

From: paintersforpeace@nubia.org
To: steven.jones7@dccmain.edu

So come.

From: steven.jones7@dccmain.edu
To: paintersforpeace@nubia.org

I'm cumming.

8.

Steven and Stela had been married only months when his book, *Yum: What Our Senses Tell Us About Human Interaction*, came out and did so well that you could buy it in Barnes & Noble. Almost immediately U of Central Vermont called and invited him to apply for an assistant professorship in life sciences. The call stipulated two important things. First, that the ideal candidate had to be able to "serve" the underrepresented ethnic communities on campus—which any idiot knew meant they were targeting a diversity hire. Second, that the ideal candidate be someone whose scholarship dealt with "controversial issues"—which likely meant there was a rich radical trustee pulling the purse strings. Or maybe that students had been protesting. Either way, the work of Dr. Steven Jones (double PhDs in biology and sociology) was mostly about plant pollination and human romance. This was not particularly controversial. In fact, secretly Stela thought her husband's work was mundane as shit.

The job call also suggested that the ideal candidate should be someone able to serve the new influx of international students on campus. This was too hard for the search committee to manage, but they figured they'd done well because though Steven was American he was after all *African* American. Plus his wife, Maristela, was Caribbean. America's Caribbean, but international enough. Stela didn't even know what the fuck to think about that.

Two weeks before his campus callback, an acquaintance on the faculty sent Steven an email assuring him that he was their front-running candidate. They wanted someone who wasn't taking the position as a leg up to something flashy in New York or California. Steven's love of Vermont was documented. He had dedicated *Yum* to its hills and mountains.

There was a formal interview process, whereby two other candidates who had no hope were also interviewed and made to present the interview talk. At Steven's lecture, graduate students asked big questions that were really about themselves, not the work of Professor Jones.

9.

Now Stela and Steven were at a fancy welcome dinner at the university dean's house. The other candidates long forgotten, the UCV faculty swollen-chested over their new acquisition. Bernie Sanders was back to being a senator, and everyone was pretending to hate the new American president, except for Steven, who was drunk enough that he was telling someone right now that he'd voted for the man because "America first" was a progressive ideal. Everything in the world was unfair and made no sense, but Steven was satisfied with it all. The unfairness of it was fair, the nonsensical nature of it made a brutish sense. Steven had struggled. He was smart. And Vermont was his home. The other candidates, both Latinas, had other places to go. Latin America, for example. They didn't, he was sure, have the history and the aftermath of that history his people had had.

Maristela was trying to stay quiet beside her husband and voice no opinion either way, until a white professor of African musicology came up to her and Steven, joking that Stela looked so young she would get mistaken for an undergrad. Stela had laughed back, heartily, and then ate a pork-stuffed roll off a server's silver tray. She hadn't eaten pork since high school, when eating it had made her think of human flesh, her then-boyfriend's flesh, to be exact. But now she did that: cursed like a whore, ate pork. And also, she didn't draw, she didn't paint.

Because it was true that she was still young. Stela had been an undergrad herself just three fucking years before. She'd left her first-ever boyfriend on a ski mountain, returned almost entirely to celibacy, and then hooked on to Steven as soon he'd eyed her. Her American friends called her a serial monogamist. Her Caribbean friends wondered what was wrong with serial monogamy. Her best friend, LaToya, had only dated one person her whole life and was married to him. The American president had been married three times. Now at the dean's house, Stela slipped the silver pork fork into her purse. A souvenir, she decided, in case she never returned.

After the dinner, Maristela and Steven went to the faculty cottage they were renting. Steven tried to rip off his tie, but succeeded instead in getting it more tightly wound around his neck. "Stela," he called. And she came over to him and slowly undid the knot. She still disliked the way "Stela" sounded in his mouth. She preferred when he called her Maristela. Stela was how her Caribbean friends and family back home knew her. Even to the state-sider Saint Tomians she was always the more formal Maristela. Now her American, Trump-voting husband called her Stela when he wanted help. And she hated the clipped, Yankee inflection of it. He wasn't white, like her old boyfriend had been, but sometimes it was almost as bad. Sometimes it was worse—Stela couldn't help but always expect better of Steven.

He sat on the couch, a large fluff that came with the cottage. He reached his hand out to Maristela and pulled her down beside him, the way he knew she liked him to do. She liked it when he was commanding. Like an island man. But it wasn't really Steven's way. He hadn't even been raised among African Americans. Now husband and wife sat beside each other, her leaning into him a little. He sighed. "I'm not sure we're doing the right thing here."

He hadn't meant to say it. He hadn't meant to say anything. He'd hoped maybe they would make love and this time he wouldn't give her the pillow to cover her face. He would let her shout into the cavity of the cottage. Now he'd gone and screwed that up. He felt her raise off his body and off the couch.

She stood and looked down on him. "But Steven. This here was your idea. Vermont always been your fucking idea."

He nodded—her cursing was sexy to him, had been that way since they met. "It's just that I feel they might have picked me because I'm safe. Plants, you know? The Cuban woman's work was about how modern abortion is more moral than modern childbirth. I just don't know." They didn't say what was really between them. The ocean. And the mountains. And Malaika.

◆ ◆ ◆

Steven fell asleep in the dark living room. Maristela had left him there. She'd felt sick to her stomach, and so had gone into the bedroom and opened the curtains wide. She went to her big handbag, rummaged through until she found the paintbrush she'd lifted when Malaika wasn't noticing. The initial that Stela had thought was a brand, but no. Custom-made brushes with an *M* on them. The bitch had her own brushes. Stela ran the brush over her legs, over her belly. Again and again until she came.

◆ ◆ ◆

The next morning is this morning. Maristela awakes to the heat of the Vermont sun. Her whole body, naked, as she'd taken to sleeping since Malaika, covered like a stone with sunshine. She lies in it for a moment and daydreams of home, her island. Of the beaches. Of the descent into water. Of how it takes you easily, like a good lover. Without resistance. That thought leads again to thoughts of Malaika. Not, Stela notes surprisingly, to Johann. Not anymore. Though true, just noting her not thinking of Johann is a way of thinking of Johann. Still, Stela lies there in the sun and daydreams of her first time with Malaika.

Maristela had laid the back of her hand between Malaika's small breasts. She smoothed her hand down Malaika's chest. Toward the low soft mound. For a moment Stela felt a little shame. Malaika was perfect. Her little hilly breasts. The tight skin around her thighs. The sharp valleys of her waist that supported a round backside. Stela looked around and saw an empty easel erect in a corner. She wished she had a dick. She wanted to be inside this bitch of a woman.

The first thing to do, she figured, was discuss STDs. Something she hadn't even done with her husband, but with Malaika Stela was sure laying it all out was the womanist-feminist thing to do. But Malaika scoffed: "I've had them all except for the ones that will kill you." To her, the STDs were like the scrapes of a great mountaineer—proof that Malaika had been places and done things and lived to tell. "But what you have," Malaika had said, "is a pulse in your wrist." She reached toward Stela's hand.

And there between Stela's thumb and index finger a little pulse was indeed ticking. "It's like something alive, pressing its way out of the ground of your skin." Which, Stela was sure, was the most beautiful thing anyone had said to her in years. "Can I kiss it?" Malaika had asked. And Stela had nodded.

Later she and Malaika noted each other's bodies—the similarities. The clipped but unshaved pubis, the brown skin, the dark eyes, the thicker hair at the back of the neck. The sharing made this thing with Malaika feel more intimate, more true. But still, Stela never mentioned that she and Malaika also, sort of, had painting in common. The withholding made this thing with Malaika feel also a little like a lie.

◆ ◆ ◆

At the same time Stela is daydreaming, Steven is actually dreaming. Still sleeping in the cool of the Vermont cottage living room. He is dreaming of his last afternoon with Malaika. It is a fearful dream. He knows he is dreaming. He hopes, in his limited sentience, that he doesn't scream out Malaika's name. He doesn't understand this pretense of keeping her a secret from Maristela. Steven knows that Maristela knows about his indiscretion; she must also know that he knows about hers. But he also knows he does not want to wake just yet.

That last day in the dusk of her little studio apartment, Malaika had told him that this would be their last time together because she was leaving. "Back to the motherland," she'd told him, using those words exactly. Malaika hadn't acted as though she knew he was also leaving. Even though she must have, if not from him then from Maristela. Malaika seemed the same full, fervid self as always. He wondered which leaving was the real reason for the end—his and Maristela's or Malaika's.

She and Steven had lain in her bed tugging and pulling at each other. She hadn't let him in, not yet. It was a game they always played. She didn't seem much saddened by their affair coming to an end; she didn't seem much changed.

"You cannot have this, silly sweet Steve."

"You are mine," he said, feeling a strange desperation in the words that he used to say to her with confidence.

He grabbed her by the tiny fluid waist. She raised her hand and slapped him in the face. The clap was loud and satisfying. He turned and she slapped the other cheek even harder. "You can't get this, Steve." The heat from her waist was still there in the palm of his hand. "It's mine," he said. "Angel, you mine. Open." She pinched her legs together and he used his elbows to spread her knees. "I'll show you who the man is in this," he said. "I am," she said and then used her nails to twist his nipple. "Bitch," and he released her. She pulled herself up and began a furious crawl away. He grabbed her legs and brought her chest slamming to the ground—her hands just barely bracing herself so her chin did not split open. She twisted to face him, legs in the air to push him. He took her feet, her vulnerable little feet, and raised them into the air until her legs straightened. Then he spread her as though ripping cloth and he pushed himself into what felt like a storm. And she sucked in her breath hard, as though she were not expecting his sudden triumph. And then she bent her legs, bringing him closer, making him lose his vigorous rhythm. "I'm drowning," he cried with something like water in his throat. "Don't worry," she shouted over the tumult as he sank deeper into her, "I'll save you."

10.

Now Steven wakes up. It isn't the slow waking that he most enjoys. It's a jolting thing, as though someone has splashed ice water on his chest. He sits straight up in the darkness. It takes him a few seconds to realize that the odd lumpiness is the couch, and that he's in Vermont and not D.C. Across the room is the computer that came with the cottage. It has free internet access. He watches the computer for a while, its little light retreating and advancing like a searchlight. Then he goes to it, to find Malaika.

This is something he's done before. After the first time he'd fucked the angel he looked her up—he wanted to be able to talk art with her, not just sex. But he is at a different computer, one that doesn't know him. The landing page is all about the brilliant psychopath president, but Steven doesn't let himself get sucked in. He does a search and then research; he is a professor, after all. Instead of being satisfied with the first pages the search engine spits at him—dates for her shows in D.C., a blog she herself wrote, her website—he opens an academic search engine. He logs in with his new university's password. He searches Malaika's full name and "visual art." In some thrilling way, he hopes Maristela will come up behind him and they can face this or be done with it together.

There are dozens of articles dedicated to Malaika, as though she is someone of encyclopedic proportions and not just a painter who screwed both Steven and his wife. There is a review of a show in Johannesburg. An Australian art critic claims Malaika is the leader in a new movement of art in Ethiopia. There is a scholarly paper written in a Scandinavian language Steven can't decipher. There is an academic book chapter in English dedicated to berating her artistic movement as manipulative and psychopathic. There is an online article praising it as truth telling and brave. There is an entire monograph on Malaika alone by a professor of material culture at the University of Cape Town. There are South African newspapers claiming that Malaika is South African.

It is over, he knows. But still Steven is looking for some kind of proof that says Malaika was born in Kenya, as she'd told him. Or raised in Kenya. But nothing. He opens a tab to Wikipedia, but Wikipedia can't confirm. A few blogs say the San Francisco Bay Area, a place Steven has always imagined was without history. Even the articles from proper newspapers don't agree. They can't all be true, but how can news be fake? When he clicks on the full monograph, the scholar only calls Malaika a "transnational African." Right now Steven, a scientist, hates the arts and humanities. Right now Steven wonders whether it is he or the entire internet that has been given the wrong information.

He goes back to try a fresh Google search. He clicks on a thumbnail of Malaika's newest work. The picture uploads in sections but Steven knows immediately, even though it's the back of her head, that it's a nude of his own Maristela. He feels a coming on of grief because he'd hoped it would have been of Malaika herself. He's not so sad that it's not Malaika as much as he's disappointed in himself for hoping it was Malaika and then getting Stela instead. He doesn't wait for the image. He leaves the computer with tabs open to this website and that, all of Malaika and Malaika's paintings and this last one of Stela slowly revealing itself. He doesn't wait to see that at the bottom of the painting is his own naked body, prostrate and kissing the palm of Stela's hand.

Steven walks into the bedroom and lies down beside his wife. He watches Maristela's back in the yellow light, all golden now. He thinks of Malaika's body. But only to wonder why he doesn't tell Stela that she's so lovely in all her parts. Why it's so hard for him to give Maristela that little magic offering of "I love touching your collarbone," for Christ's sake. It had been so easy to do with Malaika. Easier, even, than with the woman from before.

It's hot in this room and he feels sweat begin to bead in the bowls of his underarms. Normally this would drive him from Stela, but he knows things are not normal with them. He looks about, not sure what choices they have. On the nightstand, right at his eye level, he sees a paintbrush. Stela's? No. She once mentioned she used to like to paint, but he's never seen the evidence. Without getting up, without going closer, he knows it's the angel's. Something she's given his wife, or something his wife has taken.

"Maristela," Steven says, knowing she's awake. "Do you want to come hiking with me?" It was the kind of thing, like a baseball game, he might offer her for the sake of offering and hope she would reject.

Stela turns toward her husband slowly, her naked breasts facing him now. "That sounds nice," she says with ash in her voice. It's the first thing she's said out loud this morning.

"And our first anniversary," he continues. "It's around the corner. Is there something you really want to do?"

They look at each other across the ocean of the bed. Maristela catches a little of her lower lip in her teeth.

"I'd like to go home. To the Virgin Islands, I mean. See my dad and them. You know they love-love you. But we could spend a night in a fancy tourist hotel. If you want."

"No," he begins. "I mean, yes. A trip sounds right. But I was thinking maybe I'd have to go to Africa. For research, you know. For my next book." He is following Malaika, he knows. He wonders if Stela will follow, too.

Maristela wants to be brave. She sits up and pulls her legs to herself. "I'd come if you want me."

Steven reaches across the continent of the bed. "Of course, Stela," he says. "I always want you." And it is the bravest thing he has ever said, even though it isn't true.

And Maristela wants to say something to this man who has been her partner for a year, who has shared meals and email and even a lover with her. She wants to share this terrible new thing with him: "I was in love and now my fucking heart is motherfucking breaking." But instead she allows his wet body to fill her like earth.

STELA AND FLY

Metaphors are our lives.

—Salman Rushdie, "The Firebird's Nest"

SESTINA

Spring 2020

It was inevitable: the scent of bitter almonds always reminded him of the fate of unrequited love.

—Gabriel García Márquez,
Love in the Time of Cholera

1.

Maristela. She who was named after what is most luminescent above our heads and what is most looming below our feet. She is, however, disappointingly to herself, neither in the heights nor in the depths. Stela is a girl born on a small group of small islands called the Virgin Islands of the United States, a place most people from the United States are sure does not belong with the United States, though it does belong to the United States. Maristela's mother, orphaned, was raised in an orphanage. Maristela's first father, abandoned, raised himself. Her second father's father was dead before the son could even be sure of his name. Stela's parents are most afraid of being left alone. And so Stela is afraid of the same thing, inevitably.

And there is Fly. He who was not born Fly, does not know how to fly, not literally, anyway. Fly was born Earl, though on the North American continent—a place where earls are not born. And if they ever had been born, a brown boy wouldn't have been one anyway. Still, Fly can claim the engendering of global music as his legacy—gospel and hip-hop, if the reader knows little of African Americanah; jazz, pop, rock and roll, if the reader knows a little more. The only real things that Fly's parents have in common is that they love music and they are each parent to Fly. Fly is someone his parents love because he belongs to them, but someone they each feel disparagingly of because he also belongs to the other. Fly's father is mad, his mother is mad—but each in their own way. Fly comes from two people who have not yet climbed out of their respective pits of bitterness.

Grown-up Fly and adulting Stela. She's been online, on the dating apps. Who isn't? Well, he isn't. Fly doesn't even own a cell phone. His only computerish thing is his PC, but he uses it only to type his grad school papers. Fly and Stela meet in New York City, but they don't just fall in love. That never just happens—readers know this by now. They meet sitting on the same park bench or at the same café table or on the same grass at an outdoor concert. Whatever. They meet, but they have an ancestry's worth of broken hearts between them. This day in history, Stela and Fly sit as hundreds of people walk by. It's New York City, so there is nothing unusual about this. What is unusual is that a few people are wearing actual surgical masks, so no one can see if they are frowning or smiling despite this too-perfect spring day. But Stela and Fly smile. They laugh, they exchange air and thoughts and pheromones. They talk about books she's read and ones he's half read. To Stela, a man of her generation who doesn't have a cell phone is kind of mysterious, so she gives him her physical address, an act that itself is mysterious. Then they kiss—a sweet one, with only their lips touching. Because see, when two people (good-looking, young, mysterious, in a big city) are lonely and find each other they are bound to give in to their curiosity, pretty much always.

But Fly needs a sign. A sign that will allow him to make love to this woman and then fall for this woman, or maybe in the opposite order. She is familiar to him—with her accent that reminds him of his father's voice when his father was hearing voices. She is also straight strange to him, the way she sometimes stares at mundane things—like his hands, his hair—but then shrugs when he asks about it. And her constant cursing. In their first conversation he'd counted seventeen curse words. To his ear, they sounded percussive. Fly doesn't have a history of falling for rational reasons—such as compatibility or kindness. No, Fly requires metaphor. There is, he's been told, a labyrinth in a park down the way that may yield such metaphorizing. Sure, another guy would have looked up the location of the labyrinth before leaving his place, but that is not Fly's way. Fly hasn't even paid for an internet connection in his apartment. He bounces out of his building, a paperback of *Invisible Man* rolled into his back pocket. He has bought or found a dozen copies by now—kept in a row on his one shelf in his one-room apartment, right next to his old jar of marbles. The marbles are just the same ones he's had since he lived in his parents' house. He wears this paperback copy with the cover facing out, so it can be noticed and considered. On the cover is an image, a collaged face that sets the eyes apart—so Fly figures he has eyes in front and back today. He'll just stumble onto the labyrinth if he wanders through the park thinking of it, or the labyrinth will rise up before him because his thinking makes it so. Fly is so sure that he stops searching altogether when he gets to the park and sees a crowd gathered before a stage. A female actor is on a balcony. A male down below. *Romeo and Juliet*, Fly supposes. Must be that Shakespeare in the Park. But "Ste-la!" the actor onstage shouts. Which can't be what Fly just heard. But then the man shouts it again: "Stela!" Fly's heart opens up like that mouth, and just then a couple separates from the crowd, like they themselves are voices coming forth. They are wearing those surgical masks over their mouths and noses—perhaps they both have a cold. "Too many people," the man offers to Fly, his voice muffled. The guy is dark brown-skinned like Fly, and the girl is lighter, like she might be Puerto Rican or something, but they both have eyes that are Asiatic. They are beautiful, which Fly is certain means they are wise. "You gonna need just your one person for the foreseeable future," the guy says to Fly as he keeps walking by. These words are so obviously a sign that if Fly doesn't obey, it would for sure be a sin. The girl looks back at him and Fly can tell, from her beautiful eyes, that she is smiling. Fast, Fly spins out of the park. He is going to need a cell phone, some way to call his Stela. Romeo had shouted her name, the wise masked man had said to go find one person, and so Fly knows that Stela and he are fated.

For Stela most things lately are about her dad. Maristela's dad is sick, again. Cancer back. But Stela can't fucking bear her dad being sick these days, because maybe this time his "about to dead" might be "really going to dead." So she can't be bothered to figure out what's going on with that rando Fly guy. Stela has been in love, been coerced into sex, and been married—which is more than a woman needs to see that men are things to be seriously afraid of. And so Stela is shitting scared. The one man who has never left her is maybe about to die and, well, leave her. So fuck all of them. Men. She might fuck Fly, but if Fly's got feelings for Stela they are, at this point, unrequited.

From her apartment, she calls home. "You father is fucking fine," her mother says at pickup. Cursing is the language this mother and daughter share now. Fucking-fine Dad comes to the phone in coughs and wheezes, though the cancer is not in his lungs, not in his chest. "Dad, I'll be home in a few months to help. Just wait and stay the fuck alive, already." When the coughing is over, he sighs. "So what you trying to say is, I ain going to meet my grandchildren, because as yet, you ain find a man worthy of your love."

2.

In response, Stela is quiet. She is mad at her dad for his crass joke. She has no idea that in just a few weeks taking a flight will be too dangerous, that she could kill her father just by deboarding a germ-ridden plane and arriving home to care for him. But she still feels her own failure. Giving her dad grandchildren would be one big something to do for him. Stela is so quiet that even over the phone she can hear her mother, Mermaid, cursing over something in the background. "She just watching her soap suds," Dad says now, trying to lighten what he made heavy, but going heavier still. "You know how them shows is. All rape, divorce, true love."

Stela breathes deeply at his list, how the order seems inevitable.

She tries to think of something else to talk about, while her father wheezes quietly.

"Yes, my girl," Dad says finally, filling the space before she gets the chance. "That is your mother. Hot mouth whether she sweet or she bitter."

The receiver is hot against Stela's ear, like the phone has a fever. "Dad," she says, but then she has nothing to say. "Stela," Dad says in response, "you really should come see me. I going die soon for true. You know. Is fate."

Then the silence is inside her. The phone is hushed, but Stela's body also feels hushed. There on the phone with him—this man who has been her father for as long as she remembers—she imagines the cells in his prostate fusing. Not a love fusing, but a fight, a failing. She knows this has been coming all along, always.

3.

And just then her door buzzer rings. "I have to go, Dad," Stela says. She wants to tell her father, "I haven't done all I can for you. I haven't yet thanked you enough for being my father. I am sorry I have not been there to make you breakfast or keep you out of the sun. I am sorry that I have been thinking about following a vapid romantic love instead of coming to you." She wants to tell him, "Don't die." She wants to tell him, "I love you most and always."

But he gets to it first, as with any decent dad. "It's you I love, sweet Stela," he says. "Sweet Stela," which is what he called her the day he met her in a basket beside her mother. "It's you I more love," she says, playing their game. He finishes; the finale: "Oh, sweet Stela. It's you I most love."

At the buzzer to her apartment the voice is garbled, like someone is crimping paper into the microphone. Normally, Stela would ignore it—perhaps it's a burglar, or a con man claiming to be from Con Ed. But today, right now, Stela is running from her father's leaving, and so she buzzes the stranger in. It's in the middle of the day; perhaps it's just someone delivering Thai to a lower floor. But then there is a knock on her own door. Stela's chest flushes hot. She thinks of her father's soap opera list: rape, divorce, true love. Shit, shit, shit. She opens the door, and it's that guy Fly, like fate.

Stela blinks. Sure, she and Fly hung out once or twice. But for most of that hanging he talked about being a musician, and she daydreamed, barely registering what instrument he played. Now standing in her doorway with Fly before her, she knows she's been conjuring another prince to be her saving grace. Another boy, not Fly. Her first love, the one who used to save her—Johann. Which is to make clear that despite this story we are telling, Stela falling for Fly is not at all inevitable.

Still, Fly has turned up in place of that bright blond boy with whom Stela often flew off a cliff. True, she is disappointed in herself for even thinking a thought about Johann. Johann has moved on. Married someone else months after she left him, like marriage was a necessity. Stela doesn't bother considering that she basically did the same thing, marrying Steven. Johann and his wife are still married, with their second baby in his wife's belly. Stela and Steven are quite divorced. All Stela considers is her own bitterness.

Now she makes a smile of her face, and opens the door wider for Fly to come in. Why not? And doesn't Fly look like someone in her history anyway—six foot and with a fade? Not like Johann—fuck Johann. And not like her ex-husband, Steven, who kept his hair fluffy and unlined, like someone raised by white people. Here is a beautiful Black man, showing up at her door. A gift. Is love even required?

4.

Stela has her life together. She has friends. She has a good job. She's a Black girl with a balconied apartment twelve stories up in Harlem. The elevator almost always works. But when it comes to intimacy she doesn't know what to want or request.

With Fly here, she goes easy into her caregiver role. She shows him into her living room/kitchen combo and offers him tea. She makes it with loose tea leaves and water boiled in a kettle. She's like that. She takes care. Taking care has been her way, always.

"How much sugar you want?" she asks Fly, but his face goes blank, and his mouth slack. Stela is sure he is being funny. She laughs. But really, Fly is stunned by her mundane question. He knows sweet tea and unsweetened tea, and he isn't sure what to do with more options. "I'll give you three sugars," Stela says, and smiles. Fly smiles, too, but only to follow her lead. He asks, "How many spoons do you usually like?" He wonders if the three he accepted might say something he doesn't understand about himself. "Shit, I'm not typical," Stela says. "I take mine black and bitter."

She sifts the tiny tea leaves into their pouches. She turns on the kettle to boil. She chooses their cups carefully—the one for Fly says WNYC, hers BITCH. Fly is here and he is handsome, healthy and handsome. Stela says this again and again in her mind. Those are things, she hopes, she can love.

"Have you seen the Karate Kid movies? The original ones," Fly asks. This is odd, but it is what Stela expects from a real artist, even if he works in music and not in paints.

"Love it," she says, even though she can't really remember any of the movies; she's not sure if she ever watched them or just knows about them.

"Is that where you learned about tea?" Fly asks her.

"From the movie?" she asks, wondering if he's serious.

"The tea scene," Fly says earnestly. "You know? The part where the Asian woman makes the Karate Kid tea and then they know their love is, you know, inevitable?"

"Sure," she says, because she does, now, remember that scene. This boy reminds her, maybe, of Malaika, the way simple things always seemed rich with meaning for that woman. Stela had been like that, too, back when she was an artist—back before she gave up on all that. So now Stela turns and turns Fly's teacup before passing it into his palm, like the way the young woman did in the movie. She wants to say something artful and true, so she tries: "To movies from the eighties, I am fateful."

5.

Fly turns his cup, too, which he remembers the kid does in the movie. He and Stela are making a scene that feels weighty, feels meaningful, even though it's not theirs alone. He takes a delicate sip of his tea, and tries to think of what comes next. Fly wonders if he misheard her line—did she say she is fateful or faithful?

But, most important, does she smoke weed, eat gummies? And would it be weird to ask? "So music," he says out loud because that is what he knows. Stela raises her eyebrows at him, which Fly decides is an encouragement. "We need music for this. It's, like, a prerequisite."

"Oh shit, okay," Stela says, feeling giddy. She gets up to get her computer going, and Fly starts drumming his thumbnail against his cup. Stela realizes that she has the BITCH on her cup facing herself; he hasn't seen it yet. She sits back down, sips her tea, keeps the bitch to herself. "Music," Fly begins again, as he taps, "is tangible. You know?" He bends his ear to his shoulder to demonstrate. "We don't just hear music but we actually feel it. In the ear and so in the body. Right? But it's always feeling at the basic level of it. It's just, like, a delusion that it's not feeling." She wonders if the tea is making him high. He is studying music theory, she remembers correctly; getting a PhD, she remembers wrongly. Maybe, he might motivate her, move her. What she is thinking is simple, but what she is feeling is ineffable.

"Do you hear that?" Fly asks. Because he can hear music coming from somewhere, maybe down the hall from another apartment. Maybe from the streets outside and below. Stela doesn't know this game. It's Fly's. Something to impress her. "That is Kirk Franklin," he says now. "'Looking for You.' Circa 2005." He likes saying "circa." "Hmm," Stela says, because as a Caribbean Catholic, that type of church music has never been her thing. Besides, she can't hear the music Fly seems to be hearing. But then whoever is playing the music turns it up. "Oh, wait. Actually," says

Fly, realizing he'd been wrong but self-correcting, getting it right, "it's not gospel. It's um, like R and B. Those sexy girls." He looks at Stela shyly. "I mean sexy women. Zhané." Which all feels so right. Makes Fly feel like sexiness, sex itself, is now available, right now, because of the music. "Do you smoke up?" he asks Stela and puts his pinched thumb and forefinger to his lips. Stela shakes her head, and instead picks up her phone and speaks some biblical-sounding words into it, magic words, and she faces the phone toward her balcony where the music is coming from. The phone responds unmusically: "Patrice Rushen. 'Haven't You Heard.' First recorded. Nineteen seventy-nine." "Can't be," says Fly in his own defense. Stela shows him the phone, and there is Patrice, her braids beaded like jewels. Then he feels stupid, like always.

But Stela thinks his dumbstruck face is endearing. She wants to hug him right there, take his cheeks in her palms and tell him it's okay. "I don't smoke, but you can if you want." She says this wanting to protect him from his feeling of shame. Stela is falling in love with Fly, or she is realizing that Fly is someone she can love, or she is realizing that she wants to feel it, love.

It's an awful feeling, the desire is; she hates it—hates herself just a bit.

6.

Stela goes to sip her tea and realizes that there is no more tea. She pretends to sip anyway. "Maybe we should try something African," Fly says. Because that is what he is studying at school and he wants to be smart. He starts speaking about gqom music, but he runs out of things to say, so he switches again and asks if Stela has any highlife records. "I can look it up," she says. Thanks to her study abroad, she knows what highlife is. At her laptop she spells it "hi-life," and Fly, emboldened, leans beside her and types in FELAKUTI—he types like a fish might, like someone not made for anything of this plug-in world. When the music comes, it is nothing Stela has heard before and yet she loves it instantly. It's too easy to connect loving the music she hears to loving the man beside her. "Afrobeat," Fly tells her and then tents the tips of his fingers in a way Stela has seen Malcolm X do on a college dorm poster. She goes to her kitchen counter and mixes Fly and herself each the only cocktail she knows how to make—cheap whiskey, off-brand soda; but she's a Caribbean girl and so has the good Angostura bitters.

When Stela hands Fly the glass, she notes the tender lunula of his nails, the distal edges, the muscular folds of skin at his knuckles. She wonders what those hands could hold on to, could sustain. She may paint his hands, if he lets her. Imagine that. It's been so long since she's painted anything, she didn't realize it was something she would even allow herself. She and Fly clink glasses. She doesn't think about what the right thing is to say; she just says it: "To that bitch called fate."

She sips her old-fashioned. And Fly laps his, which he hopes appears manly—her cursing makes him want his own fierce thing. Her phone pings with an odd ping, so Stela doesn't ignore it. "Ugh. School is canceling," she says out loud. "But that's great," he says because it means school is canceling for him, too. He takes out a spliff, lights it and pulls. Stela stays looking at her phone for a minute, then two, then three. Then she pitches the phone onto her small couch. "Looks like I have to go in next week though," she says. "To learn some new online teaching shit. They acting like it's the end of the fucking world." He offers her a smoke, but Stela sighs. She walks them out onto the balcony, because that seems to best suit the moment. Fly stubs the spliff and shoots the drink down his throat, just to get the performance of drinking and smoking over with. The balcony is a Juliet, but enough for two people. The sun is setting in pinks and purples. Stela doesn't often come out for the sunset, and she imagines that this can't be a normal sunset, stunning as it is. "Wow," she says. He says: "It's like we're *in* the sky." It is spring and the night is balmy and they are in New York City—a place fantastic and foreign to them both. New York is actually a place foreign to its own country, as these two are as well. There are sirens going, and somewhere they can hear a newscaster suggesting that a quarantine is likely. But there is also the music from her computer streaming out, and they have been drinking alcoholic drinks, and it is beautiful, and this, everyone knows, leads to making love.

"You curse a lot," says Fly. "Fucking true," Stela says, and feels strong saying it. "But if I kiss you, then you can't curse," Fly says. And Stela doesn't know what to say to that, so she says nothing. And Fly can't believe he even said what he just said, it was such a cool thing to say, and so he figures, well, he better kiss her. And so there is kissing. There is the taste of the tea and there is the taste of the cocktail, with the tender bite, a nibble, of the bitters. There on the balcony it's as if Stela's soul is on the edge of a cliff, with a boy beside her soul. Her eyes are closed and she feels, sees, the sea. But there is no actual sea below. Below is a street in Harlem, but it makes no damn difference because she feels what she feels. Out there is the real New York City skyline—the beauty so easy and ubiquitous that for a real art lover a replication would never be required or requested.

Just standing on the balcony is like being a piece of art, a play; and isn't beauty the point of art anyway? The music coming is, indeed, R&B—a 1980s mix. Sex music, for certain. And that sea-star boy of Stela's past is far, far away. Stela opens her eyes to beautiful NYC and sees this boy, Fly. The beauty in both is what she needs right now, and maybe for always.

They are high up enough that pedestrians cannot see them, and it is getting dark enough that her neighbors across the way would have to be paying some serious attention to figure them out. Stela's thinking uncontrollably turns to her dad dying, but she lifts that thought away by lifting her own shirt over her head. Fly, too, lifts off his shirt. They are stripping and kissing. Then they are doing it so fast they are flailing. The danger is inevitable.

Inevitable, bitter, always, fate, unrequited, love

7.

Fly's thinking uncontrollably turns to his dad fucking, but he lifts that thought away by lifting naked Stela up with his own hands, gripping her with his own fingers. He perches her on the narrow steel of the balcony so he can lick her, which he knows is the true way to a woman's heart. He read that in a men's magazine, because he's not only into porn, not anymore. He reads now. And he's sure that this trick could have held Suzanna to him if he'd known better back then. But in Stela's mind, Fly's tongue in her vagina doesn't feel like it is doing magic on her heart. It's not how Johann used to do it, with her looking out to the ocean. She feels some things more mundane—that the view of Fly's head bobbing is not so lovely, and that her ass is unstable on the ledge. Now Stela feels scared. She holds Fly's shoulders. "I have you," he says into her thighs. "Trust me, I have you." And because he has said the words with conviction, to Fly it all now seems inevitable. He *will* have her. He *will* be trustworthy and trusted. He feels something hard shift behind his breastbone; it hurts just a little. But he swims his tongue on and around and in. He's seen this in a magazine—eating pussy on a balcony. And here he is doing it right now. The pain in his chest recedes.

Stela, though, is trying hard not to worry about being so high up on the edge of a balcony, about being naked outside on a balcony, about the loop on her belly of a gentle roll of fat. This moment should be poetic and passionate. This moment should be like jumping off a cliff at seventeen years old. It's reckless and real; this is how to be young and alive, while you are still young and alive. Which makes Stela think of dying. Then she thinks of her dying dad. The song coming from a neighbor's now seems to be a requiem. The taste of the cocktail surges bitter in her mouth. Then she is seeing the mattress. The concrete floor. She is hearing, remembering herself saying, "Stop. No." And Edi going go. She is daydreaming, but the dream feels beyond her control. Here on the balcony, she feels her body breaking out in tiny boils. They rise on her skin like so many red lights. She wants to be off the ledge. "Stop, stop now," she tries with Fly. It is a whisper, like it had been that time before. But Fly hears her.

Fly hears her and stops. Halts right there. "Are you okay?" he asks. "What do you need?" Which, Stela realizes, is what she always has needed—the ask. "I want my bed. I want us in a bed." He moves from her gently. His hands ease her down. His hands are former basketball-playing hands, but she doesn't know that yet. For now she knows that his hands hold her hand and lead her to her own bed.

Afterward, after Fly has slept some and then left, Stela is out on her balcony again. Another old-fashioned in her hands. And she is doing her daydreaming—calmer now, in control now. She is thinking that being with Fly is something new. Somehow. She wishes she understood it all. Herself, to start. She still has no answer as to why she broke the heart of the first boy she ever loved, and no answer for why she married a man she didn't. And no answer for her dad dying—that one she knows will never have an answer. She looks at the city. It isn't a church. But it is, in a way, an ocean. Sirens go blaring, but they could be church bells or the songs of whales. Then, as if fated, actual church bells go blaring, too. There is, right now, a sinking happening in the city, and in Stela. She sees herself in the belly of the whale. She sees it all like a picture she will paint.

Fly is walking across town because, it turns out, they live only twelve blocks apart. He is whistling as he thinks about being with Stela, being in her. Holding her naked body with his own hands. He whistles until he starts to sing. Then he feels a hard thing behind his breastbone again. He sings a belting sound, and he feels the hard rattle, rolling. The marble, he thinks. It scares him, a little. He looks around to see if anyone sees him and indeed there is a line of people standing outside a 7-Eleven. A line of people, which is strange enough, but they are all looking at him, and some are wearing those doctor's masks again. So Fly stops singing and settles on a scat and hum. The people in the line look scared and he feels a little scared, too. His fear is added to his joy and he loses some of his cool. The sum of this seems to be a soft but charged music coming from inside him. "That better be a requiem," someone from the line calls out, which does seem to be the right equation.

When Fly opens the door to his studio apartment, he goes to his little canister of weed that is right on the table, the kind of canister other people might use for pencils or coins. Stela had used hers for tea bags. On that table are also his textbooks, his *Invisibles*, his marbles, his flute, and a camera, an SLR. The camera had been his dad's. But were there digital SLRs back then in his Dad's young days? If there were, his dad would have had one. It dawns on Fly now that maybe it was the same camera his father used to take that picture of the woman he first loved. Fly rolls the joint and takes a pull and another. The idea of taking pictures of Maristela with this camera feels so perfect. He sucks the spliff again. His body is calm now, and there is nothing hard and round rattling inside him. He looks at his hands open on his knees.

He picks up the camera, balancing it in an awkward-fingered grip, like a musician with a new instrument, and takes a picture of his own open hand. His mother calls on his landline, because he has one of those, and she pays the bill for it and in fact she is the only one who has the number. "New York is going quarantine," she shrills through the receiver. "Earl, you have to make your way home to me. True, this may seem like a sci-fi movie, a TV show, but it's for sure real, and it's right now." To say she sounds panicked would be to say an ocean is a drop of rain. Which is a good metaphor because it's raining outside right now. And Fly is so high that as he listens to his mother from the phone he has between his shoulder and ear, he also holds the camera awkwardly and takes another picture of his own hand. And then another. He takes them until he has a good one. A beautiful one. One that he loves.

MEETING THE MONSTER

STELA AND FLY

New York City

Summer 2020

The day the detectives came it was just beyond midnight and it was cold. First, they knocked on the door, but Maristela and Fly were making love on the living room floor of her apartment. Right now, Stela could hear nothing but her and Fly. Fly could hear the groove of Mary J. Blige coming through the walls from the neighbor's apartment. Everyone was always playing music these days. When the detectives called out, "Open the door," Fly didn't lose his rhythm. He asked, "Who's that?" but softly, into Stela's ear so that the question wouldn't disrupt his thoughts—which were of Stela, sort of, but Stela with the ass, legs, and mouth of a woman he'd seen, studied, favorited to be true, on one of those sites that had found him when he should have been doing research for a paper.

But Stela always focused on Fly when they made love. If she didn't do this aggressively, she might instead conjure up Edi and that night, which would make her pussy go dusty. She was vigorously thinking only of Fly, and now, with the voice and the knocking, she just looked at him, her body stilling. So, he tripped to the door after tugging on his pajama pants. "Put a mask on," she called from behind the couch. To be wary was her way, cloying or caring. But Fly just opened the door, no mask at all. That was his way.

There were three white men—cops, they were plainclothed but they showed their badges. One wore a mask over his mouth but not his nose; the others didn't bother. One of them without a mask spoke, and that one asked for Maristela Jones. A woman who didn't exist any longer, since she'd already changed her name back to the one she was born with. Already left that Maristela Jones behind.

Fly could have told them that he didn't know any Maristela Jones. Or better, that she wasn't here anymore and no, he didn't expect her back. Closed the door on these men, he could have. But that didn't seem possible to Fly. Cops were killing people, or spraying them with tear gas, or punching them to the ground, right now somewhere in New York City. He tried to think what could be the correct protocol. Should he put his hands up to the cops? Or would that be too sudden a movement? He was nervous because he knew his body—foot tapping, knee shaking, picking at the palms of his hands. Sudden movement was basically his thing.

Fly couldn't hear the neighbor's music anymore. The neighbor had turned it off, probably listening. That was something everyone did now, too—spy on each other. But all Fly could see was that there were three white police officers at the door, just like the three white officers who had visited his house when he was a shamefaced teenager. And he wasn't that boy anymore; he was a man. Stela's man. He'd told her—asked her, actually—to please never call him her boyfriend. But these cops were asking for Fly's own girlfriend, his woman, by another man's name, and Stela was naked behind the couch. All this was in Fly's mind. So his body remained at the door, floating in the moment. Fly, whose name wasn't really, not officially, Fly, was from the South—Georgia—and so it didn't take a stitch of imagination to see that he was a Black man and nothing else for the moment. A fly in the milk of America.

◆ ◆ ◆

On the couch there was a throw flung over the back, seemingly for style but really to cover a stubborn stain. This Stela tugged from the couch and wrapped around herself. She walked to the bedroom, running her fingers nervously over the face of Fly's djembe drum as she passed it, making a soft music—doing this all in plain sight and sounding. He'd left this drum at her place once and now it lived here. Slow, she commanded her heart. Slow the fuck down, as she put on a T-shirt and jeans. They had masks made of kente and batik. Fly had one that said I CAN'T BREATHE, and she had one that said BLACK MEN ARE DOPE. But the ones she chose for them now were the surgical kind. The kind that said "You are safe from me" and nothing else.

Fly was here and alive. So it could not be Fly whom the officers were here to tell her about. If one of her brothers was sick or dead, Mermaid would have called. Besides, it wouldn't be right, not right at all, if she lost another family member so soon after Dad. But, shit, where was Steven? He was the man who had given her that last name and now there were three large white men at her door calling her by that name. "Misses Jones?" the youngest one asked, when she returned to the living room. He was the only one of the cops wearing a mask, but it hung loose around his mouth, the tip of his nose out obscenely. It reminded Stela of how hood kids used to wear jeans around their asses. A youthful defiant style. This cop was thick-bodied but short, with a round head and thin hair. He looked, Stela could not help thinking, like Charlie Brown. In the original cartoon Charlie Brown had seemed old, his head balding. Charlie Brown had his old-man depression and inability to kick a football. His melancholy mood always ruining everything good, just like this detective was surely about to do.

Was Stela's ex-husband hurt or dead? Anything was possible. Her dad was dead. Lots of people were. They were dying from the virus and from racism. And why not Steven Jones, a Black professor in very white Vermont? Was Stela, as ex-wife, still somehow Steven Jones's next of kin? Dear fucking God, she prayed in her mind. Dear holy shit Jesus and motherfucking Mary. The TV news of dead Black boys had just been news. The people protesting in the streets had just been news. Now maybe it was life. Stela had ordered a Black Lives Matter tank top, but hadn't gone down to protest. Hadn't even worn the tank top once, to be true. She didn't worry now about white Johann at all, except to note that she wasn't worried about him.

Outwardly Maristela nodded at the name of her ex-husband, Jones, and at the Charlie Brown who used it, hating that nodding was the right thing to do. Stela didn't give Fly the mask she'd chosen for him. Instead, she turned to him and fastened it over his face, trying to look him in the eyes the whole time, but his eyes were unfocused. Once she had adjusted the straps and secured it comfortably, she smoothed it over his face, and then tapped here and there, fidgeting with it like a nurse with a sick but sweet patient. She looked him in the eye, an affirmation. Then she stepped forward into the threshold. Fly, inexplicably, stepped back into the apartment.

Stela wanted to tell these men: *You are going to fucking ruin my spanking-new relationship. Just by making my stupid heart beat hard over my ex-husband's name. Just by stoking my man's insecurity.* But what could she really say when they had already opened their wallets and shown their detective badges? "Come in," Maristela said and waited for what they would offer, for what they would take.

"Ma'am, we're here to ask you about May thirtieth. Do you remember what happened on May thirtieth?"

Stela closed her eyes and did not even try to remember. She breathed a heavy breath of release. "Oh, Jesus fucking Christ," she said out loud and wondered if cursing was illegal. "I'm here thinking someone was hurt." She turned to look at Fly, wondering if he could see the guilt on her face. After all, she'd been thinking about another man, not him. Fly looked at her blankly, and she knew then that he could see and did. He nodded at her and at the officers, then withdrew to the pillows behind the couch, where she'd just been making love with him.

"It's just . . ." She looked back at the men who were staring at her. Charlie Brown now had a file open. "It's just that I thought maybe it was one of my brothers or something." The half lie felt infidelic in her mouth. But still. Thank you, Lord, she prayed silently and quickly. Did she even care about Steven at all? She hadn't thought so, but she knew her body's secret, how her heart had been skipping in her chest.

"Is your brother in trouble?" asked the eldest-looking, a man with greasy hair and a loud Brooklyn accent. He looked not like a detective but like someone playing a detective on a TV show. Charlie Brown and the TV detective. The third one, tall with porcupine hair, hadn't spoken yet, so she couldn't place him in the picture.

"No," Stela started, trying to say something that would ground her. Trying to call the name of a man who would not threaten Fly. "My younger brother, Everett, he's in the Virgin Islands. At the university. It's just that he's my baby brother. It's just . . ." She shook her head and smiled, hoping the smile looked real. Was this real? Had she just been making love with a man and now there were cops in her apartment? And were these cops really in her apartment without masks, even though sneezing could kill people these days? "I'm sorry. What you need again?"

Then, despite the Novel Coronavirus 2019, which was decimating the city and cities around the world, and despite Black men and women dying under the knees of men who reported directly to men like the ones in front of her, Stela did something wild—she welcomed the three officers in.

They all stood around the coffee table. Her biology textbooks were in a neat pile. She didn't have to teach this summer, but she was doing training for online teaching—a requirement for the teachers at her school, even though they were all going back to in-person education; the mayor had promised so. Fly's graduate-school books, with their eager academic titles, were spread out in a jumble. His school was going virtual, Zoom, Zoom all the time. This man who had barely understood how to plug in a computer now used it all day long. Almost never turned away from it. Fly's flute lay on top of all this, like it was still the crown of it all. There was also her one book of labyrinths teetering on the edge. And a hardcover of one of his many *Invisible Man* novels on the floor. He had a dozen of them, it seemed. Always had one on him. The tallest cop nudged this Ellison with the toe of his shiny shoe. Pushed it under the table. Charlie Brown cleared his throat. "Do you remember going into the Cell-U store on May thirtieth?"

Maristela shook her head. She knew that it was almost midnight but it was only now registering to her that even if this wasn't about her brothers or her ex-husband, it must still be something bad. What she knew clearly was that her boyfriend, her man, was rustling behind the couch keeping company with his small djembe. Was Fly scared? Had he done something? Did Stela want him back there, safe from the officers? Was she safe? Either way, she was facing these three white cops on her own, and one had spittle on his lips. She could see this all clearly, as if she had painted the image herself. And it wasn't good, the image. She felt ashamed that she was even thinking about painting right then.

"Ma'am. We have video of you stealing a cell phone."

"Excuse me?"

"Listen, we know you did it. The clerk saw you take it. The cameras caught you fingering the phone. You're in the Cell-U system as a customer. They have your address and phone number. Hell, they have your whole life. If you just admit it, it will be easier for us all." That was the TV detective, mean and loud.

Stela could feel herself blinking and she knew from the teacher training for managing plagiarizing students that she should not be fucking blinking. Blinking was a sign of lying. She shook her head to clear her brain; she tried to steady her voice so her immigrant-sounding Caribbean accent didn't edge in, so her usual cursing didn't come bursting through. "Sorry, wait, what are you talking about?" They had a video of her? How would they even know if it was her? She never went into stores without a mask on.

"So you're saying it was not you at Cell-U on May thirtieth?" Charlie Brown spoke in an easy voice, as though it was really a question. She knew it wasn't really a question. She shook her head again. It felt as though something was pinched behind her eyes. She couldn't see clearly at all.

"I don't remember. I had no reason to be there. There is so much going on. I don't remember." She turned around the room and reached her hand out to Fly. "Baby, I need you over here." But it was as if Fly hadn't heard any of what was happening. He got up, his face as blank as before, and stood there where her hand had reached. She pulled him to her and tried to hold on to him.

"Don't give us a hard time," the tallest one said, in a deep impatient tone. This was the first thing he'd said. Each of these fuckers, Stela thought, was big in a different way: stout, loud, tall. "You don't think we'd come all the way to stinking Harlem for a cell phone if we didn't know you did it, do you?" He was too tall for his suit jacket, which ended short of his wrists. He was the only one who didn't seem like a caricature, and for that he was the most frightening. Fly was tall, six feet, about, but this man was taller.

"I'm sorry, I don't know." Stela could feel Fly's arm in her grip. It felt loose. Not a muscle clenched. She looked at him, trying to see if he could tell her something. Explain what really was. But he was just staring.

◆ ◆ ◆

Fly stared at the men. He was pretty sure that this was what you were supposed to do. Keep calm and don't blink and don't show fear. Isn't that what his father had taught him about interacting with the police? But then again, what did his father know, unwell as he was? Fly could tell that Stela was afraid. He wished she would stop acting afraid. Afraid could look dangerous. It all, somehow, translated that way. She was acting as though she'd stolen a diamond from Tiffany's. As though she was a lying thief for sure.

But there was something to the danger. Had Fly ever felt dangerous? Maybe that May 30? Maybe then. It had been a strong feeling. But if he was too respectful now, he might look submissive. Fly knew that *submit* wasn't a manly word. And anyway, these officers were going to consider him aggressive, tall and brown as he was, no matter what he did. He might as well get the benefit of the feeling. And ah yes, here it was coming on him again. A calmness. A steadiness. It felt like manhood.

Carefully, without shifting his eyes, Fly thought again about the packet of marijuana he'd just slid into the pages of an *Invisible Man*. He'd bent the book in half and tucked it into the body of the small djembe drum. On the cover of this copy, the man was made of shadow, and lightbulbs were raining down on him. This book was now making invisible the thing Fly was sure these cops would catch him for.

He calculated how much bud it really was. Was it enough to be a misdemeanor or a felony? The laws were changing so swiftly. Was it enough to get him arrested right here? To get him jail time? Would Stela maybe get a thrill out of having a thug for a man? She didn't know he'd been to the protests on May 30. She'd told him it was too dangerous, that he'd bring the virus back to their home. But he'd gone anyway. Just hadn't told her. Had to go. Felt the absolute of it in his chest.

And when there he had yelled and shouted, and even once actually thumped his own chest. Mostly he had kept his right arm up and fisted for over an hour. In his mind it hadn't felt like much, but in his heart it had felt like everything. He took a shower as soon as he arrived home, hoping that would keep the virus off him. Stela was already gone to the funeral, and he told her not a thing. When they spoke by phone he asked how the service was going, and she asked how his research was going. She told him the military was doing the most, and he told her the library was closed to visitors but that he'd stood in line to get his books through a walk-up window. Told Stela he got stuck on the subway coming back from the library. That they were both withholding key information, they never quite knew. He hadn't felt in danger at all during the rally. Actually, he'd felt like he was the danger. He'd read somewhere that Black people were immune to the virus anyway.

But he wasn't immune to three white cops. The chunky balding cop, who seemed to be the one in charge, turned to Fly now. "We're taking her to the station either way. Sorry—you can't come."

Fly remained silent for another moment. He wasn't sure if he had heard the white man right. He replayed the sentences in his head. So. Wait. The cops didn't see *him*, *Fly*, as the criminal here at all? They didn't see him as a threat? With his eyes on the man's glinting forehead Fly stood up straight, to his full height, and responded. "But I'm her partner," he said, because suddenly saying "I'm her man" felt ridiculous, and he did not want to be ridiculous. The officers flicked a glance from one to another to another. Fly was sure he felt the power shift his way. "I'm not letting her go out with three strangers at midnight by herself." Fly said this firmly. Manly as muscle.

But the older man just laughed a little, spit forming on his bottom lip. A wet giggle. "It doesn't matter if you're her mother," he said to Fly, almost shouting, the spittle spraying now. "It's against policy. And she's not going with strangers. She's being escorted by the NYPD. Here's the address. You can meet us there." He flicked Fly a business card. Then, "Get some shoes on," the officer said in Stela's direction. "We're tired of waiting."

Fly was confused, though. He'd been firm. He'd been clear. And now the mean tall one seemed to watch Stela's ass as she turned. Was Fly imagining that? This was definitely racism. Right? Fly was taller than this man, but he felt himself slouching for the man's benefit. He hated himself for that little curling motion. Hated Maristela for making him do it, to be real. Fly held the card and looked down at it but couldn't, for some reason, read it. It looked blurry, as though underwater in his hand.

Fly felt Stela let go of him as she went to find her shoes. With her gone he faced the men. They didn't seem afraid of him. Not at all. "A phone?" Fly snarled at the white men. "Three of you come up here for a cell phone past midnight? I mean. People are dying in the streets. And police officers are doing nothing. Or they are doing the most." Fly paused here to let that sink in, and also because he wondered if he'd gone too far. "How much does a cell phone cost, really? Like, a dollar twenty-five. Made in China." Fly felt proud, angry, proud of his anger. "This is some capitalistic . . . nonsense." He'd wanted to say bullshit, but couldn't manage it. He could feel the wetness from his own lips moistening the inside of his mask.

"If it was your buck twenty-five," the loud detective began, as if Fly hadn't just said a smart thing, "you'd want it, right?" This detective was so close to Fly that Fly felt the man's spit, just a light mist of it, on his cheek. He wanted so badly to recoil, but he knew that wouldn't look manly at all. This man stepped forward as though perhaps he was the one in charge. Perhaps he had the other two in training. He had a thick accent that seemed to Fly's ears to be native. He couldn't place it exactly—Brooklyn or the Bronx—except to feel as though this man knew more than he did. This white man from New York had a say, a run of the place, that Black Fly from Ellenwood, Georgia, didn't. Couldn't.

Stela came out in flip-flops and a jacket. She'd switched out her mask to one of the sterile paper ones. She looked sick, as though she was heading to an ambulance. Her eyes looked weak, like she'd been crying. Fly wanted her to look strong. She wasn't doing her part, with that scared look in her eyes.

"If that jacket she's wearing was stolen, you'd want your buck twenty-five back, right?" continued the officer, his voice bounding so loudly. Loud enough for maybe a neighbor walking down the hall to hear. Fly stepped back to avoid the officer. Maybe the man knew he had the virus; maybe he wanted to get them all sick on purpose. "If those pants you're wearing were stolen," the officer pressed on, "you'd want your buck and a quarter back, right?" Fly's pants, which were pajama pants, did not cost a buck and a quarter. At least, he didn't think so. They were silk, and Stela had bought them for him, a set. He wanted to tell the cop this, but instead he finally and fully noted that the detectives didn't seem to smell the marijuana in the room. They weren't here for him at all. They were here entirely for Maristela. And her stupid phone. Fly had warned her about these sorts of devices.

Stela came to him and took his hand. She gripped it hard but he didn't grip back.

"If it was your cell phone," the cop said now, looking Fly right in the eyes, "I mean if it was your brand-new cell phone with all your fresh beats and mixes, you'd want it back, right, man?" The cop kept looking Fly in the face, but Fly looked down at the card in his hand and tried again to make out what it said. Could he even read anymore? He tried to focus so his fear would turn to calm. Or turn to rage, why not? But he was too stunned, because how did this dude know that secretly Fly had been making beats on Stela's laptop? He had been thinking maybe someone would notice them, see that he was a musician. No one had, of course. The beats were just buried treasure on the hard drive. But this cop knew! They had seen him at the protest! They were tracking his moves on the computer! Somehow, they were doing this. So Fly couldn't find the fight.

Charlie Brown snapped plastic surgical gloves out of his pocket. He put them on so slowly and carefully that it was terrifying. "What are you doing?" Maristela asked, her voice muffled.

"I'm arresting you," he said, and used his gloved hands to take her by the arm.

"I can tell she did it," the real New Yorker was heard saying as they walked Stela down the stairs. "I can tell by the way they're acting, the both of them."

◆ ◆ ◆

The car seemed like a regular car. There wasn't the usual New York traffic, and once during the ride, the driver, the tall mean one, flashed the lights that were the colors of the American flag. The car in front of them had its turn signal on in the wrong lane. They didn't pull the car over. Stela hadn't been inside a car in weeks. Cars, enclosed, were unsafe, and she felt this now, felt the reality of them all, despite her protective mask, inhaling each other's breath. Because that was the nature of this virus—that just doing the thing that kept you alive was enough to kill someone else. And she'd read the numbers; regardless of Fly's conspiracy theories, she knew Black people were dying too—dropping like under a firing squad.

But honestly, despite all this, their cop car was just a regular vehicle—a detective car in disguise. They went up and around and looping, as though confusing her was one of their tactics. And Stela was scared of the car and confused about where in the city they even were. And also she could not fucking believe she was in the back of a cop car. She began to pray the Hail Mary, but she was misremembering it. Could it be that you actually wound around, saying Mary's name again and again? Stela was getting lost in that, too.

Through all the winding the detectives talked to each other. When they talked about visiting hospitals they called the victims "mine." They claimed the beat-up woman from her asshole boyfriend. Claimed the raped girl from her pedophile father. "Mine," they said. "Mine had a broken shoulder blade. If I hadn't asked the nurse, I would never have believed mine was even alive." They hadn't cuffed Stela, but in the back seat she sat on her hands anyway. She wished she had gloves, because the car felt cruddy. And also she was fucking freezing. It took some time for her to realize that her feet were cold. She was only wearing the flip-flops and it was a too-cool summer night.

The young one, who wore the mask and made her think of melancholy Charlie Brown, was sitting beside her in the back seat and she could see now that he was very large, despite being short. He still had on his gloves. He wasn't in charge at all. Here he was, shunned in the back with her. Protecting himself from COVID like a chump. Probably in training. She felt bad that he looked uncomfortable. She tried to give him a comforting look. "We could have handcuffed you," he said to her when she met his gaze.

Fucking hell. Was this shit for real? Stela wasn't sure if she could keep from crying. For the first time, she tried to think, really think about a cell phone from Cell-U. But she couldn't recall being there. Yes, that was her cell phone company. Yes, she and Fly had their joint account there. She paid for it. She'd even purchased Fly a cell phone and set it up for him herself. Though did he use it? No. But she'd done it all anyway. Like she always did—took care of every-damn-body. And now her own cell phone company was fucking her. She had other choices for cell service—didn't they always say *Thank you for choosing us* when she called? Didn't they say *Welcome to your communications home* as soon as she walked into their store? Would your homie do you in like this shit during a fucking pandemic? "Can't I just give you the money they say I owe?" Stela now said quietly to the man beside her. People were losing their jobs and there was a rent strike in her building, but Stela and Fly, tethered to schools, were okay. From the passenger's seat the TV cop slapped the dashboard as though he'd nailed her. "If you didn't do it, you would never just give up money."

She looked out the window. New York was naked of its people. The only souls out were those known as essential workers—at this late night–early morning time that meant building cleaners, security guards. Mostly Caribbean Americans, like Stela. Everyone with a mask on their face that muzzled them. She knew people were protesting downtown in Battery Park, but even they were holding signs, standing six feet apart. The days when it was nothing in Manhattan to get shoulder-checked by a stranger—gone. The world was mad enough, but somehow things were even crazier for her now. Here she was, sitting in the back of a cop car, as they drove past a plastic dome huge as a house. "What the hell is that?" asked the driving officer.

The tall one in the passenger's seat shrugged. "Wasn't there when we drove in."

"It's a morgue," said that cop beside Stela. The other two looked at him through the rearview mirror but said not a damn thing.

So. New York had built a morgue in a matter of hours, and Stela was being picked up for a fucking cell phone? And stealing a cell phone just wasn't even like her. Too concrete and cold. Not her style at all.

At the station Charlie Brown walked her upstairs and downstairs and around corners. She'd never find her way out. Cops smiled at each other. And most of them weren't wearing masks, so there the smiles were. They made jokes about how much coffee they'd drunk. Didn't seem to even realize Stela was there. She was in close proximity with more people, real flesh-and-blood people, than she had been in weeks. Stela and the cop walked up and around and down until he opened a door and told her to wait in there. *In there.* And then she saw the door close and heard him lock the bolt. The room had the one locked door. The room had no windows. She wondered who had been in here last. She wondered if they had sneezed, and if she was inhaling the virus right now.

Stela sat there. Alone. Did people really go to jail for stealing cell phones? Didn't they get stolen all the fucking time? This was bullshit. It was one a.m. Stela was dreaming. She must be. She was a high school biology teacher who was spending the summer learning Google Classroom and tutoring summer students via Zoom. Yes. She was quarantined with a man who smoked a bit too much and sometimes watched porn instead of fucking her, but he was handsome and educated. Good. The world was going to shit with the strong men in office and the dumb women who voted for them; and people were dying and dying because of a virus that, when under a microscope, looked like the life-giving sun. No way that could add up to our sweet Stela being in actual jail. Not now of all times. No, nah, nope.

Her father would kill her. Would have killed her. But he was dead. And Mermaid? Mermaid was alive. But Stela didn't think she would ever tell her mother about this. Sure, Mermaid was always telling stories about her own childhood at the orphanage. And about that one girl who was like a sister to her—Darleen. The girl who stole everyone's baby teeth and wore them around her neck in a pouch. That shit was creepy and weird. Weirder because as a child Stela had found a tooth on a necklace in her mother's jewelry box. Knew immediately that her mother had stolen it from the sister, but Stela had never let on. Instead, she'd just check on that tooth pendant periodically. Make sure, every few months, that it was still there and not some story she'd made up in her own head. And then her mother had worn it at her father's funeral, like no big deal. Stela wished so badly that she herself had a sister. A sister was someone you could safely steal from. A sister was someone Stela would tell this story to.

The door opened and Charlie Brown offered Stela a cup of water, which she wanted but didn't want him to know she wanted. Police officers were her enemies. They had dragged her out of her apartment at midnight, when life was hard enough—goddammit. She had to be at school to co-lead an online teacher training in the morning. Was there internet service here at the precinct, and would they let her at least send her principal an email? Stela was supposed to be live from the science lab, presenting on asynchronous breakout rooms.

And worse, these police people had called her by another man's name and she had known that it still meant her, maybe always would. Like she would never outgrow her past. She said no thank you to the water, and instead, "Can I get something to draw with? A piece of paper, pencil?"

"We don't have that here," the cop said. "We have water."

She took the cup of water but waited for him to leave before she drank it. Instantly, she had to pee. She wondered if this was why he had offered water. So that she would have to pee and then be desperate. Stela passed ten minutes daydreaming about banging on the door and begging for the bathroom while Charlie Brown snickered on the outside. She imagined herself squatting in the corner with the detectives watching and jeering at the stream of piss. And wouldn't that be something? A respectable high school teacher peeing in the corner of a jail. What a disappointment she was to her father. Of course, he'd died on her. She couldn't even take care of herself.

◆ ◆ ◆

Since the pandemic there'd been a curfew over the city, though you could be out if you were masked and running to the grocery store for food or to the drugstore for medicine. It wasn't clear who was sick and who was out getting something for a sick person. Though it was clear that there wasn't really a difference. The virus was so contagious that caregivers were guaranteed an infection of their own. Fly, young, healthy looking, and alert, looked just enough like one of that caretaker league. So no one had questioned him while he rode two trains to get to the station. Walking now from the subway stop he noticed the VOTE!/¡VOTA! stickers on electricity poles. A few KEEP AMERICA GREAT signs in small shop windows. Fly didn't expect to see those there, but it was true that Fly himself did admire the candidate behind that slogan. The man was brash and unapologetic—maybe a little racist but strong. All those not-Fly things, things he nevertheless shamefully desired. Still, Fly never imagined he'd find people here in New York who would show off their support for that guy. In Georgia, sure, Fly expected it. His own dad had voted that way. Then Fly remembered that the brash candidate was, in fact, from New York. No matter. Fly hadn't voted at all. Not his thing.

But there was a whole thing going on about if Black lives even mattered, and if Black men could even go for a jog, or bird-watch, or sleep in their cars or do anything at all, without risk of being killed. And now how would it look, Black Fly showing up to an actual police precinct in sweats and sweating at midnight? Fly was anxious. He had a marble in the hand-warming pocket of his sweatshirt. He hadn't grabbed it special; it was just that these days, since the pandemic, he supposed, he always had a marble on him. This one was hard, a steely, and felt like it could be a weapon. He rolled it around and around his fingers.

Also in his pocket was his cell phone. He'd delayed so long getting one. Was his the very phone she'd boosted? Was there a tracking device on it? Is that how the cops had found her? Fly should have filmed the cops. That is what a real man would have done. Not that it would have helped if he had pulled out his cell phone. That might have made the cops shoot him, and then Stela would be on the news crying about her dead boyfriend rather than locked up in a Midtown jail.

On the street, Fly turned himself around and around, trying to find his way. He went up streets and down streets and around buildings. This Midtown wasn't like Harlem at night. There were some young drunks but no old crackheads. There was techno music and boys in bright colors walking in pairs—groups of more than ten were not allowed. Harlem at this time would be quiet, until there was a fight, then that would be loud. Then the sirens might or might not come.

When Fly finally walked into the police station he realized that he had never before walked into a police station. It was a Black male statistic he had avoided all his years. But here he was. He sat down in the front room, which had some chairs on one end and a huge desk with a cop behind it on the other end. An open space spread between like a kind of protection. Fly sat, the cop's tall desk in his periphery, thinking that someone would come to him. How can I help you, they would ask.

The police station smelled like pesticide, which Fly knew well on account of his dad, and which he also hated on account of his dad. He tried to calm down, even though he felt his skin itching. Was it an anti-roach chemical? Or was it an anti–Black people chemical? He'd read a poem once, or part of a poem, or heard it on the radio—he couldn't remember—where Black people and roaches were made the same in some metaphorical way. Though in the metaphor the Black people were the roachy heroes—the ones who could never die despite all the attempts at extermination. Now that Fly thought about it, maybe he'd made up the Black people roach metaphor himself. Dang, it was a good one. Maybe he'd write a song about that. Just thinking about his own creative intelligence made Fly calm down.

He looked around. No one from behind the tall cop desk asked him what he needed, what he wanted. He needed and wanted so many things; if they would just ask they would know. But as he sat there he could not, *Jesus*, could not help imagining Stela behind longitudinal bars. Fly was wearing his same silk pajama pants. The expensive ones. And the hooded fleece jacket that he had slipped off his head when he walked into the station—he didn't want to look like a criminal. Some asshole had killed a kid back in the day and blamed the hoodie and gotten off Dred Scott–free. Fly fingered the steely in his hoodie pouch. Fingering. That was the word the cops had used. Sounded crass. But it was kind of a good word, too. Fly felt sick with it all.

His own phone pulsed in his pants—he forgot he'd put it in there. He touched it, felt its smooth metal hardness. He waited until the phone stopped—it wasn't Stela, so it didn't matter who it was. Instead of pulling it out, he pulled out the steely. Rolled it over his knuckles, wondering if anyone was watching him. He did it faster and faster, then caught the marble in his hand. Switched hands and did it again. He imagined the cop behind the desk looking at him. He caught the marble and looked up. No one was looking at him. He put the marble back in his pocket. He should have brought one of his *Invisibles* instead; that would have been better. Or a Bible, that would have been best.

Fly watched other detectives bring in different kinds of women. The cold air bursting in each time. These were women who Fly might give spare change to, or women he would cross the street to avoid. A woman wearing a BLACK QUEER LIVES MATTER T-shirt, her own blond hair straight and dry as straw, came in struggling with the officers. Despite himself, Fly had a fierce desire to whisper to this woman as she passed: "Control yourself! Get yourself under control and they won't hurt you." A skinny almond-skinned woman was escorted in. She was coiffed, made up like a model. She was wearing a bikini bathing suit top and tiny jean shorts. Her face was haughty, but with tears streaking it. "Don't be afraid," Fly said to her in his mind. "Don't be afraid and it will be okay." He saw women again and again. They all seemed to be seeing him, seeing him seeing them. Was it that they were all looking for a sign from him? Was this what it felt like for his father? The voices in Dad's head? Was Fly, right now, coming into his wicked inheritance? Finally losing his mind?

Fly sure wished he had a song for the women. A hymn. A gospel. He shook his head, unable to give them the music they needed. You'll have your woman vice-president soon enough, he wanted to say—but maybe it wasn't true. Maybe it wouldn't be so, would never be soon enough, would never be enough at all. Finally, after almost an hour Fly shivered himself into action. He stood up and went to the counter. "I need to see my girlfriend." The desk was up high like pharmacy shelves used to be. Fly had to stand straight, had to lift his chin to look the officer in the eyes.

And when that man, whose protective blue mask only served to make him menacing, looked down and asked for his woman's name, Fly had to use "Jones." The ex-husband's name. Flipping Doctor Steven Jones.

But they couldn't find her. It had been two hours since she'd left the apartment, but now they couldn't find her. Fly's first thought was that Stela had broken out of the jail, but this was absurd. His second thought was that he had come to the wrong station. He dug into his pockets, trying to find the business card with the address. He turned to pat himself down. A door across the waiting room opened and the younger detective now led Maristela out and into another room. Stela's hands were behind her back as though bound, and her mask was down cupping her chin. He could have called out, but it suddenly felt as though she did not belong to him at all. The two of them, Stela and that man, turned down a corridor.

"That was her," Fly said quietly up to the cop at the desk. "That was her who just went down there."

"Right. She's going to get printed. Then you can go see her. A minute or so."

It was another hour. When she passed back into the room and out again, she wasn't wearing a mask. Fly pretended he didn't see her. He didn't want to meet her eyes. Not yet. Maybe not at all. Maybe never.

◆ ◆ ◆

When Fly was finally let into her little room he was offered the water also, and Stela wanted to tell him not to accept, but he said yes and swallowed the water in one gulp. He leaned against the wall and stared at the ceiling. Stela stared at him; he remained masked even though it was just her, only her breath by now. He looked exhausted; he looked, frankly, worse than she felt. And she felt despondent. She wanted to hold him and protect him from this. From her. She tried to hold his hand, but Fly would not grip back.

So they sat here. With her finger, Stela traced a labyrinth into the dust of the tabletop. At the center, not the heart of Jesus as she'd been taught in Catholic school, but the open mouth of a whale—she'd taught herself that. They'd made her take off the mask when they took her picture and now she was exposed. Fly sat still, his mask safely on his face. He stared at the walls and thought of all the women downstairs. He counted them in his mind like sheep.

◆ ◆ ◆

By the end it was five in the morning. "Good people do bad things," Charlie Brown said, "but the cell phone companies are cracking down on . . ." There was a pause. "The people." He coughed behind his mask. "Me and the guys were in Harlem for some other stuff. You know what's been going on. You been on my to-do list a month and some. You know. Easy as American pie. No biggie to me. Them companies will screw you. They screw us all."

The cop was being kind now. And Stela, well, she longed for it, even if it was a trick sort of kindness. The cop had let her go but she'd have to report to court. She'd get something in the mail telling her when. Now she and Fly walked out of the station together. She'd lost her mask in the station but there was a box of disposable ones in the precinct lobby. She asked first, afraid to steal from the police, but the man at the high counter had scowled when she asked. Fly had taken one and said, "Thank you, sir," as they walked out. But once out, Fly put money for the subway in Stela's face and walked ahead. She felt like a whore and hugged herself tightly to bear the morning chill. When they sat on the platform bench, she tried to press against her man, but he closed his eyes and folded his arms—his dead pharaoh style. She needed him to give the care, or give in to her cloying. But neither was coming.

◆ ◆ ◆

The tiny steely in Fly's sweatshirt pocket was like a weight he was lifting—he was so strong that it felt like nothing. He pressed the tips of his fingers hard to it, and imagined he was pressing Stela's face down—like he sometimes saw in the sex videos, but hadn't yet tried, was too scared to try with Stela. But he would now. He would press her face down into the pillow. *A cell phone, Maristela!* He could have bought that for her.

But no, no, he couldn't actually. He could barely cover his rent. He couldn't buy his woman anything. Fly took the steely out and pitched it onto the train tracks. It made a noise too loud for its size. A noise that felt about right to Fly.

Stela tensed, startled by his violent movement and by the clanging metal sound. The train came, and they stood, then boarded. Stela reached for Fly's hand, but he didn't remove it from his pocket for her. She knew she should think. But Stela didn't want to think about May 30. Not with her man sitting there beside her and sending all the signals that he was rejecting her, didn't even want her loving. What had happened in May? That's what the cop should have asked her. Instead, he just kept asking her about that one day, May 30. He never asked about what had preceded that day, or what had followed. Death. Funeral. Her father had been sick her whole life, always something small and silly ailing him: an ingrown toenail that mysteriously turned to gout; a cold that twisted into the flu that bloomed into bronchitis. Until it wasn't small at all. A urinary tract infection had turned into the Big C. Cancer. Then remission. Then the cancer's steadfast return. Stela had left New York on May 30, despite the news, despite America being on fire, to make it home in time to help her mother with the funeral planning and all the paperwork. The funeral had been awful and beautiful. The army didn't do much right, but they knew how to do a funeral. Lots of practice, Stela guessed. But what had Stela done the morning she left? She'd prepared herself to go home, that's fucking what. She saw herself packing. She saw herself crying alone on the sofa after Fly left for class. She saw herself remembering to pack her cell phone and its charger. Simple, lonely things.

Now on the subway she couldn't think straight. Her father was dead, she was on her way home from jail, and her man was sitting here, but his body was a board beside her. She thought of Fly's slack hand in hers at the station. His loose arm in hers before at the apartment. He wouldn't hold her hand now. Wouldn't even look at her.

Fly didn't walk Stela to her door. He left her at the front of her building. He walked the dozen blocks with his head low, hoodie up. One person walked by with a plastic helmet covering his entire head and face and fastening at his neck. He looked like an astronaut on the moon.

Inside, Stela went to the sink and washed herself standing there. She wanted to pray but she was too pissed off, too ashamed. She put on her teacher clothes, walked out to work. Turned back because she'd forgotten her cell. That fucking thing.

In his studio apartment on the other side of uptown, Fly took a shower, where he sang a low, deep something without words into the jets of water. He thought about the man with the astronaut shield. Thought about how the earth had become foreign and hostile to them all, how it might as well be the moon.

◆ ◆ ◆

That afternoon Stela stepped off the train and felt the hot outside air lick her face and chest. It felt disgusting. She was disgusted. Her own presentation had been a mess; she'd shared her screen and said a few things about rooms and doors and the purpose of windows—which she knew made no sense given that the virtual rooms they were working with didn't have doors or windows, though maybe they did theoretically. Either way, everyone smiled along, and the principal directed everyone to use the clap icon to show their gratitude. The questions afterward were not about the usefulness of online breakout rooms, but instead were about how to use the basic elements of the platform. These Stela could answer. She spent most of the time looking at her own square on the screen among the squares of her colleagues. She looked tired, but did she look like someone who had spent the night in jail? She looked sad, but did she look like someone whose boyfriend, the only person she interacted with meaningfully during this quarantine, was breaking up with her?

Walking to her apartment now she was feeling the exhaustion from the all-nighter and the humiliation of not being a good presenter, and the wet heaviness of the air, but in her stomach she felt something fast and metallic—a panic. The panic was that Fly would not be in her apartment when she got there. He was always there, going back to his own place just to grab something, maybe take a call on the landline his mother kept paying for, nap and smoke, but then be right back with Stela. He'd had a key since the quarantine started. If she ever left she'd usually return to him reading or banging drums—recess, he called it. But after last night, Fly would fly. Stela knew this. Fly was his name and that was his nature.

And so now what? Stela didn't have Steven—he was getting remarried; he'd told her on the phone when he'd called to give condolences. She didn't have Johann—he'd been married for years with two daughters old enough now to talk. Stela didn't even have her dad or her first father. She'd never been an orphan herself, but now this orphaned feeling was the all of her.

From the subway stop Stela took a series of detours to get home. She was so very tired and her back hurt, but she stopped to roll up her jeans, and then she walked past the bodega where she knew Fly sometimes got rolling paper for his marijuana. She walked past the pickup truck that was now a fruit stand. The dark-skinned Dominican man had his mask around his neck and was calling out: *Papaya, papaya, fresh papaya.* When someone came up to him he lifted his mask up to cover his face and began chopping the sweet fruit into a plastic zip bag. Stela was pretty sure that what he was doing was illegal, given the quarantine. The man was risking getting sick because he needed a few dollars. The world was so fucked up, she needed to get inside. But when Stela saw that she was close to her apartment building, she veered away again. She passed the deli that didn't sell sandwiches but always had stale M&M's. It was closed now. The sign on it said: STAY SAFE NEW YOURK.

Steven Jones would have held her hand on the subway, wouldn't he? After her father's viewing Johann had shown Stela pictures of his daughters—all blond and gray-eyed. Inside the church sanctuary the few of them gathered together all wore masks, but outside, no one on island seemed to think it necessary. Stela had stared at the picture he showed her, the sunlight casting a glare that seemed pretty, then she'd said, "I always thought you'd have brown babies." She'd been sad enough that she didn't even care how it sounded. "Me, too," Johann had said back. Everything had felt absurd. People were dying by the thousands in New York from a virus that hadn't existed in this form a few months before, but here in Saint Thomas her father had died of the same cancer he'd had for a decade.

Now Stela passed the Chinese restaurant where you had to be buzzed in and still there was bulletproof glass between you and the couple you ordered from. These days there was a wide window that had a little revolving door. You put in the money, they turned it and counted, they put on a box of kung pao, and turned it back to you. There was a bottle of hand sanitizer taped to the window. Stela went to it, pressed it, wiped her hands with the cool gel. Didn't order a thing. She wondered if she was stealing. She passed the pizza place that had been owned by the two Kittian women with British accents. It was boarded up.

When, finally, Stela walked into her own apartment building, she'd worked herself up into a misty sweat. She knew she and Fly were doomed as the devil. She was a divorcée, after all. And a Catholic one. She'd been doomed before Fly even came into the picture. His mother, he once confessed, blamed Stela for keeping Fly in New York and away from home.

And Stela's mom? Please. Stela's mother still held a fucking torch for fellow orphan Dr. Steven Jones. And Mermaid still loved Johann, too: "Like a son to me, that boy," she'd said after he'd left the repast on the funeral day. "Especially since you and your damn brothers all wanting to live stateside." Stela had put her head in her mother's lap then and cried and cried.

Stela and Fly should not be dating at all. She was a cheat and a klepto; that was all out in the open now. He was a pothead and a perv. He said he'd thrown the magazines all out since they started dating, but his internet porn was worse. The advertisements had started popping up on her computer—"black dick fucks mullatress pussy" and "primitive African girl learns to suck her chief's cock." Fly and Stela were just stereotypes after all. They weren't good for anybody but Jesus.

Stela was daydreaming all of this as she stood at her apartment door. She realized she was crying, just as a neighbor walked by. Eyes were so important these days; it was all people had—so Stela looked down. She watched a teardrop hit the ground, and imagined what it might be like to draw it. The neighbor disappeared into his apartment. Stela breathed in a deep breath, the mask flushing into her nostrils, which made her cough. She walked into the foyer. And fucking hell. She could hear djembe drumming coming from her own apartment. The drumming something soft and gentle. It sounded tired, like maybe Fly was just winding down from a loud and wild session. All the things she had been thinking, the ways she had readied herself for the end, convinced herself of it. Now gone. Stela was just so grateful that he was here. And she was confused by her gratefulness. She put her forehead to the door.

Fly was on the other side of the door, on the inside of the apartment. He'd awoken in his own apartment, but had awoken missing

Stela. He smoked to get high but mostly to get the coming-down clarity. The clear question was what kind of man did he want to be? Did he want the verb, to fly; or did he want the adjective, to be fly? Which kind of man was he? What kind of man did Stela need?

He'd taken a copy of *Invisible Man*, this one a hardcover he tucked under his pit, but left his place and started back to Stela's. He wasn't sure what he was going to do or say when he got to her, but he was home-pigeoning, the verb, for now. The twelve-block walk felt more winding than usual and he felt for a marble in his pocket to fidget with, but he had forgotten to grab one. He realized he was going a different way than normal, passing by the hospital, which was a mistake. The one time he'd passed before, there was a line of nurses, fully in scrubs from the head covering to the feet covering, all smoking cigarettes as if they were junkies. He'd heard that nurses and doctors were regularly doing two and three shifts back-to-back. Their faces all looked haggard, like they'd been smoking since they were ten.

But this time he heard them before he saw them. Their sound was rhythmic, and he heard the rhythm before he understood the words. It was maybe twenty nurses this time. And they were gathering in a bunch in front of the hospital. They weren't wearing scrubs, so maybe this was a different group of nurses or maybe they were doctors and dentists in there, too, or maybe there was a different dress code for rallying: "White coats for Black lives," they yelled. Some had machine-made signs that said the same thing. Some had it on a pin that they'd fastened to their collars. They were all races, but mostly some type of Indian or South Asian.

Fly nodded at them and held up his fist as he walked by—which caused them all to cheer, though at him or at themselves he wasn't sure. He'd been trying to remember who he had been when he'd been his best. So when the *Invisible* slipped from under his arm, he caught it in his hand. He looked at it for a second. Then he passed it to the doctor, a South Asian–looking man, who was closest to him. "Thank you, my man," the doctor or nurse or orderly or whatever said.

"It was never mine," Fly said back and felt perfect, just perfect about how he'd performed it all. He went on now with a fly-boy swag in his walk.

His father, Fly was sure, would leave Stela. His father was a runner, a driver, maybe, but same thing. Fly wanted to move but he wanted to move toward something. To face the thing, be brave in the face of it, and keep on moving to the next fight, no flying. Like Pastor John the Baptist. Why not do that with Stela? But where was the blueprint, the map? Maybe that stupid class where he'd learned the hero's journey. Or maybe tenth-grade Greek mythology. Theseus. Fighting the minotaur. This was a test, a metaphor for the man he wanted to be. Fly stood at Stela's door and lowered his head in prayer. He didn't know any Greek or South Asian prayers, though those might have kept the metaphor intact. So he prayed the one he knew best from his childhood: "Though I walk through the valley of the shadow of death, I fear no evil." He had the key to Stela's place—he thought of it like a sword for slaying. He let himself in.

Yes, he'd done this a hundred times before. But this day he entered her apartment and decided he was conquering something. "Amen," he said as he closed the door behind him. The prize was Stela, a woman to be his for life, he felt sure. But just so we are sure, though he knew Psalm 23 by heart, he had less command of the Greek myths. He settled in and began to play his drums.

◆ ◆ ◆

Now, in Stela's crib, cave, valley, labyrinth what-have-you, Fly gets an alert on his phone. Months ago when the pandemic started, he'd installed dozens of apps in the initial frenzy of having a cell and having nothing else to do. When he first realized what the finder app was, he'd watched Stela, a bubble on the map, move over and under the city running errands, heading to her school to pick up supplies. Felt like watching her from the sky. Like a god. Wasn't Theseus a god? But back then Fly had also started playing the games with bubbles to pop, and then there were bubble butts in apps, too, and then apps that were whole naked bodies and not bubbles at all. And, well, he hadn't thought about the finder app in months. Stela and he were always together anyhow.

But he is using the app now, and it tells him that Stela has arrived at her apartment. It tells him she is there on the other side of the door, though he is pretty sure he would have sensed this now even without the technology. He feels her there, in some magical, mystical way. Because Stela is his woman. And he feels that thing that men supposedly always feel, that this woman will be his wife, his life. He feels it like the hard ball behind his chest bone. Fly scrolls through the pictures on his newly fabulous phone, looking for the one he wants. He finds it among those he'd uploaded from his digital camera. Presses Send.

Outside, her forehead to her own apartment door, Stela hears that there is nothing to hear. The neighbor has gone. Fly has stopped drumming. Maybe he knows she is there. He has those kind of magical, mystical knowings sometimes. She coughs into her mask again. She wonders if she is finally getting sick. If she will die of this virus, if she will join her father and do like everyone has always done—leave her mother lonely. Stela hears Fly cough on the other side.

Fly coughs and feels the hard smooth thing rattle in his chest.

Stela listens and listens more closely, but Fly doesn't come to the door. He doesn't come for her. She leans back and reaches into her bag for her keys. Her phone dances in her bag and against her hand. She looks at the face of the phone and then clicks on the message. It is a picture. It opens slowly, so slowly. So slowly that Stela doesn't hear anything from inside her apartment. Doesn't hear Fly breathing.

Fly in fact isn't breathing. He is feeling something hard and round rustling in his chest, or in his back. It's in his lungs either way. But he can't think straight because he can't breathe. But then, grace, the coughing comes. Coughing, coughing. Fly's lungs release like a window broken. The voice in his head comes unbidden and it is his father's: "You know I don't like being rushed." Fly's coughing clears. His lungs release. His heart.

Stela hears Fly now. It sounds like he is crying and retching. Which he sometimes does in his sleep. Usually, when it wakes her, she will wake him and then he will tell her about his dream, which is always about his father, about Fly's fear of going crazy like his father. Now she presses her ear to the door to hear if he is indeed sleeping or waking or what. She waits, and while she waits, she looks down at her phone. The picture Fly has sent her is a picture of his hand. It is not a well-balanced photo. It is not, by most standards, a piece of art. It is just Fly's open hand. And she has always loved the lines in a man's hands. Now Stela puts her hand over Fly's hand. She holds it. The door opens.

NOTES AND THANKS

Thanks:

Thank you to everywhere that published parts of this. I mean, really. Thanks especially to Billie Geraldi, Morgan Parker, and Erin Stalcup for very early editorial interventions.

Thanks to Dee Brown who first invited me to read from "Belly of the Whale" at a Community Foundation of the Virgin Islands event.

Thank you to my New School students in the novel in stories/linked story collection reading group, for the smart discussions we had. Thank you to my colleagues, administrators, and students at Wesleyan University—you will always be home to me.

Thank you to Emory University—the badass members of the English Department and Creative Writing Program, in particular the witches of the coven. Could a novelist or poet hope for a better institution? Nope.

Thank you to the Squaw Valley Community of Writers where I worked on revisions of this. Thank you to the Hugo House in Seattle, which invited me to write the story that became "Monster in the Middle" and inspired the whole novel. Thank you to Troutbeck: The Poet Society, where I wrote the last chapters of this book.

Thank you to the Bread Loaf Writers' Conference, and to Jen and Lauren, and to all the writers and readers who have lived through Bloaf and who have written through it. For me, there would be no books without the mountain.

Thank you to Katie Freeman, my friend and my champion.

Thanks to Elise Capron for her never-ending dedication. I love you. Straight up.

Thank you to Sarah McGrath for her faith and fortitude, and to Alison Fairbrother for her generosity and grit. Thank you to Delia and Ashley—what the fuck, you are brilliant. Big up, Riverhead!

Thanks to Darleen Albert and her husband for driving me around Vega Baja, so I could swim at the beach where my grandmother first learned to swim. Thank you to Loretta Collins for introducing me to Darleen and for being a poet feminist mother/example to me.

Thanks to Asa, Adina, Courtney, Jennifer, Nelly, and Whitney for talks about this book. To Nick Helbich and Anton Nimblett for in-depth talks and guidance.

Thank you to musician Imani Wilson for her sharp intelligence and deep generosity. Thank you to Stephanie for her savvy and to Nat for her wisdom. Thank you Erica, sister, for holding me as I finished this book. Thanks to my cousin Mike Smith, and to Jamey Hadley for feedback on Memphis. Thank you to Hashim, who read the whole book and wrote in just about every margin. Shark, I am prouder of this book in large part because of your intelligent guidance. Thank you to Jericho for being my fierce leader and brave example. Thank you to Pastor Michelle Lewis for literally and figuratively giving me a quiet holy space in which to write. Thanks to Seth Markle, my old friend, who lent me his story and stayed supportive even when I pivoted and did what the hell I wanted . . . as I do.

Thank you to Shaan and Pabatso, the caregivers who gave me time. Thank you to Moses for being my co-parent through the early developments of this book. And Big Daddy—sneaking in a thanks to you just because I think it will make you laugh.

Thank you to my fellow mermaid, Hannah Appel, for her life and love and story. As well as to her partner James, and her/my children for giving Han the space to be in it all with me through this project. May we swim these oceans together as long as there are oceans.

Finally, and always and for every single thing—thank you to my grandmother.

Notes:

When Fly considers that roaches might be akin to Black people, he believes it is a connection he makes all by himself. The poem from which this connection actually came to me (and therefore to Fly) is Jericho Brown's "Beneath Me."

The section where Fly sees the arrested women in the police station was inspired by a poem called "A Fact Which Occurred in America" by James Allen Hall, which was itself inspired by a painting by George Dawe titled *A Negro Overpowering a Buffalo—A Fact Which Occurred in America, 1809.*

The Lorraine Motel, where Gary and Eloise visit and where the Reverend Martin Luther King Jr. was shot and killed, is indeed now the National Civil Rights Museum of the United States. However, it did not become a museum until 1991. Which tells you how people can change spaces over time.

The beach where Mermaid learns to swim in Vega Baja, Puerto Rico, is called Playa Puerto Nuevo. The strange geography of the beach is exactly the same today as it was in 1938. Which tells you how space might resist our changing, regardless of time.